Girl
in Snow

A NOVEL

Danya Kukafka

Simon & Schuster

New York   London   Toronto   Sydney   New Delhi

Simon & Schuster
1230 Avenue of the Americas
New York, NY 10020

This book is a work of fiction. Any references to historical events, real people,
or real places are used fictitiously. Other names, characters, places, and events
are products of the author's imagination, and any resemblance to actual
events or places or persons, living or dead, is entirely coincidental.

Copyright © 2017 by Danya Kukafka

All rights reserved, including the right to reproduce this book or portions
thereof in any form whatsoever. For information, address
Simon & Schuster Subsidiary Rights Department,
1230 Avenue of the Americas, New York, NY 10020.

First Simon & Schuster hardcover edition August 2017

SIMON & SCHUSTER and colophon are registered trademarks of Simon & Schuster, Inc.

For information about special discounts for bulk purchases, please contact
Simon & Schuster Special Sales at 1-866-506-1949 or business@simonandschuster.com.

The Simon & Schuster Speakers Bureau can bring authors to your live event.
For more information or to book an event, contact the
Simon & Schuster Speakers Bureau at 1-866-248-3049 or
visit our website at www.simonspeakers.com.

Interior design by Ruth Lee-Mui

Manufactured in the United States of America

1   3   5   7   9   10   8   6   4   2

Library of Congress Cataloging-in-Publication Data is available.

ISBN 978-1-5011-4437-0
ISBN 978-1-5011-4439-4 (ebook)

For Doris Kukafka

Day
One

WEDNESDAY
FEBRUARY 16, 2005

Cameron

When they told him Lucinda Hayes was dead, Cameron thought of her shoulder blades and how they framed her naked spine, like a pair of static lungs.

––––––––

They called an assembly.

The teachers buzzed against the far wall of the gymnasium, checking their watches and craning their necks. Cameron sat next to Ronnie in the top corner of the bleachers. He bit his fingernails and watched everyone spin about. His left pinky finger, already cracked and dry, began to bleed around the cuticle.

"What do you think this is for?" Ronnie said. Ronnie never brushed his teeth in the morning. There were zits around the corners of his mouth, and they were white and full at the edges. Cameron leaned away.

Principal Barnes stood at the podium on the half-court line, adjusting his jacket. The ninth-grade class snapped their gum and laughed in little groups, hiking up their backpacks and squeaking colorful shoes across the gymnasium floor.

"Can everyone hear me?" Principal Barnes said, hands on each side of the podium. He brushed a line of sweat from his forehead with his sleeve, squeezed his eyes shut.

"Jefferson High School is in the midst of a tragedy," Principal Barnes said. "Last night, we were forced to say good-bye to one of our most gifted students. It is with regret that I inform you of the passing of your classmate, Miss Lucinda Hayes."

The microphone shrieked, crackled.

In the days following, Cameron would remember this as the moment he lost her. The hum of the overhead fluorescent lights created a rhythm in time with the whispers that blossomed from every direction. If this moment were a song, Cameron thought, it would be a quiet song—the sort of song that drowned you in your own miserable chest. It was stunning and tender. It dropped, it shattered, and Cameron could only feel the weight of this melody, this song that felt both crushing and delicate.

"Fuck," Ronnie whispered. The song built and built and built, a steady rush.

It took Cameron six more seconds to notice that no one had a face.

He leaned over the edge of the bleachers and vomited through the railings.

———

Last night:

Almond eyes glaring out onto the lawn. A pink palm spread wide on Lucinda's bedroom window screen. The clouds overhead, moving in fast, a gray sheet shaken out over midnight suede.

———————

"The nurse said you threw up," Mom said when she picked him up, later that afternoon.

Cameron nudged the crushed crackers and lint on the carpet of the minivan, pushing them into small mountains with the side of his snow boot. Mom took a sip of coffee from her travel mug.

After the initial drama had simmered down, everyone had gathered outside the gymnasium to speculate. The baseball boys said she was raped. The loser girls said she killed herself. Ronnie had agreed. *She probably killed herself, don't you think? She was always writing in that journal. I bet she left a note. Dude, your fucking throw-up is on my shoe.*

"Cameron," Mom tried again, three streets later. She was using her sympathetic voice. Mom had the sort of sympathetic voice that Cameron hated—it seeped from her throat in sugary spurts. He hated to imagine his sadness inside her. Mom didn't deserve any of it.

"I know this is hard. This shouldn't happen to people your age—especially not to girls like Lucinda."

"Mom. Stop."

Cameron rested his forehead against the frosted window. He wondered if a forehead print was like a fingerprint. It was probably less identifiable, because foreheads weren't necessarily different from person to person, unless you were looking at the print on a microscopic level, and how often did people take the time for that?

He wondered how it would feel to kiss someone through glass. He'd seen a movie once about a guy who kissed his wife through a jail visitation-room window and he'd wondered if that felt like a real kiss. He thought a kiss was more about the intention than the act, so it hardly mattered if saliva hit glass or more saliva.

Since he was thinking about lips, he was thinking about Lucinda Hayes and hating himself, because Lucinda Hayes was dead.

When they got home, Mom sat him down on the couch. She turned on the television. *Get your mind off things.* She emptied a can of chicken noodle soup into a bowl, but over the whir of the microwave, the voice of the news anchor blared.

"Tragedy struck in northern Colorado this morning, where the body of a fifteen-year-old girl was discovered on an elementary-school playground. The victim has been identified as Lucinda Hayes, a ninth-grade student at Jefferson High School. The staff member who made the horrific find offered no comment. The investigation will continue under the direction of Lieutenant Timothy Gonzalez of the Broomsville Police Department. Civilians are encouraged to report any suspicious behavior."

Lucinda's eighth-grade yearbook photo smiled down from the corner of the television screen, her face flat and pixelated. The remote dropped from Cameron's hand to the coffee table—the back popped off, and three AAA batteries rolled noisily along the table and onto the carpet.

"Cameron?" Mom called from the kitchen.

He knew that park, the elementary school down the block. It was just behind their cul-de-sac, halfway between his house and Lucinda's.

Before Mom could reach him, Cameron was stumbling down the hall, opening his bedroom door. He couldn't be bothered to turn on the lights—he was ripping the sheets off his bed, he was pulling his sketchbook and charcoals and kneaded eraser from their hiding spot beneath his mattress.

He ripped out the sketchbook pages one by one and spread them in a circle around his bedroom floor. It took his eyes a moment to adjust to the dark of his room, but when they did, he was surrounded by Lucinda Hayes.

In most of the drawings, she was happy. In most of the drawings, it was sunny, and one side of her face was lighter than the other. The left, always the left. In most of the drawings, she was smiling wholly—not like in the yearbook photo, where the photographer caught her before she was herself.

Lucinda's face was easy to draw from memory. Her cheekbones were high and bright. The lines near Lucinda's mouth gave her the appearance of effortless happiness. Her lashes were thick and winged outward, so if Cameron skewed the shape of her eyes or set them too deep beneath her brow line, you could still tell it was Lucinda. In most of the drawings, her mouth was open in laughter; you could see the gap between her two front teeth. Cameron loved that gap. It unclothed her.

Cameron pressed his eyes to his kneecaps. He could not look at Lucinda like this because he had missed her most important parts: The way her legs flew out when she ran, from all those years of ballet. How her hair got frizzy at the front when she walked home from school in the heat. The way she sat at her kitchen table after school, listening to music on her shiny pink MP3 player, drumming white-painted fingernails against the marble. He always imagined she listened to oldies because he thought they fit her. *Little bitty pretty one.* Cameron had missed the way she squinted when she couldn't see the board in class, the creases at the corners of her eyes like plastic blinds she had opened to let in the sunlight.

He couldn't look at Lucinda like this because now she was dead, and all he had were the useless things—a smeared charcoal iris. A pinky finger drawn quickly, slightly too thin.

"Oh God, Cam," Mom whispered from the doorway. "Oh, God."

Mom stood with her hands on the doorframe, taking in his ring of drawings, looking like she might crumple. Her pink, striped sweater looked fake and sad, and Cameron wanted to melt her right into him so she wouldn't look so old. The way Mom's hands clung to the doorframe reminded Cameron of when he was a kid and Mom did ballet in the basement. She used the dirty windowsill as a barre and put her Mozart tapes in the cassette player. She whispered to herself. *And one and two and three and four. Jeté, jeté, pas de bourrée.* Cameron watched through the railing of the basement stairs. Her old back never straightened, and her old toes never pointed, and she looked like a bird with a body of broken bones. It made him sad to watch her dance because she looked so fragile and so expressive and so happy and so fragmented, all at once. Mom looked like herself when she danced; he had always thought so.

Cameron wanted to tell Mom that he was sorry for all of this. But he could not, because of the horrified way she was looking at his collection of Lucinda.

Cameron put his head back on his knees and kept it there until he was sure Mom had gone.

———

Things Cameron Could Not Think About:

1. The .22-caliber handgun in the lockbox underneath Mom's bed.

    Gandhi was assassinated with a Beretta M1934—three bullets to the chest. Lincoln took a bullet from a .44-caliber derringer. A .30-06 hunting rifle killed Martin Luther King Jr., and John Lennon was murdered with a .38-caliber pistol. The only famous person shot with a .22-caliber handgun was Ronald Reagan, who came out of the ordeal just fine. This made Cameron feel a bit better, like maybe if he or Mom were to use the pistol, the chances of actually killing someone were less than if Mom had, say, a 9-millimeter.

2. Dr. Duncan MacDougall.

    Dr. Duncan MacDougall claimed in 1907 that the human soul weighed twenty-one grams. Cameron had read this statistic a few years back, after Grandma Mary died. He calculated exactly where he was at the moment she passed: in the kitchen, washing crusty macaroni off a plate. There had been a functioning body on earth and now there was not—didn't it have to be subtracted somehow? But after Grandma Mary died, the earth weighed twenty-one grams less and Cameron had gone on washing. Nothing had felt lighter.

    Cameron tried to calculate exactly where he was last night, when Lucinda died on the playground. He couldn't fathom it—like when you tried to remember what you had for breakfast, and in the process of fishing for the truth you only pushed it deeper down, until you could have had pancakes or pizza or a five-course meal, but you'd thought about it so much you'd never know.

3. Hum.

Lucinda was probably there now, standing in front of the blue-painted door, wondering how any place could be so peaceful.

4. The strips of translucent hair on Lucinda's shins where she forgot to shave.

———

Before Mom picked Cameron up at school that afternoon, Ronnie and Cameron had walked together to history class. Ronnie wore what he'd had on since last Thursday: A pair of forest-green sweat pants and a plain white T-shirt with yellow armpits. An oversized black ski jacket, unzipped. His head stuck out the top like a cardboard box balanced on a #2-pencil neck.

"Dude," Ronnie said. "This is some seriously crazy shit."

Police officers milled around at the end of the hall. From this distance, they looked like ants.

Cameron had turned fifteen last month, but he wouldn't take driver's ed. He would never learn to drive. He didn't want to risk getting pulled over and having to look a police officer in the eye. *Hey*, the officer would say. *Aren't you Lee Whitley's son?*

It didn't help that they looked similar. Cameron and Dad were both wiry, with long arms that swung when they walked. They had the same light-brown hair. (Cameron grew it out, because Dad had a crew cut.) Pointy nose, pasty skin, hazel eyes. Narrow shoulders, which Cameron hid in various versions of the same baggy hoodie. Knees that bowed in a V shape, pointing naturally inward. Shy feet.

People used to say that Cameron and Dad had the same laugh, but Cameron didn't like to remember that.

Ronnie had talked all the way to class, and Cameron had ignored him. Ronnie Weinberg was Cameron's best friend—his only friend—because neither of them knew what to say or when to say it. Ronnie was obnoxious, while Cameron was quiet, and no one else spoke to either of them.

Beth DeCasio, Lucinda's best friend, had decided a long time ago that Ronnie smelled bad and Cameron was weird. People tended to believe Beth DeCasio. Beth once told Mr. O—Cameron's favorite teacher—that Cameron was the sort of kid who would bring a gun to school. Aside from dealing with the administrative mess that followed—the interviews with the school psychologist, the calls home to Mom, the staff meeting—Cameron had the same nightmare for four months straight. In the dream, he brought a gun to school and he shot everyone without meaning to. But that wasn't the worst part. In the dream, he had to live the rest of his life knowing those families were out there, missing their kids. Mom had lots of meetings with the school's counselors, and after, she'd come home vibrating and angry. *Unfounded and unprofessional*, she'd say. She'd make Cameron tea and assure him that he would never do such a thing, and besides, it was physically impossible to accidentally shoot a whole school of people.

Cameron still thought about it sometimes. Not in a way that made him want to shoot anyone—still, he felt like a toxin in the bloodstream.

Now, Beth DeCasio walked in front of Cameron, arms linked with Kaylee Walker and Ana Sanchez. She wore purple, Lucinda's favorite color. This made Cameron think of Lucinda's diary—the cover was purple suede, with a white elastic band holding it shut. The girls cried, their shoulders hunched, tissues bunched in their palms.

Usually, Lucinda left her house between 7:07 and 7:18 a.m. Sometimes, her dad would take the morning off from his law firm and they would go to breakfast at the Golden Egg, but this generally happened less than once a month, and Cameron always factored in the odds. It occurred to Cameron now, as Lucinda's friends cried in front of trophy cases, that this morning had been different, and he hadn't even known—Lucinda had not been walking down the street, behind or in front of him. She had not brushed her teeth over the bathroom sink, she had not eaten a croissant or yelled at her mom, she had not wrestled her arms into her yellow down coat.

Cameron felt genuinely sorry for Beth, Kaylee, and Ana, though he didn't think anyone had a right to be sadder than anyone else. A girl was dead, a beautiful girl, and there was tragedy in that. And anyway, some types of love were quieter than others.

"I bet it was some kinky shit that killed her," Ronnie said as they took their seats in history class. "Like, strangulation or something. Everyone's talking about her ex-boyfriend, that soccer player—Zap. Douchebag looks like he's into the nasty shit." He made a choking motion.

Ms. Evans flicked on a movie about the Hundred Years' War and shut the lights.

Cameron was afraid of the dark. It came down to thinking and unthinking. Once he imagined the possibilities that accompanied absolute darkness, he would convince and unconvince himself of all sorts of horrors: A stroke in his sleep, and the subsequent paralysis. Sleepwalking to the drawer of steak knives in the kitchen. All the awful things your own body could do to itself. He'd twist in circles around his miserable brain until he exhausted himself and fell asleep or lifted the screen off his bedroom window and ran. Neither option helped much.

"Excuse me," said a gruff voice from the doorway. The smell—Dad had smelled just like that. Tobacco, coffee, rusty chains. "May we speak with one of your students?"

"Of course," Ms. Evans said.

"Cameron Whitley?" The police officer was silhouetted in the crack of fluorescent light that streamed in from the hall. "You'll need to come with us."

Jade

I have a theory: faking shock is easier than faking sadness. Shock is a more basic emotion than sadness—it's just an inflated version of surprise.

"The details have been released," the vice-principal says. He claps his hands together, all business. "The victim was a student here at Jefferson High, Lucinda Hayes. The ninth-grade class is currently in the auditorium, where Principal Barnes is delivering the news. There will be a memorial service on Friday. Counseling will be available in the front office. We encourage you all to stay alert."

He strides out of the classroom, a swish of khakis.

I pinch the bridge of my nose. I look stupid, but so does everyone else. Half the class looks genuinely sad—embarrassingly sad—and the other half bounces with the sort of glee you only find during a drama like this.

I imagine how the shock must look on Zap, but I don't dare turn around.

Zap has this way of sitting. He leans back in chairs, spreads his knees wide, lets his limbs do what they want. It's not arrogant or lazy. It's intentional. Comfortable. Zap leans back and lets his body occupy that space, as if he commanded the chair to assemble beneath him and it listened.

Today, Zap sits at the broken leftie desk by the window, three rows back. He wears a red sweat shirt and corduroy pants with holes in the knees. They're too short at the ankles because Zap grew five inches last winter. His glasses are still fogged up from walking across Willow Square in the biting February cold.

These are things I know without looking.

The rest is up to my imagination—how the shock of Lucinda Hayes sits carefully on him. All wrong at first, loose on his frame. But it will sink in. The shock will move from Zap's shoulders to his neck, to the birthmark on his second left rib. From there it will spread to all the places I can't see.

Shock is just sadness that hasn't reached the gut.

———

Of course, I already know that Lucinda Hayes is dead.

I find out before school this morning, over a naked Toaster Strudel. Ma throws away the frosting packets so we won't get fat, leaving our strudels an unassuming brown, bare oven tracks running across their backs.

"Sit down, girls," Ma says. She taps ash from her cigarette into the kitchen sink. A hiss. In the morning, the wrinkles on Ma's face are canyons.

Amy totters to the kitchen table and swings her gigantic purse onto my chair. Amy recently decided backpacks were immature for a seventh-grader, so she carries a brown faux-leather purse instead. Her math textbook is so heavy she walks with a limp.

"It's about Lucinda," Ma says. "I'm so sorry, sweetheart. She's—she's passed away." Ma sighs in her pitying way (usually reserved for the post-office attendant and the boy in Amy's class with recurrent cancer).

Amy's bottom lip quakes. Then a shrill, gravelly cry. She stands dramatically and backs into the sliding door, spreading her pink-painted fingernails against the glass and suctioning them there like starfish.

Ma puts out her cigarette on a pizza-stained paper plate and crouches in her sweat pants next to Amy, who slides to the floor. Ma strokes her hair, unknotting the tangles inconspicuously.

"I'm so sorry, honey. They'll make an announcement at school today."

Ma is sorry for Amy. She is not sorry for me. I've never cried like that, so frantic and choked. I'm not trying to be brave or stoic or anything. I've just never liked anyone enough. Ma knows this. She glares at me, Amy's head still in the crook of her elbow. A runny line of snot drips from Amy's nose onto Ma's freckled arm.

"Jesus, Jade," she says, shifting her gaze to my stomach, which pudges out from the bottom of my Crucibles T-shirt, bare under my unzipped army parka. "Go put on a real shirt. You're taking your sister to school today."

I lean over the kitchen counter, resting my elbows on an outdated phone book.

Emotions shouldn't have names. I don't know why we bother talking about them, because emotions are never what they're supposed to be. You could say I feel ecstatic, or guilty, or disgusted with myself. You could say all of the above. Amy sobs, but I identify only this foreign lightness: like someone has sucked the weight from my legs, taken the terrible thoughts out of my head, softened some sharpness jabbing at my ribs. I don't know.

It's so calm.

———————

"Are you even human?" Amy asks.

Madison Middle School is a rectangle in the distance.

"Alien," I say. "Surprise."

"You're not even sad."

"Yes, I am."

"You're not. Ma says you have serious issues with 'empathy' and 'self-control' and 'sad tendencies.'"

"The word is 'sadistic,'" I tell her.

"Lucinda is dead," she says, "and you don't even care."

Amy hitches up her purse and her leopard-print coat spreads open in the front. Amy wears a 32AA bra, and no matter how she is feeling, Amy is always quite cute. It's the product of a fortunate combination: Amy's red hair and the millions of freckles that dot her cheeks like grains of sand.

"It's pretty fucked up, Jade," she says. She pauses before the word "fucked" to consider. "We've known her our whole lives, and now she's dead, and you're not even pretending to be sad."

I pump the tip of my tongue through the silver loop in my lip. I do this when I want someone to stop talking. It always works.

Amy stomps ahead, hugging herself close, shoulders bobbing as she stifles more sobs. Always the drama queen. She's never been close with Lucinda, only Lucinda's little sister, Lex. When we were young, Ma subjected us to weekly playdates—Lex and Amy would spend hours playing princesses in the Hayeses' basement, while Lucinda and I were forced to sit there awkwardly until Ma came to pick us up. Lucinda would braid friendship bracelets, and I would read comic books, and we'd pointedly ignore each other while our sisters played make-believe. Lex and Amy used to be inseparable, but now they only hang out when Ma arranges it.

I wonder how Amy would feel if I died. Maybe she'd sleep in my bed some nights. Maybe she'd make a blanket out of my old T-shirts, which she'd keep in a box to show her children once they turned sixteen. Maybe she'd feel relieved. I'm suddenly aware of the ten feet of space between us, the four sections of sidewalk that separate Amy and me. I almost run to catch up with her. But just as unexpectedly as it comes, the desire passes again, leaving a faint, pulsing hatred somewhere I can't touch.

WHAT YOU WANT TO SAY BUT CAN'T WITHOUT BEING A DICK
A Screenplay by Jade Dixon-Burns

EXT. PINE RIDGE DRIVE—BROOMSVILLE, COLORADO—EARLY MORNING

CELLY (17, slouched, dyed black hair), and SISTER (13, her opposite), walk to school. Celly hums a bouncy, upbeat song.

                       SISTER
Are you even human?

                       CELLY
Alien, surprise.

                       SISTER
You're not even sad.

                       CELLY
No, I'm not.

                       SISTER
That's fucked up.

                       CELLY
How can you claim to be sad? You barely even knew her.

                       SISTER
Who cares how well I knew her? It's not a popularity contest.

                              CELLY

        Everything is a popularity contest. This

        sadness you're referring to. I know how it

        looks. You'll go to school today and you'll

        accept knowing hugs from all your pretty

        little friends. You'll tell them how Lucinda

        let you borrow her nail polish once, five

        years ago.

Sister walks faster, away from Celly.

                           CELLY (CONT'D)

        No one will call bullshit on you. All your

        pretty little friends will cluster around,

        trying to get closer to the wound.

Sister turns a sharp corner, nearly running now. Celly calls
out after her.

                           CELLY (CONT'D)
                             (louder)

        You'll smile in spite of yourself. The

        teachers will let you skip your assignments.

        Tell me it's not a popularity contest. Tell

        me, Sister. Go ahead.

Sister practically sprints up the school's front steps. Celly
stops walking and watches her sister disappear into the
building.

                           CELLY (CONT'D)
                             (sotto)

        Tell me about my sadness.

———

Zap used to have a constellation map taped to his ceiling. I would lie on his bed and stare at all the black space between pinpoint stars, thinking how half an inch on the poster was a million miles in reality. I would imagine floating through space on a continual supply of fake oxygen. That way, you could forget that back on earth there's this stunted, superficial way of existence. I think about this as I try to tune out the girls by the mirror—about how living would feel without air, and how that non-air would feel without people. Quiet.

"I heard Zap went home. Didn't say anything, just walked right out after first period."

"He must be so devastated."

I flush the toilet to let the girls know I'm there. It doesn't make a difference. They carry on, their voices like roosters crowing, waking me from a zombie sleep. I focus on the frayed laces of my fat black shoes until the door swings open—a sliver of chatter slips into the bathroom from the crowded hall outside. The door shuts. Cavernous silence.

Zap loved that poster. His favorite constellation was Libra, because it looked like a kite, which reminded him of when he was little and he lived in Paris. He remembered the Seine, he said—he had this red-and-blue-checkered kite he flew down by the riverbank on summer days. He gave me a seashell years ago, from a beach on the French Riviera where he'd gone on vacation. *One day, we'll get out of here*, he told me. *It's a big world out there; you'll see.* The shell is a rippled beige, shaped like an ear. I used to keep it under my pillow.

His name isn't really Zap, of course. It's Edouard, pronounced with the emphasis on the second half. His parents are French—they both moved to America at eighteen. They met in the French Undergraduate Society at Yale and they've been in love ever since—real love. Mr. Arnaud buys Mrs. Arnaud flowers on his way home from work, and sometimes they hold hands in public. His mom is like a woodland creature, slight and green-eyed.

No one can pronounce "Edouard"—he's gone by "Zap" since the fourth grade, because one day he came to school dressed in a gigantic lightning-bolt costume he'd made from a cardboard refrigerator box. It was the week after the flash flood of '98, which killed three people in Longmont, the next town over. He painted the lightning bolt yellow and harnessed it on with a pair of suspenders. All day he went around saying *zap, zap, zap,* passing out fun-sized candy bars. He was a force of nature, he said, but the kind that brought joy instead of harm. I thought this was so great. Everyone did. After school, he and I went to the field behind my house and watched the clouds roll toward the mountains in surrender.

That summer, Mrs. Arnaud brought hot chocolate in thermoses and Mr. Arnaud carried the camping gear—we set up sleeping bags in the middle of the field to watch meteor showers. Scratchy grass poked through nylon. It was too cloudy to see any meteors, but we didn't care. The sleeping bags smelled like the Arnauds' house: Laundry detergent. Christmas candles. We laid on our backs, and Zap recited all these useless facts about outer space, like did you know you can see only fifty-nine percent of the moon's surface from our shit spot down on earth?

Thinking about Zap makes me sick. I bend over the toilet and make a series of violent gagging noises. They sound forced. Someone opens the bathroom door, hears me, and leaves again. Nothing comes up.

At the sink, I debate splashing water on my face, but I'm wearing too much makeup. The black around my eyes will smudge—it will look like I've been crying, and I can't cry today. My eyeliner is extra dense, just the way Ma hates it.

Usually, I avoid mirrors. But today I'm hoping that the sight of my own body will help me place myself in the newly shifted universe. My arms are still doughy. My skin is still sickly white. Pustules burst from every surface, despite Ma's prescription medication and my monthly trips to the dermatologist. *Stop picking,* Ma always says, but I like the way my skin peels. I like exposing the red, glistening part underneath.

Russ

Why did you become a cop?

It happened when Russ was a child, he says. An incredible act of violence. He refuses the details. People nod sympathetically, but Russ takes no satisfaction in that head shake—awe, respect, the necessary driblet of pity.

In truth, Russ became a cop because he couldn't afford college and he had been told about the benefits of carrying a gun.

———

Russ gets the call at 5:41 a.m.

Hello? he says.

His teeth are fuzzy with sleep's film.

Russ, the lieutenant says, crackly in the speaker, we've got a body.

———

Russ picks yesterday's boxer shorts off the floor. Wriggles them on. Usually, he would roll over Ines on the way to the bathroom—he allows himself three seconds of that familiar warmth, hot salt skin beneath her ratty cotton nightshirt. Ines always sleeps through this, so Russ takes some time to hate himself in the shower as he lathers his body with dollar soap.

Today, Russ rolls out of bed on his own side.

We've got a body. Russ has never heard these words before. Well—in cop shows. Thriller movies. And of course, he heard these words in his head all through recruitment, through his time at the department's local academy, and all through training for the Broomsville police force. Back when his job still glimmered with potential, before he knew he'd be spending ninety percent of it watching cars whiz past at five over the speed limit.

By 5:54, Russ is in his squad car, radio stuttering. It's still night. His hands are numb and the steering wheel is icy leather.

Russ runs his tongue over his teeth. Regrets it. Plaque: his mother used to say it like a swearword, the corners of her lips turned down in disgust. He has forgotten to brush.

———

6:03 a.m., and Russ is the last to arrive.

The body is at the elementary school. All five patrol cars are parked in the middle of the street like they've been washed from the curb in an apocalyptic flood; fire truck and ambulance flash red across the intersection. Russ parks on the corner and his tires squeak, packing down snow. A layer of new slush mars the concrete.

Fletcher, someone says when Russ approaches. It took Russ months to adjust to this form of address. Fletcher was his father. Even after a year on the force, it didn't register in his memory. Fletcher! someone would call, and Russ would keep typing case reports like no one needed him.

Now, the team is clustered around the playground carousel. They rub their eyes, bleary from the early-morning call: Sergeant Capelli, Lieutenant Gonzalez, Detective Williams, and all five patrol officers. They stand in a tight circle at the center of the black morning, backlit by a film of gray at the horizon where the sun will eventually rise.

Detective Williams ushers Russ forward, hands shoved in his pockets, asking what took him so long, he's got to see this—it's pretty bad, they found her like that, go take a look.

The body belongs to a young girl. Fifteen, maybe sixteen years old. She is covered in a thin membrane of fresh snow, and her skin is jaundiced in the glow of CSI's spotlight. Blood and snow have frozen together on one side of her head (blond, the few untouched pieces of hair by her scalp). Her neck is broken, twisted to the side at a decrepit angle. The girl's eyes are closed—postmortem, Russ thinks, because the snow has been wiped from her forehead with clumsy hands. She wears a purple skirt and black, sparkly tights, flecks of glitter dotting the nylon.

Later, Russ will see photos of this girl, alive, and she will look like teenagers he used to know. Like the girls he and his school friends thought about when they jerked off in the early afternoon, listening anxiously for the grumble of the garage door. Child hips.

Lucinda Hayes, someone says from behind.

It's Detective Williams. He puts a hairy hand on Russ's shoulder and continues: The family reported her missing late last night. Heard something in the yard, parents checked, she wasn't in her bed. The body matches the description. We'll need you and the boys to stay here, secure the scene after Medical is done. Then take a walk around the neighborhood. Knock on some doors, ask around.

This your first body?

Russ doesn't answer. He looks down at the dead girl again. She does not seem at peace. He thinks of Ines and how she sleeps, all those shifting positions; Ines has seven, maybe eight sleeping forms she cycles through each night, indecisive about what will bring her comfort. Nothing, it seems.

The body—Lucinda Hayes—reminds Russ of his wife. She does not know how to position herself. Legs jut at an angle. She looks dissatisfied.

————

Russ was barely twenty-one when he started his job. He'd spent the three years since high school on his parents' couch, doing crunches on the carpet and waiting to be older. He attended the occasional criminal-justice class at the community college, and after dinner, his father drank scotch and told Russ about his own time in training. The sergeant pulled out the shadow box, with his old badge and his old gun, and he talked himself ruddy. When Russ's father retired, the department had rolled out the infamous meat-and-cheese platter, an inexpensive champagne toast.

When it finally came time, Russ passed all his tests at a mediocre level: civil service, written exam, oral board, psych evaluation, fitness test. Then, training, where he spent twenty weeks shadowing an older, more experienced patrol officer.

His assignment was Lee Whitley—the pale, bony officer the rest of the patrol guys whispered about, the weakest member of the Broomsville Police Department. A man who'd been given four whole years to prove himself entirely unremarkable.

————

Russ doesn't allow the memories very often. But in these rare moments of reminiscence, Russ wonders if he always knew—somewhere locked and hidden away—what would come of Lee Whitley.

They met outside the lieutenant's office on Russ's first day of training. A dreary afternoon, seventeen years ago—1988. Hair was bigger and cigarettes weren't so bad, and they all wore faded denim with white, foamy sneakers.

Lee was the skinniest thing. His gaze flitted down and to the left when he spoke. Bulky nose, turned-in feet. Hazel eyes with pinprick pupils. His concave chest made a hollow sound when you slapped it in jest.

Okay, Russ said, and that was all he could manage.

Okay, Lee said back.

Russ thumped him on the back in that jovial young-man way. Lee coughed. A crooked, impish smile. Lee crushed a paper cup in his hands, and dregs of instant coffee ran down his elbow. Russ liked him then, this scrawny pup trying to look big as coffee made its sluggish descent down his forearm.

And so it began: this brilliant, unlikely pair. Both too aware that this partnership, just minutes in, had already begun to expand into some slippery shape, water on a hardwood floor, an ever-changing mass that neither could contain.

———

Who found her? Russ asks one of the other patrol officers.

The night janitor, the officer says, then uses his middle finger to point. Russ follows the arc of knuckle, though he already knows whom he will see.

Sure enough. The night janitor.

Ivan stands with one hand in the pocket of his janitor's uniform. A cigarette dangles from the other. When Ivan puffs those massive lungs his breath is doubled and thick—nicotine, carbon dioxide. The glow of Ivan's cigarette is a lively orange, flickering against a sea of black police jackets. Dismal gray snow. Russ is not surprised by Ivan's presence on the playground. Ivan works the night shift at the elementary school—Ines asked Russ to pull some strings; Ivan was having such a hard time. So he did.

Russ loves his wife very much. Quiet Ines. But Russ does not love her brother. In fact, Russ wishes, deeply and acutely, that Ivan did not exist.

Alone with the body now, Russ lifts his radio to his lips and speaks.

The microphone is off. You there? Russ mumbles to the plastic, keeping his gaze on the girl's hair, all blood and straw. Can you hear me? Russ presses the radio to his chapped lips but he can think of nothing else to say. Ivan smiles, cheshire and mischievous, a hulking mass of testosterone, the amber-glowing cigarette dangling like a dare.

Cameron

"Y ou're the dead girl's stalker, aren't you?"

The girl in the scratchy armchair outside Principal Barnes's office was speaking to Cameron.

"Excuse me?"

"You're the freshman they're all talking about. The kid who stalked the dead girl. Right?"

Her head rested against the wall behind her chair, bored and effortless. Cameron had noticed her before. She lived in the neighborhood and she was always alone. Her jeans had chains hanging from the pockets. Her eyes were ringed in black; raven, greasy hair swooped over one eye, and she wore a T-shirt that sported the name of a band Cameron didn't know. The T-shirt was cut sloppily above her midriff, and two inches of pale stomach rolled over her waistband even though it was winter and she was probably cold. A spattering of acne spread across her chin and forehead.

The girl raised one slanted eyebrow at Cameron. He wanted to raise one back, but every time he tried, the other went up automatically, and he didn't want to look stupid.

"It's okay," she said. "I was just wondering. I don't care either way."

"Oh," Cameron said.

"The dead girl and I babysat the same kid."

"Lucinda."

"Whatever. It's illegal, what they're doing. They can't interview minors without the consent and presence of a parent. They think because there are no officers in the room they can frame it as grief counseling, but that's bullshit, if you ask me. They still had police officers walk us down the hall. Scare tactics, I think."

She nodded, satisfied with her own rebellion. Her eyes were perfectly round. Cameron loved Lucinda's slanting eyes, and these were their opposite: marbles, circular and glassy.

"I'm Jade," she said. "Like the rock. I'm a junior."

"That's a nice name."

"I got off easy." She shrugged. "My sister's name is Amethyst. And you're Cameron Whitley. Freshman. You live down the block from Lucinda. They're all very worried about your mental health, because your dad is the police officer who—"

"Please," Cameron said. "Don't."

"Didn't that happen, like, a long time ago?"

Cameron wished he were better at carrying on a conversation. He generally disliked talking to people because he never knew what to say. Even with the simplest questions, he was overwhelmed by the number of potential answers—which would sound best, or which was appropriate, or which would make the other person feel least awkward.

He could ask Jade why she dressed like that. He could ask what she thought about first thing in the morning—or why her parents had named her Jade, because it was unique and he liked it and he wanted interesting names for his kids someday, too. He could ask Jade what her favorite school subject was, but that seemed dumb and cliché. He could ask if she'd ever been in love, but he had enough sense to know that was too personal.

"Did that hurt?" Cameron finally said, because Jade was glaring at him, harsh, expectant. He pointed to the thin silver ring that wound around her lower lip.

"Yeah, it hurt a little."

"Oh."

"Want to see my tattoo?"

"Sure."

Jade held out her left wrist. The outline of a dragon had been etched in black, its wings unfurled across white skin. The ink rippled and danced where it spread over blue veins.

"Is it real?" Cameron asked.

"Usually, I would say yes. I tell most people it is. But you keep looking at me with that intense face, so, no, it's not real. I draw it on every morning."

Cameron couldn't figure out if this was the nicest or meanest thing someone had ever said to him.

"So," she said. "Did you actually stalk the dead girl?"

"Lucinda."

"Oh, I super don't care."

Cameron hated the word "stalk." He had other words for his relationship with Lucinda, but they were words no one else would understand. Words like *vibrant, frantic, twinkling, aching*—

The door to Principal Barnes's office opened and a woman with hair pinned tight against her head stepped out.

"Jade?" she said. "We're ready for you."

Jade rolled her eyes at Cameron like they were sharing some joke. As she stood up, Cameron caught a whiff of grape shampoo, and it occurred to him that he should have rolled his eyes in response, but Jade had already started to walk away. He didn't expect her to look back.

———

Cameron had started playing Statue Nights when he was twelve years old. The summer after sixth grade, he realized he could pop out the screen in his bedroom window. The jump to the planter below was doable, if he bent his knees at the right moment.

The game of Statue Nights began with the Hansens, next door. Cameron would stand on the curb outside their house for hours, watching them eat microwaved food and argue. Mrs. Hansen would put her hair in curlers like a woman in a 1950s sitcom, and Mr. Hansen would walk around in his boxers, skin sagging and drooping in a way Michelangelo would have appreciated. You could see Mr. Hansen's bones. They left all the lights on; it was impossible to avoid looking. The human eye was naturally attracted to light—a fact Cameron had read about the retina in *The Map of Human Anatomy*.

That first summer, Cameron made his way slowly down Pine Ridge Drive. If he stood perfectly still, he wouldn't be seen. Cameron documented the tiny things: Mrs. Hansen kept Mr. Hansen on a strict diet, but he stored chocolate bars in the Crock-Pot next to the refrigerator.

Next door to the Hansens, Cameron once watched the Thorntons have sex on their kitchen table after the baby fell asleep. It looked violent and out of control at first, like fighting dogs thrashing around, then close and rhythmic—a rocking boat. After, Mr. Thornton hovered on top of his wife, kissed her forehead slow. Some nights the wife stayed up late, bouncing their crying baby around the living room while her husband took the limping little dog for ten o'clock walks, ushering Cameron home with his stranger presence on the street.

As he waited to be questioned, Cameron pulled his favorite kneaded eraser from his pocket and molded it into different shapes. Mr. O had given it to him for when he needed to Untangle, which was often. He tried to mold it into a perfect square against the surface of his thigh.

Cameron had started watching Lucinda around the same time Mr. O's class started a unit on figure drawing. He started seeing mountains in people's cheekbones and spider legs in people's eyelashes and translating these into different shades of black, white, and gray. He loved the way Lucinda's face curled and rolled.

When Cameron watched Lucinda, he played this game of Statue

Nights. He liked to imagine that he was one of Michelangelo's figures, frozen on paper, etched in one position for all of eternity. But at some point he'd hear his own heartbeat or an inevitable exhale. One of these certainties would break the silence, and he'd be forced to recognize that no matter how still he stood, he did, in fact, exist.

He never knew how much time passed, but the whole point of Statue Nights was that it didn't matter.

On February 11, 2004, almost exactly a year ago, Lucinda's father opened the sliding back door. *I know you're there*, his voice boomed across the empty lawn. *I know you don't mean harm. But you need to leave. If you come back, I will call the police.* Cameron had run home, to the other end of Pine Ridge Drive, and huddled underneath his covers with Dad's tattered copy of *The Map of Human Anatomy.* He memorized the functions of the human kidney, because he imagined that somewhere near the kidney was where the body stored that hollowed feeling: guilt.

He hoped the police wouldn't ask about that night in Lucinda's yard. Cameron was awful at lying, and he couldn't tell them the truth—that he found people fascinating when they thought no one was watching. He couldn't tell them about the sincerity of life through windows—that he hated himself for it, but he couldn't stop. He didn't want to.

—————

There was this feeling Broomsville gave you, with all its short, pastel buildings and open spaces. It was voted number five on CNN's *Top Ten Friendliest Places to Raise a Family*, and no one was surprised. Broomsville was an overgrown cul-de-sac of square lawns, browned from the Colorado droughts. It was not the sort of place for white picket fences, but Broomsville had good public schools, with after-school programs you could join if you didn't have money. The average family lived in a beige house just like Cameron's, with two floors and three bedrooms and windows that faced the Front Range of the Rocky Mountains. People drove mountain cars, pickup trucks or Outbacks or Trailblazers, with bumper stickers that yelled, "BUSH CHENEY '04!"

And above, the mountains. Always watching.

Colorado air was so crisp, it stung your nostrils. Once, Mom's friend from college visited from Florida, and on the first day she passed out from altitude sickness. They called an ambulance and everything. The EMTs stuck plastic tubes in her nose to help her breathe. They took off her shirt and her bra to better reach her lungs, and her naked breasts flopped to the sides on the living-room floor. Cameron tried not to stare.

After a day or two she was fine, and they went on short hikes in the foothills—the small, rolling mountains that formed the base of the Rockies. Colorado had this specific smell in summer, like pine needles recovering from a miserable winter and hot, red dirt sliding down steep mountainsides.

You could see Pine Ridge Point from the Tree, and that was partially why Cameron had picked that specific aspen. You could lean against the smooth white bark and look up at the hill that enclosed Pine Ridge Point, where Dad first took him when he was six years old.

The sun was setting. There were plenty of natural phenomena that went unrecognized (snowflakes kissing a windowsill, fingernails dug into the skin of a tangerine), but Cameron could see why people made such a big deal of sunsets. The sunset at Pine Ridge Point always made Cameron feel so disastrously human, caged inside his own susceptible self.

Pine Ridge Point was a cliff suspended over a reservoir at a perfect ninety-degree angle. The reservoir had no waves. It waited, still and complacent, a pool of blood spreading away from a wound.

On the other side of the cliff—the side that didn't face the water—sat the town of Broomsville, all quaint boxy houses and lawns with clicking sprinklers, starkly different from the chaos of the Rockies. You could see Cameron's street, a minuscule Pine Ridge Drive, and everything else converging to this plateau. From the horizon of Pine Ridge Point, Broomsville looked like a cardboard town filled with paper people. Cameron's hands could rearrange it however he pleased.

He often daydreamed about bringing Lucinda to Pine Ridge Point. *Look*, he'd say. *Don't you see how weightless we are?*

———

"Hello, Cameron."

The social worker's hair was slicked back into a wet bun. Her eyes were tunnels. Her smile was hard.

"Hi."

"My name is Janine. Do you remember me?" She sat with a notebook in her lap, legs crossed, jiggling one of her clogs.

"Yeah."

"This is a voluntary school-conducted interview, okay? We're just checking in with our kids. You're free to leave at any time. You're free to abstain from answering anything that makes you uncomfortable. Do you understand and consent to continue?"

Once, when Cameron was flipping through a cookbook in the kitchen, he found a poem tucked inside. Lord Byron. Mom did this sometimes—put fragments of poems in unexpected places. Cameron took the Byron poem to his bedroom and taped it to the inside of his closet door. Mom had transcribed it onto notebook paper in her scratchy handwriting, with a pen that exploded in bursts of ink.

"Yes."

"Okay. Cameron, why don't you tell me about your relationship with Lucinda Hayes?"

(She walks in beauty, like the night
Of cloudless climes and starry skies;)

"Cameron?"

(And all that's best of dark and bright
Meet in her aspect and her eyes)

"That's all right. Let's start with an easier question," Janine said. "Where were you last night, February fifteenth?"

"At home," Cameron said.

"Was anyone with you?"

"My mom was there."

In truth, Cameron couldn't remember February fifteenth. Last night. *At home; my mom was there* seemed like a simple and believable answer. He had somehow lost this night—it had slipped casually into all the Statue Nights in his Collection. It scared him to lose time like this, though he was no stranger to the concept. If Cameron could get every moment of his life tattooed on his body, he would, just to prove they had all happened.

"Cameron." Janine paused, so stern in her turtleneck. He wished she would stop saying his name like that. She leaned across Principal Barnes's desk, breathing coffee too close to Cameron's face. "How would you describe your relationship with Lucinda Hayes?"

(One shade the more, one ray the less,
had half impaired the nameless grace)

Cameron often worried the beating of his heart would overpower the small space it occupied. Mom used to say his heart was too big for his chest—she meant it as a compliment, but Cameron started to imagine his heart swelled so big it clogged up his airways. He could feel it now, growing and shrinking, growing and shrinking. He was sure this would kill him one day.

"Cameron?"

He wanted to tell them how Lucinda looked in the morning. How the sun hit her face, how sleep congealed in the inner corners of her eyes, how long blond hair stuck, matted, to the back of her head. Her tan legs in their plaid cotton pajama pants as they slid out from beneath the purple comforter. He wanted to tell them how the pillow left crease marks on the side of her face, rivers on a map of an empty state.

(Which waves in every raven tress,
Or softly lightens o'er her face;)

"He's not responsive," Janine said to Principal Barnes. "We're going to need to talk to a parent. We can bring him in for voluntary questioning if they'll agree to it."

It dawned on Cameron, in an unexpected moment of devastation, why they had pulled him out of class and why they were asking these questions: they thought he had killed Lucinda Hayes.

It all happened very fast.

Cameron was standing up, knocking over the plastic chair with the backs of his knees; he was opening the door; he could have been crying, he wasn't sure, but his cheeks were hot, his skin was burning; he was Tangled, he was so Tangled.

A manila folder sat on the receptionist's desk outside Principal Barnes's office. Police officers stood in a semicircle a few feet away, talking in gruff voices. Cameron knew what the folder contained—Dad had been a police officer, after all. Cameron had seen plenty of folders just like this one. Dad used to pore over them in the den, drinking whiskey from a coffee mug, his back hunched, blinking fast with reddened eyes.

Lucinda Hayes was in the folder.

"No," Principal Barnes said from directly behind Cameron. "Don't—"

She was sprawled in terrible angles on the carousel at the elementary-school playground. Someone had hurt her, someone had really hurt her, because her head was turned to the side and her profile against the snowy red metal was mangled, twisted. One arm was tucked beneath her chest and the other was thrown over the edge of the carousel. She wore her favorite skirt, the purple one from school-picture day. Sparkly tights. And the blood—it dripped down from one side of her skull, smearing pulpy into clean snow.

This was not Lucinda—instead, some smashed and violated version of her, some sick thing he didn't recognize, a photo from his own childhood he couldn't remember taking.

Everything throbbed. Cameron was collapsing; he was converging. He did not dare to look away, though he was sure he would see nothing else for a long, long time. He could feel his heart shrinking and growing, shrinking and growing. This version of Lucinda was not aching or twinkling—he didn't understand how someone had taken this from her.

(Where thoughts serenely sweet express,
How pure, how dear their dwelling-place.)

———

One night, almost a year ago, Lucinda stood in front of her full-length mirror.

She wore only a bra and blue jeans. The bra was white, with a small pink bow sewn between triangle cups. Lucinda shifted her weight from her right hip to her left and back again. She tightened her bra straps as far as they would go, pushing her breasts together with her palms so they'd look fuller. It didn't make any difference. Cameron loved her back, naked to the window—her shoulder blades, flat and smooth. Those lungs. Humans have thirty-three vertebrae, but he counted only six on Lucinda, a range of rolling foothills, exposed and fleeting.

These were Cameron's favorite memories, and he stored them in a mental folder, special for thinking about late at night. His Collection of Statue Nights—on the lawn, looking in, stunned by the pure complexity of her form.

Lucinda had a birthmark on her right hipbone. It was the shape of a swan and the color of a red pepper gone bad left on the counter too long.

Jade

My favorite song is called "Death by Escalator." It's about a girl who falls on an escalator and hits her head on the bottom stair—her head smashes against ridged metal with every new stair that pops up.

If I sit at the right angle beneath the deformed tree in the Jefferson High courtyard, no one can see me. Today, the snow melts halfheartedly in patches, so I sit on a plastic lunch tray. Danny Hartfeld is the only other person outside. He reads *The Hobbit* with gloved hands. Danny Hartfeld and I end up in the same places sometimes, but he hates me, and that's fine.

I pull out the bologna sandwich Ma packed and turn up the volume in my headphones. I've long been obsessed with the Crucibles' first album, from 1986. It's smash punk, not quite screamo. But today, "Death by Escalator" makes me think of Lucinda's tan little body draped over the edge of the carousel. How I imagine it: her shiny nails drag in the dirt, blood is matted in her hair, her lips are frosty blue—

I yank the headphones out. I try to breathe normally, but I can't remember how normal feels. A bouncy blond girl from the freshman student council approaches Danny Hartfeld with a piece of paper. He nods. Signs.

She starts toward me. With the headphones away from my ears, "Death by Escalator" is just static noise. The bass, the drums, all of it: gone. Lost in this distant, screaming buzz.

"Hi," the girl says to me, enthusiastic. She holds out a manila envelope and a neon-purple Sharpie. "We're sending a card to the family of Lucinda Hayes. Sign to show your support?"

"No thanks," I say.

"Are you sure?" she says. "Just your name?"

"No thanks," I say. I glare until she turns away.

I've only seen photos of New York City at sunset. Waning honey light paints the buildings, a golden wash. Skyscraper lights flicker on one by one—pinprick samples of every sort of life possible beyond this one.

———

It's Lucinda Hayes's fault that I have two jobs: babysitting for the Thorntons and housekeeping at the Hilton Ranch.

People leave traces of themselves in hotel rooms. Crumpled tissues, ear-plugs covered in sticky wax, the occasional condom. Last month, I found a digital camera. Last week, a love letter.

Querida, querida,

You are an ocean, and I dream only of salt. When I wake, you are sand in the cracks between my teeth.

—Madly

They come in every Tuesday. Madly comes at six thirty, Querida follows at seven. I think they're in their late twenties, but who knows. Ma says love takes years off a woman's skin.

Every Tuesday, they check into a room—Aunt Nellie gives Madly a swipe key, smacking her gum and smiling conspiratorially. He waits in the fake-leather armchair by the window until Querida shows up, her battered purse slung over one shoulder. Querida is pretty in the way of a woman who does not try to be pretty. She wears no makeup; some lumpy knitted hat, and her T-shirts are too tight (but this seems like an accident). It's how she smiles—shy at first, as she compulsively twists a lock of long black hair. You can practically see her heart jumping out of her chest.

They walk to the elevator, shy. Madly lifts her chin carefully, with one finger, and Querida blushes scarlet. They talk at a safe distance—like they're afraid they'll burst into flame.

The night Lucinda died, Aunt Nellie and I shook our heads from the reception desk until the elevator doors dinged shut. Aunt Nellie turned to me, like she had suddenly remembered I was there.

"Jade, are we paying you to stand here and gossip?"

It wasn't gossip because we hadn't said anything, but I gathered my cleaning cart anyway. I'd spent the previous two hours constructing a pyramid out of toilet-paper rolls, and now I had to be careful crossing doorframes. The pyramid was wavering, precarious. I trundled the cart past the housekeeping supply closet and into the staff elevator, where I caught a glimpse of myself in the mirrored doors as they closed.

I was the furthest thing from a woman in love. Drowning in the folds of my maintenance polo, bleach-stained apron pulled too tight across my waist. My hair wrestled its way out of a ponytail, and makeup pooled beneath my eyes.

Every Tuesday, I push my cart into the room that shares a wall with Querida and Madly's and I hold my breath until I go half blind. I never hear a thing. I can only imagine how they sound, all gasping whispers, the careful hush of skin on skin. The night Lucinda died, I stood in a room that had already been cleaned and wondered how it would feel to be touched like that. Eager and desperate.

Ma's shrink says I suffer from a debilitating lack of direction. Most of the time, this doesn't feel as bad as it sounds. But sometimes, I'll wake in the middle of the night, terrified for no reason. Once, I dreamed of *The Birth of*

Venus and I woke up crying because of her marble skin. The hillside curve of her. I took a sip of water from a plastic cup, even though it had been sitting on my nightstand for days.

Querida, querida, I thought, and this made things better.

I like hotel rooms. Humans are disgusting, every single one of them. Even Querida. After I found the love letter in Room 304, I pulled a clump of black hair the size of a roach from the shower drain.

———

When I come home from school three hours early, Ma isn't supposed to be there. She volunteers on Wednesdays at the animal rescue down the street so she can call herself a nurse at book club.

"What are you doing here?" I ask.

The oven clock reads 12:47 p.m. Ma sits with her legs propped up on the kitchen table, reading *HGTV Magazine*. Cigarette smoke uncurls in the early-afternoon light, spiraling above her dyed chestnut hair like DNA.

"Personal day," she says. "It's all so sad. Did you come home because of the news?"

Ma stubs the cigarette out on a marble coaster and leaves the butt there, ringed in greasy red lipstick.

"News?"

"People have been calling all morning. They think they already have the fucker who did this."

"Who was it?"

"You know that boy down the street? Cameron Whitley? His dad was Lee Whitley, that rogue cop from a few years back."

She smiles. Ma loves being the one with this information. I'm disgusted by her faded lipstick, curled over yellow cigarette teeth. She wears a revealing silk bathrobe with soup dribbled down the front, patterned with Japanese cranes, the outline of her sagging breasts clear beneath thin fabric.

Often, I'm certain that Ma is the worst person in the world. Other times, I pity her.

"Oh," she says. "Chris Thornton called. He knows it's last minute, but I told him you have the night off from the hotel. Can you babysit tonight?"

"No."

"I already told him you would. He sounded rushed; you could go over now."

"I don't want to."

"That's not an answer."

"Fuck off, Ma."

"Nice work—you're grounded. And you're going to babysit. That man's wife is very sick; you know better than anyone. I don't know how I raised such a selfish brat."

"Takes one to know one."

"Go."

———

Chris Thornton comes to the door in a T-shirt and jeans. I've only ever seen him wearing a suit and tie (he works a fancy job in downtown Denver). His wife, Eve, isn't home—she's usually at the hospital, or in Longmont with her parents, or locked upstairs with the curtains shut. About a year and a half ago, right after the baby was born, Eve Thornton was diagnosed with something serious. Cancer, I think, though people always whisper when they talk about it.

"Thanks so much for doing this, Jade," Mr. Thornton says, and he gestures at the back door, toward the playground. "Ollie's daytime sitter canceled, and I haven't gotten any work done."

He hands Ollie—short for Olivia—over casually, like a jug of water, and mumbles about putting her to bed at seven; he'll be back later. He slings a gym bag over his shoulder and rushes to shut the door.

Ollie is not a pretty baby. Her face is a soft tomato, red and wrinkled like a newborn alien's, even though she is nearly eighteen months old now. When Chris Thornton's car is safely out of the driveway, I carry the baby upstairs, where the hall is still stacked with half-unpacked boxes from their move here two years ago. Puddles, their gray, loping terrier, nips at my heels all the way up the stairs. Puddles's eyebrows are so long she can barely see, and she's probably older than me. I can't imagine why you'd name a dog Puddles—especially a dog as depressing as this one. I sit in the rocking chair by the nursery window, and Ollie cries, bucking and squirming and mumbling. She toddles around the room, while Puddles stays folded at my feet. The window is cracked open; biting fresh air streams through the screen, blowing the baby-pink curtains into the room like a skirt.

Across the Thorntons' lawn, over the fence, and past an ancient oak tree, the playground sits like it always has. Now, three police officers stand by the carousel.

Zap and I used to sit in the center of that carousel. I'd wrap my legs around the red-painted pole and flatten my back against the bumpy metal surface. We'd start slow. Zap's sneakers would slap against mulch and the sky would swirl, a ceiling fan of blue and white. When we gained enough speed, Zap would jump on beside me—he didn't like to lie down. He would lean against the middle bar, his scarecrow arms stretched out to the sides, captain of his own spinning ship.

Ollie peers up at me with a saliva-slick jumbo Lego in her hand, finally calm. Her brown eyes bulge, wet and cowlike, feather eyelashes protruding from their lids.

Go on, I think. *Tell them how awful I am.*

She opens her gummy mouth and lets out another screech.

———

Around the time everything started to fall apart with Zap—over a year ago—I found a book called *Modern Witchcraft: A Guide for Mortals.* It's based in the history of pagan witchcraft, compiled by a group of reputable researchers. Now, I can't set foot in the Broomsville Public Library because the book has racked up hundreds of dollars in overdue fines. I don't have any intention of returning it.

It happened in May. Lucinda was the whole reason I had to take the hotel job, the reason the Thorntons stopped calling me to babysit. This was almost a year after everything went to shit—and still, I spent my nights combing through childhood photos, drawing Sharpie moustaches on me and Zap so I wouldn't get so sad. It was useless, I know. You can't change people. You can't stop them from growing. You can't make them look how they used to: like a gangly kid with bottle-thick glasses and an idiotic bowl cut.

The week I checked out the book, I was supposed to babysit. A ten-hour shift, and Eve Thornton was going to pay me a hundred dollars—she rarely coordinated babysitting, but she would be out of the hospital for a few days and could use the extra hands. I was happy to spend a Saturday out of the house, where Ma was on a tirade about the electricity bill. That morning, she'd shattered a plate against the mantel.

While I was walking to the Thorntons', the family cell phone Ma lets me use for work buzzed. A text message from Eve Thornton: "NVRMND. DOUBLE BKED. U DONT NEED 2 COME 2DAY. THX."

As I turned to leave, I crossed Lucinda coming up the Thorntons' driveway. She smiled as we passed each other, all straight teeth. Lucinda had one dimple, on the left side of her face. Even when her smile was fake, it dotted her cheek. A button. Of course the Thorntons preferred Lucinda Hayes—she probably knew how to put Ollie to sleep without a fit. I bet she was certified in CPR.

"Hey," she said, the way you talk to an old acquaintance you know you should remember but don't.

The air she floated through smelled like strawberry shampoo. I rounded the corner, stomach rolling like I'd eaten something bad. It was like that night all over again, like I was standing in that narrow hallway, listening to fireworks pop over the lake and letting Lucinda Hayes take everything from me.

Later that night, I set the whole thing up, just like it said in "The Art of the Ritual," the sixth chapter of *Modern Witchcraft: A Guide for Mortals*. Step by step. The candles, the herbs, the altar.

I don't regret the ritual, not even now that Lucinda is actually dead.

I wished her away.

———

Mr. Thornton pays me in cash, a fat wad with two extra twenties thick at the heart of it. This is probably accidental—the only thing I've done tonight is put Ollie to sleep and eat the raw cookie dough from his refrigerator. I couldn't find the leash to walk Puddles, so I carried her to the corner of the back fence and stood guard while she peed, ready to scoop her up if she tried to make a break for it. I leave before Mr. Thornton notices the overpayment.

When I get home, the house is quiet. 10:19 p.m.

Usually after babysitting I'd go to see Howie—the homeless guy who lives behind the library. But tonight, I'm too curious. I change into a pair of men's boxer shorts and a clean Crucibles T-shirt. Roll my plastic desk chair to the window. I turn off the lights and use my pink lighter to ignite the chamomile candle on the nightstand. Ma says it's a fire hazard because my room is so cluttered. I'm not allowed to light candles until I get rid of all the useless junk, but I'm terrible at knowing what's irrelevant.

I pull a CD from the middle of my stack, which wavers at the foot of my bed. They're homemade mixes, burned to fit different moods—this one is titled *Night Walks*, which is scrawled messily across its matte-finish face. The track list: Misfits, Green Day, Bad Religion, the Crucibles, and Blink-182. "Letters to God" by Box Car Racer comes on, and when the nasally singer starts to whine, I allow myself just a twinge of satisfaction.

I sit at my window like always, but I know Cameron won't come tonight. The hood of his sweat shirt always gives him away, distinguishing him from the shadows—the white drawstring across his chest is illuminated in the moonlight. Lucinda's back lawn slopes upward from where her house sits at the bottom of the small suburban hill; from where Cameron stands by the fence we can both see into her bedroom.

It's been almost twenty-four hours since Lucinda Hayes disappeared and tonight, the grass is still. A police car idles with its lights off, whirring sneakily by the side of the house. The Hayeses are in their living room, but from my desk chair, looking down across the short alley of grass between our houses, their faces are visible only in passing. They have relatives visiting already—grandparents, aunts, uncles—who shuffle in and out of the kitchen with steaming cups of tea and food that no one touches. A steady rotation. Lex sits on the floor with her back against the legs of the couch; she looks like her younger self, like Amy's twin princess-sister in their game of pretend. Except now, she is wearing a pair of rhinestone-spattered jeans and crying quietly as their grandmother braids her hair.

I search for the white of Cameron's sneakers and instead I find the roots of the bushes that line the back fence, ropes uncoiling across a midnight lawn. For an ignorant moment, I'm afraid I'll get sucked into that endless dusk.

Lucinda is gone. Cameron will have no one to watch. No one to make his hands shake. No one to think about before he falls asleep, as he watches the cracks in the ceiling or counts Orion's elbows.

———

How Zap used to look at me:

With eyes open wide, like someone surprised by a camera. Often quickly. In passing. In longer moments, which stretched beyond their appropriate span. *What?* one of us would say. *What do you mean, 'what'?*

Nothing.

You're looking at me funny.

I'm not.

What are you thinking?

Did you know Mars takes six hundred eighty-six days to orbit the sun?

That's not really what you're thinking.

Prove it.

Shut up.

Russ

Russ and two other officers are told to knock on every door on the block. They start with the houses lining the playground, the houses with fences that overlook the carousel.

Did you hear anything last night?

They speak to Greg and Rhonda Hansen, the older couple doing calisthenics together in the living room. They speak to Lucinda's ballet instructor, who insists on serving tepid tea. They speak to Chris Thornton, who struggles to keep a squirming toddler on his hip. They speak to Kelly Dixon-Burns, who wears a silk bathrobe and looks Russ too long in the eye as she takes a hefty pull of her cigarette, and to Sherry DeCasio, who sobs the moment they say Lucinda's name. In this case—as with the Weinberg family, the Sanchez family, and anyone else who has children at Jefferson High—Russ asks: Can we come back after school? We'd love to have a word with your child. Most nod solemnly.

———

When Russ gets back to the police department it is late afternoon, and he does not expect to see the boy.

Cameron's middle-school yearbook photo hangs on a bulletin board where they've already tacked up the faces of early suspects. He looks strikingly like his father. No one comments on this. No one mentions Lee at all.

But those hazel eyes: a snake writhes in Russ's gut. Nostalgia, a dagger.

The entire Broomsville Police Department has been summoned to the main conference room to be briefed on the case. If anyone remembers that Russ is related to the janitor, Ivan—another suspect pinned to the bulletin board—they don't say anything. Maybe they've forgotten about Russ's brother-in-law. More likely, they don't care.

The case is already making national news, the chief tells the room of officers and sergeants and receptionists. You are not to make any comments to the media.

A short list of suspect individuals:

Ivan Santos, the janitor who found the body.
Edouard Arnaud, the victim's ex-boyfriend.
The parents—Joe and Missy Hayes.
Howard Morrie, the homeless guy squatting in the park behind the
   library.
Cameron Whitley, the stalker boy from down the street.

———

Russ went to visit Ivan in prison—only once. No warning. Ivan, six foot two, was gargantuan on the other side of the metal table in the visitor's room. Russell, Ivan had greeted him, with a firm handshake, sliding comfortably into his chair. My brother.

In prison, Ivan fought no one, made no friends. Instead, he read books: Latin American philosophers, combined with texts from a freshman liberal-arts syllabus Ines found online. These were the sort of books Russ couldn't get through if he tried. Plato's *Symposium*, Foucault's unintelligible French lectures about power. José Martí, Juan Montalvo, Leopoldo Zea, and the writings of Sor Juana Ines de la Cruz, whom Russ Googled and found to be the first Latin American feminist writer. Ivan copied the entirety of the New Testament onto legal pads, which Ines purchased and mailed in bulk. In the end, the only evidence of Ivan's time in the slammer was this homemade New Age–Christian religion, an impressive combination of scholarly philosophy, Catholicism, and motivational speaking. And one sloppy jailhouse tattoo—a bleeding Virgin of Guadalupe on Ivan's right wrist, a bouquet of four-petaled flowers drooping by her side.

A free man now, Ivan delivers winding philosophical sermons to the Spanish-speaking community that occupies plastic chairs in the one-room church on Fulcrum Street. He preaches in a clean white button-down and pressed slacks, encouraging them to further their spiritual exploration by reading, and instead of the Bible, he gives them Plato's *Symposium* and speaks of emancipation.

Believe in your own goodness, Ivan cries. Trust your own goodness. Confíe en su propia bondad.

Ines sits in front. She sings with proud, open eyes. The old church women cook food for Ines and bring it to the house; while Russ is at work, Ines walks across town to return the empty pans. Often, Russ wonders if Ines misses that side of Broomsville, with its lopsided houses and peeling-paint cars and all those women who return her rapid-fire language. Sometimes, in her sleep, Ines mumbles in pleading Spanish. Russ keeps a pen and paper in his nightstand so he can write down words and phrases to Google in the morning.

When Detective Williams questions Ivan in the room at the back of the station house, Ivan has none of that messiah fury. Russ briefly watches from behind glass as Detective Williams pulls every interrogation trick he knows. They question Ivan for six hours, and Ivan gives them nothing but

a resounding calm that terrifies Russ, who pictures the hundreds of legal pads—Ivan's handwritten Bible—stacked next to a twin mattress on the floor.

I don't know anything, he says, over and over again.

I just found her, he says, over and over again.

Confíe en su propia bondad.

———

Russ and Ines met in summer. Colorado summers are dry—heat presses down, slow and unbearable, a curtain lowered over a blazing stage. Red dust. Chlorine. White-hot cement.

It was Russ's day off. Girls wore strappy dresses and walked barefoot through the park, where boys threw Frisbees and let the sun drench through their shirts.

Russ parked his car and watched the crowds under the wide, cloudless tent of sky. He had intended to take a run up the mountain, but it was too hot, so he stopped at Main Street Park. He couldn't go back to his house, where he'd roast in front of the television, drinking Bud Light. It was not uncommon for Russ to go his full forty-eight hours off without talking to anyone but the pimply pizza-delivery boy.

So he had gone to the park for the push and squeal of other people, the existing fact of them. The day smelled like a sunscreen dream, and Russ meandered down the walking path, until he passed an ice-cream cart. He got in line, ordered a snow cone, and walked toward a half-empty bench.

The snow cone melted faster than he could eat it, cherry sugar dripping from the paper cup and over his knuckles, dribbling on his khaki shorts and flowering through like little blossoms of blood.

Here, she said.

Ines was sitting next to him on the bench, a book open in her lap. She held out a miniature wrapped packet of tissues.

Thank you, Russ said as he mopped himself up.

You're welcome, she said. She had an accent. She was shiny in the sun, the pages of her book a blinding white, and she wore a pair of denim shorts and a baggy T-shirt.

What are you reading? Russ asked.

She held up the cover. *Love in the Time of Cholera*, he read aloud, stumbling over the word "cholera" because he could not remember what it meant or how to pronounce it. She had marked all over the open page in pencil. Russ could not recall the last time he read a novel. He wasn't sure he'd ever finished one.

Is it good? he asked.

Yes, she said. I read it many times in school, but this is my first time reading it in English. It's quite different.

How so?

The turn of phrase, she said. That's what you call it, right? When a sentence twists in different ways?

Yes, Russ told her. That's what you call it.

Look at this, she said as she flipped through the book, then tore out a page.

A Band-Aid–ripping sound—before Russ could protest, she had handed him the page with its raggedy edges, a single sentence underlined. He squinted to read.

"He was still too young to know that the heart's memory eliminates the bad and magnifies the good, and that thanks to this artifice we manage to endure the burden of the past."

Nice, yes? she said.

Very.

He moved to give the page back—as though she could reinsert it into the book—but she waved him away. When she smiled, he wondered if Ines was flirting. He had not flirted in years.

Keep it, she said, before lifting the book to her face and settling back into her seat, burying herself in words. Russ stuffed the page in his pocket and

stood to throw away the snow-cone wrapper. He loped back toward his car, wishing she had asked him to stay, or that he had the courage to do so anyway.

———

Detective Williams is nearly as old as Russ's father, who had served as a mentor to the detective back in the sixties. Ah, Fletcher, the detective is always reminiscing. Your pops really got me my start in law enforcement, you know that? He believed in me when no one else did.

You don't want to be on patrol forever, right? Detective Williams often asks Russ. You want to move up eventually?

Russ cannot imagine being a detective. He likes the quiet of his patrol car, in the soft veil of a graveyard night. The slice of headlights on paved, sleepy streets. The whir of the heater and the vast blackness surrounding him, the only one awake, the only one alive.

Of course, Russ always says. Of course I want to move up eventually.

After Ivan's interrogation, Russ watches his peers file out as Detective Williams places a hand on Russ's shoulder. Leans his weathered face close. His breath like salami.

Pay close attention to this case, Detective Williams spits into Russ's neck. You could learn a thing or two.

Truth is, Russ does not want anything but what he used to have, and he wouldn't give up his patrol job for fear of losing even the smallest memory.

———

Ivan is gone before Lucinda's family arrives. There isn't enough room, and they cannot legally keep him—he has cooperated with patience. As Ivan leaves, he gives Russ a small salute. Russ cannot gauge its sincerity.

They interview Lucinda's father first. Russ observes from the other side of the one-way mirror.

Joe Hayes sits across the conference table, facing Detective Williams and the lieutenant. His gray hair reflects the fluorescent light, thin and wan. He swipes a palm over his eyes like a rag—Mr. Hayes's plaid button-down shirt already looks like a remnant of an earlier version of himself, a self before his daughter died. The shirt of a man who took pleasure in pouring coffee in a thermos before getting in his car to drive to work. He wears wire-rimmed glasses, which he takes off intermittently and folds in his hands, giving them something to do. Russ knows that tragedy is a thief. It will eat Mr. Hayes's days, his months, his years alive.

Detective Williams asks, Is there anything you know that might help us with the investigation?

Lucinda's father tells them about the boy last year—the boy in the yard. The boy they caught standing by their fence, the boy they told to leave and never come back. The boy they often felt, a presence lingering outside the house. But by the time the lights flicked on, the yard was empty, night after night.

Do you know this boy's name? Detective Williams asks.

He was in Lucy's class, the father tells them. Cameron Whitley. The other neighbors have seen him too, walking around late at night.

Even the sound of Cameron's name brings Russ places he'd rather not go. The name said aloud: Whitley. A quicksand sort of sinking. Rapid and unsalvageable.

———

Lucinda's mother twists a silver ring around her pointer finger, hands shaking so hard she can't hold the paper cup of water they've placed in front of her. Her hair is the same shade of gold as both her daughters'.

Detective Williams asks, Is there anything you know that might help us with the investigation?

Some combination of shock and grief comes spewing out. An unintelligible moan, a short fit of hyperventilation. A social worker sits beside Lucinda's mother, rubbing her back in methodical strokes.

Russ has never felt something so strong. Category eight. The other patrol cop backs away slowly, embarrassed to be spying on such a miserable spectacle. But Russ is not embarrassed. He is fascinated, hooked, and in some incomprehensible way, jealous. That grief—so pure.

———

And last, the little sister. While they interview Lex, her father slumps in the chair beside her, head bowed.

Lex wears a rainbow-striped wool hat with a pom-pom on the top. She keeps her ski gloves on, tenting the fabric away from each finger, pinky to thumb.

I love my sister, Lex says, eyes wide and wet. She does normal high-school things, I think. She spends a lot of time in her room and texting on her cell phone. I don't have a cell phone yet, but I'll get one when I turn fourteen, like Lucy—

Lex's voice cracks, and her father stands up.

That's enough.

Detective Williams thanks them and ushers them out, wringing his hands like they've gone numb in the cold.

We've got nothing, he mutters to Russ, absent.

———

Russ gets home late.

Ines is in the chair next to the fireplace, legs crossed beneath her. There is a switch next to the mantel that would ignite the gas flame, but in three married years neither Russ nor Ines has ever flipped it on.

Ines's pale nails maneuver her knitting needles—they clack against one another, the only sound in the big house. A tangled braid hangs across her left breast. Usually when Russ comes home, Ines is at the computer in the corner of the living room, smiling to herself as she reads an e-mail from one of her sisters, laughing out loud as she types back in Spanish written with no accents on Russ's English-language keyboard.

Russ and Ines live in a permanent bachelor pad. The living room is bleak, with outdated beige carpet, a couch, a chipped coffee table, and too much unfilled space. The furniture is from before they were married. The only thing Ines has put up for decoration hangs by the front door: a framed photo of family members standing in a garden, a tangle of happy arms. Out the window, the mountains are toy peaks—frosted white, minuscule.

Russ throws his jacket over the shoulder of the couch.

Hi.

Hi, Ines says, knitting.

Do we have any beer? he asks.

Check the fridge, she says, and Russ realizes that Ivan has not called his sister, that Ines has not switched on the television today.

Russ finds half a can of Bud Light in the refrigerator door. He downs it quickly, but the carbonation is long gone and it is watered down, yeasty. Usually, Russ would ask how tutoring went, but today is Wednesday, and the kids get Wednesdays off. Any other day, Russ would ask about Ines's favorite student, the girl who tells funny stories and can't pick up a word of Spanish. Any other day, Ines would talk animatedly, repeating teenage gossip in an exaggerated fake American accent, like an annoying teenager at the mall. Oh my gaaaad, she says.

Russ wishes he could speak to Ines in Spanish. Maybe then, she'd look up from her knitting. He can remember a bit of the mandatory conversational Spanish class he took at the police academy, and he bought a Rosetta

Stone when Googling proved fruitless. But his high-school transcripts made it clear that Russ was no scholar. He memorizes word after word—*la mesa*, *el coche*; *ocho*, *nueve*, *diez*—but by the next day, it's like Spanish has a completely different alphabet.

Ines's favorite student has a name that sounds like old-time television. Russ had recognized it first thing this morning: Lucinda. Russ does not tell Ines about her brother, found at the scene of another crime. He prefers her just like this—knitting.

Cameron

Things Cameron Didn't Like to Remember:

1. Dad's scalp. How his hair thinned at the front, creeping back toward the crown of his skull, a gradual reveal of pink.
2. The bones of the finger. The distal, intermediate, and proximal phalanges, and how Lucinda's were especially long. Especially thin.
3. The second-grade talent show—the only time Cameron ever performed onstage.

   Cameron had practiced for weeks. He'd plunked away at the piano in the den, perfecting "Für Elise." But at the talent show itself, in that anticipated and terrifying hour, the stage in the gymnasium felt too foreign. Cameron hated all those eyes—his hands slipped off the keys, they were so sweaty. He played five notes, the beginning trill of "Für Elise," before the wave swelled forward and caught Cameron in its froth. He blacked out.

   The teachers said he was great. The break between the chorus and the bridge was moving, he had a natural sense of lyricism. They said he was so caught up in the music, his whole body was swaying—he had to stick with it, he had real talent. When Cameron stayed silent at dinner that night, Mom and Dad said, *Cameron, what's wrong?* He didn't know. It wasn't Cameron up there, playing "Für Elise." Someone else. A body uninhabited.

Those three minutes had escaped him, in all their glory and panic.

———

When Cameron came home from the Tree that evening, he lay on his bed. His toes were frozen blue in wool socks. Mom had gone back to work, even though it was *against her better judgment,* and did he promise he'd stay right there on the couch?

The Tree was Cameron's sacred and secret space.

The Tree took on the general shape of a man, and that was why Cameron had picked this specific aspen: thick trunk, like a torso, and about six feet tall. When Cameron squinted, he could imagine the spine, vertebrae stacked on top of one another, inconsequential as a tower of blocks. He could picture the heart—the aspen had a knot of bark in its chest, with a protruding nub in the exact location of the aorta. Usually, this was where he aimed. Sometimes, when Cameron felt particularly Tangled, he aimed for both kneecaps, but this was the cruelest thing to do, and remembering it—remembering how real those legs had been in his head as he'd squeezed the trigger—guilt seeped through him, spreading and blotting through his body like ink.

Today, Cameron had set the .22-caliber handgun on the ground like a sacrifice, the barrel resting in a patch of dirty snow. Cameron liked to think they were in Hum, all the imaginary people of the Tree, those figments of his mind to whom he'd done real hurt. And now Lucinda was there, too. He hoped in the morning, the birds would chirp their gurgling songs for her.

Now, safely in his bedroom, Cameron's thoughts were like the string of a forgotten yo-yo—knotted up on themselves, twisted in inconvenient patterns. The psychiatrist he had seen for a few months after everything happened with Dad had given him a safety word for times like these, times that bordered on clinical panic attacks but felt different, so specific to Cameron and the jumble of his insides. Untangle. These eight letters used to calm him—they used to scare away the blackout, which felt like fainting, though if you asked any witness, Cameron was usually conscious. Untangle. Walking around, talking to people, playing the piano or whatever he'd been doing before, just with a brain so overwhelmed it had shut off entirely. Untangle.

Gradually, the safety word had lost its meaning. He'd overthought it, like when you stared at a word for too long and it stopped looking like a word and became an alien formation of letters with no real significance.

Untangle wouldn't bring Lucinda back to life, and it wouldn't numb the badness of the Tree. He wanted to remember how charcoal faded across Lucinda's jawline. Her symmetry on a nine-by-twelve pad of paper. Urgent. Cameron reached between his bed and the wall, where he hid the porn magazine Ronnie gave him back in December (Rayna Rae in the centerfold, with jet-black hair that barely covered her nipples).

Reaching beneath his mattress, Cameron's thumb brushed against something solid, caught between the bed and the wall.

Before Cameron pulled it into the dim afternoon light, he knew exactly what he was touching. The suede was unmistakable. The elastic band held it shut, an accusation whispered in his ear before he'd even seen the thing: *You have done something wrong*, it said to him. *You have done something very wrong*.

Cameron laid it out, a body on a coroner's table. He stood over his bed, examining the strange combination of synonymous shapes: the rectangle bed frame, the rectangle sheets, the rectangle comforter, the rectangle pillow, and there, in the middle, Lucinda's rectangle diary.

Untangle wouldn't explain how Lucinda's diary had ended up in his bed. Untangle wouldn't tell him what to do with it. Untangle wouldn't help him remember the night of February fifteenth—last night. It wouldn't bring her back to life.

Twenty-three minutes passed, and Cameron could only think: he had never been so close to her.

Cameron would not open the diary, but he knew that whatever she wrote had probably been recorded with meticulous effort. He remembered from her school notes how Lucinda's ys and gs curled underneath the blue line. Cameron stretched the elastic to the side, thinking that he had only ever known Lucinda through windows and in gym class, smiling over her shoulder in her Jefferson High School shirt, "LUCINDA" Sharpied in block letters across the stomach.

Cameron had taken a liking to the Hayes family—to the way they chopped their onions for dinner and rubbed their eyes in the morning. Combed their hair after a shower. Father washed the dishes; younger sister dried. Cameron refused to form an opinion about the millions of little ways they chose to move around their house; that wasn't his job. He was only a witness.

The purple diary was the only thing left of Lucinda. Cameron shouldn't be the one to open it. It didn't seem fair. So he put the diary on the top shelf of his closet, along with the Collection of the Pencil Bodies and the Collection of People Who Did Terrible Things, both manila folders hidden behind a stack of winter sweaters he had long outgrown.

Cameron had lots of different Collections, all hidden on the top shelf of his closet. The Collection of Pencil Bodies, the Collection of Pens, the Collection of Photos from When Mom Was Young. The only one hidden in his head was the Collection of Statue Nights—this was his favorite Collection, because it was full of Lucinda.

Cameron didn't hide the diary because he was afraid of getting caught. He simply didn't want to ruin her.

———

Mom was always tired after work. Her days were long, because she spent them arguing with bored old women about the price of yarn and cutting fabric against the special measuring tape at the craft store.

Tonight, the refrigerator door whooshed open and closed. The silver-
ware drawer rattled the forks and the knives. Cameron listened until Mom
knocked softly on his bedroom door.

"Why are you on the floor?" Mom said, creaking it open.

She held a plastic plate of apples cut into smiley faces, with a glob of
organic peanut butter scraped onto the rim.

"I made you a snack," Mom said. "Come outside. You look like you
need some air."

Cameron put on his coat and hat and followed Mom to the driveway.
They sat on the drying porch steps. Mom's jacket was pastel purple. She'd
worn it every winter as long as Cameron could remember, and her hat was
a striped department-store beanie. It didn't look very warm.

"I know this has been a hard day," Mom said.

She bit into an apple slice. Cameron loved to watch people eat fruit.
Peaches, especially, looked like kisses. Sloppy and sticky.

"I need to talk to you," Mom said. "About last night. When Lucinda"—
she tilted her face up to the sky and closed her eyes, like when she had
a headache—"when Lucinda was killed. Remember how Principal Barnes
pulled me aside when I came to pick you up today?"

"Yes."

"He asked if you were home last night. I told him you were. The police
asked us to go in to the station, but I wanted to talk to you first.

"Cameron, honey, look at me," she said. "You weren't home last night."

Cameron tried to take her words and form them into a shape he could
better understand: *You weren't home.* If he wasn't home, and Lucinda was
dead—Mom would never lie.

"I was home," Cameron said.

"I was so afraid of this," Mom said. She pressed her fingers to the bridge
of her nose. "I heard a noise from your room. You weren't there, but the
window was open. I know you've done this before—walking around at
night. I chose not to worry."

Cameron coughed, because it felt like the logical thing to do.

"Mom, I was home."

"Sweetie."

He couldn't look at Mom, because he could tell from the way her head was bowed that she was crying. He'd dragged her out to the driveway and made her say those horrible words—*You weren't home; you weren't*. Cameron felt the beginning of Tangled coming on. His head could barely hold itself up; his insides were swollen and angry. The perimeters of his vision were a dusk, his breath like cement in his chest. He pressed the heel of his hand so hard into the sidewalk that the tiny bits of gravel lodged themselves in his skin, sending stinging lines of pain through his whole arm, and he felt a little better.

"Where was I?" Cameron said.

"I was hoping you could tell me that," Mom said.

"I don't remember," Cameron told her, and this was the truth.

"You can't have forgotten," she said. "It was only last night."

"I don't remember anything," Cameron said, and he couldn't tell from Mom's face—which was the most scared and pitying he'd ever seen—whether she believed him.

Mom's nose was dripping, a small river above her mouth, but she did not move to wipe it. She picked up Cameron's sticky hand and interlaced her feathery fingers with his. Cameron was embarrassed because he was too old for things like this, but he liked the feeling too much to let go. It was like someone had pressed a shaky bow to a violin string and played one long, vibrating note through his ribcage and through hers. They were both very still.

Cameron had not consciously let himself cry in nearly three years, because he was afraid of the floodgate: once he started, he'd never be able to stop. So instead of crying, Cameron let the sadness spread across the inside of his throat, let it melt into his glands, burning thick. He and Mom were both hunched over, they were numb on the drying concrete outside the beige house, they were clinging to one another so tight their palms were sore. This sort of grief was unbearable, but it was nice to share it with someone, even if it made his neck impossibly heavy.

———

Cameron had considered keeping his Collections in Dad's closet instead, because Mom would never go inside. It was down the hall, outside their bedroom. The closet smelled like Dad: worn leather, the pages of the morning newspaper. Dad's closet was the place Cameron went when he was most Tangled—since Dad left, Cameron had gone into his closet only twice, when the missing felt too big. He'd stood among scratchy shirts and pants folded on hangers, wondering how it felt to put on these clothes every day, how it felt to be someone bad.

The Collection of People Who Did Terrible Things was a manila folder. On principle, Dad belonged in there, even though Cameron felt so morbid sticking him in with Andrea Yates.

Everything started with Andrea Yates. *You hear about that woman from Texas who killed her own kids?* someone said in class. *Drowned them all in the bathtub. Thought she was saving them from the devil.*

Cameron had looked it up on the family computer. He printed everything he could find: news articles, blog forums, family photos. He simply wanted to know how such a love had been chronicled, to possess it somehow, if only to feel sad for the dead kids and sad for the husband and even sad for Andrea Yates. Even though it made him nauseous, looking at all the terrible things this woman had done, he wanted every detail. He wanted to know what the kids ate for breakfast that day, what they were wearing, and how the husband felt when he found all their tiny bodies laid out on the king-sized bed. If the kids had shampoo in their mouths, if it bubbled between their baby teeth, if they tried to scream but only gurgled. If Andrea Yates did something so awful for love. If you could count a love like that—five gangly bodies, soaked in murky water that leaked through to the mattress. One was an infant, he read. He wondered how a love like that drowned. Or worse, how it dried.

So the Collection of People Who Did Terrible Things began with Andrea Yates, and once he started looking at all that, the rest of the collection came quickly and with the same burning curiosity. Next was the sorority-house murderer from the South. Then, Jack the Ripper. And in the back of the folder, Dad.

With the Collection of People Who Did Terrible Things spread out on the floor, Cameron started to feel Tangled. He pulled the eraser from his pocket and kneaded it against his palm until it was pancake flat. His thoughts were like cartoon hummingbirds, making circles around his head, pecking at his earlobes, nudging his shoulders. They wouldn't leave him be. Usually, he was thankful for their company, but Lucinda's diary was in his closet, and she was dead, and here Cameron was, sitting on the floor with Dad and Andrea Yates.

Cameron popped the screen out of his bedroom window and let the February air lick his cheeks.

———

The neighborhood was dim with shock. Snow, mostly gone. Lucinda died last night, and shadows seemed longer. Headlights were blinding. Cameron observed from his invisible places.

The Hansens were watching television. Their faces sagged, blue light flickering against their gooey skin.

Mr. Thornton sat alone in the living-room armchair, baby Ollie's toys scattered across the rug. Usually he would walk the dog around this time of night, pulling the bright-blue retractable leash from a hook by the door. When Mr. Thornton clipped the leash onto the dog's collar, Cameron always started walking home; he did not like to share the shadowed street's refuge. But tonight, the dog was sleeping by Mr. Thornton's feet. He'd left one light on—the stained-glass lamp in the far corner of the living room.

It threw his details into silhouette: the ridge of his suit jacket, still pressed. The folds of his ironed shirt. The tie, hanging around his neck like an abandoned noose.

Once, the school counselor asked Cameron if he was happier on his own than with other people. This was a dumb question. Other people were not trying desperately to stay Untangled, they were not thinking about their Collections and the complexities of the bodies within, or about Lucinda Hayes and the individual strands of her hair with little glands at the tips, secreting waxy oil. They were not picturing Rayna Rae's hipbones in the centerfold, or the flat space between those hipbones, like the clean inside of a marble sink. Even when Cameron was with other people, he was alone, and this made him feel both cosmically lucky and useless to the world.

Lucinda was dead, and the fact settled over the houses like last night's snow. It fell gently at first, and soon it would melt carelessly into the way of things. But not for Cameron: Lucinda was dead, and the reminder slapped him constantly, freezing ocean waves against his thighs. He could only wade deeper. Deeper, until the truth bubbled into his mouth, salty, miserable. Deeper, until it was pointless to search for shorelines because he knew Lucinda would not be standing on them.

Day
Two

THURSDAY
FEBRUARY 17, 2005

Jade

Cameron pulls an apple out of a paper bag. Bites into it, tentative. Even from the courtyard, I recognize that familiar self-consciousness as he sits alone at a table by the window.

People have been whispering about it all day: the cops are just looking for evidence now. He was obsessed with Lucinda. Her stalker.

I don't think it was like that, with Cameron and Lucinda. They were friends. Really. And those people don't know how he looked, standing pathetic on her back lawn every night. Melted gazes. Adoring.

Once, I heard Beth shrieking some ridiculous taunt about Cameron—she and Lucinda were walking arm in arm down the science hallway when Cameron passed with his head down. "Psychopath," Beth hissed, loud enough for him to hear. Cameron camouflaged himself easily, disappearing nimbly into the swarm of students.

Lucinda stopped walking, wriggled her arm free, and pulled her notebook protectively to her chest; it had a printout of a Degas painting plastered to the front. A ballerina perched on a bench, tying silky ribbons, with a tutu sprouting from her fairy waist.

"You don't even know that kid," Lucinda told Beth. "Leave him alone. He's not crazy."

―――――

WHAT YOU WANT TO SAY BUT CAN'T WITHOUT BEING A DICK
A Screenplay by Jade Dixon-Burns

INT. JEFFERSON HIGH SCHOOL—CAFETERIA—NOON

Celly approaches FRIEND (15, social pariah) at a cafeteria
table. He looks up at the mass of her, doe-eyed.

                         FRIEND
                       (startled)
        Uh. Hi.

                         CELLY
        We met yesterday. In the principal's office.

                         FRIEND
        I-I know.

                         CELLY
        Can I sit?

Friend stuffs his half-eaten apple into its paper bag, blushing
as Celly sits across from him.

                    CELLY (CONT'D)
        I'm not going to tell on you. For what I saw
        the other night.

                              FRIEND
                          (stammering)
          I don't know what you're talking about.

                              CELLY
          The night Lucinda died. I saw you on her

          lawn. I always see you there.

                              FRIEND
          I don't—

                              CELLY
          It's okay. You didn't kill her.

Friend looks around, then into his lap.

                              FRIEND
          You don't even know me.

                              CELLY
          I've got this theory, you know. Every person

          is just a conglomeration of observations and

          insights. You can't ever know someone, not

          really. Anyway, I don't think you would hurt

          Lucinda.

Friend swallows, hard.

                         CELLY (CONT'D)
          I've observed. You're not the only one

          capable of watching people.

```
Friend stands up quickly, crumpling his paper bag into a ball.
He looks back at Celly.


                    FRIEND
          Thanks, I think.


Friend rushes away, leaving Celly alone. She laughs, shaking
her head.


                    CELLY
     God help me if I've turned into an optimist.
```

———

I don't approach Cameron. Instead, I sit under the tree in the courtyard, tracing a smelly chemical Sharpie over my tattoo. A dragon with a spiky tail and swirls of fire.

Chapter Two of *Modern Witchcraft* is all about signs from the dead. You get three signs if someone is contacting you from the afterlife: the Image, the Dream, and the Token.

A man in Oklahoma lost his wife to a serial killer. She sent him these three signs, over and over again, which he recorded carefully on his blog: the Image, the Dream, the Token. The Image, the Dream, the Token. *Signs from the dead*, he blogged, *are really just signs from your own mind. It isn't possible.* They continued, in sets of three, until the man in Oklahoma finally called the cops. Surely someone was fucking with him.

The cops found him hanging from the ceiling fan, one of his wife's old-lady nightgowns wrapped around his neck. From the placement of the noose, they confirmed it was not a suicide. But all the doors to the house were locked from the inside.

When I first read this chapter I was sitting in my bed, on top of a mountain of dirty T-shirts, reading by the light of my chamomile candle. Everything in my bedroom was suddenly a sign: My moon charts. Troll dolls with wiry pink hair. My obituary collection. My collection of rocks that look like other things (hearts, dogs, Jesus). The Image, the Dream, the Token. The Image: a visual representation of the deceased. The Dream: just as it sounds. And the Token: something of yours that the deceased has claimed for themselves. How can you be sure to recognize a sign when it comes? A fist knotted in my chest—a silly, paranoid fear.

My only reprieve: I'd never known someone who died.

The first magic spell I did was on Amy. I wanted her home from school so Ma wouldn't notice if I cut class, so I mixed a bag of herbs and hid it in Amy's laundry, just like *Modern Witchcraft* said to do. The next day, she woke up with a fever. I promised never to practice magic again. Of course, that only lasted so long.

The warning bell rings, and I leave the second half of my peanut-butter sandwich under the courtyard tree so the birds can pick at the remains. On my way out, I consider going over to Cameron's table, playing out this unlikely scenario I've imagined. But real life doesn't swell like that, in waves you can predict as they roll, as they peak. Neither does love. I don't know how love goes, but my guess? Something else altogether. Avalanche.

———

Everyone talks about Zap too, of course. But by default, he isn't as suspicious as Cameron—Zap is not awkward or greasy or small. No, Zap shines too bright for that sort of public contempt. In a year and a half, we'll all be graduated, and Zap will be at some big college, playing soccer. Though I've vowed not to think about college until next year, when I have to—writing scholarships are hard to get, and Terry doesn't make enough money to send me anywhere good—I find some relief in this image. We'll all be in dorm rooms, drinking cheap beer, with shiny new lives. Maybe in the muddle of distance and time, everyone will remember Zap for who he really is.

I have witnessed Zap's truest cruelty. I've seen the slate gray of him.

I've seen hatred in Zap Arnaud's eyes—and I've deserved it all.

————

WHAT YOU WANT TO SAY BUT CAN'T WITHOUT BEING A DICK
A Screenplay by Jade Dixon-Burns

INT. JEFFERSON HIGH SCHOOL—MUSIC WING—AFTERNOON

Celly sits on a piano bench in the corner of the practice room, instruments strewn around the space. BOY (17, lanky and handsome) wipes the mouthpiece of his shiny trombone with a clean white rag.

Celly watches him.

                    CELLY
        Remember when we were little, and heartbreak
        was something reserved for pop songs and
        dead pets?

Boy doesn't react.

                CELLY (CONT'D)
        When we were so young and stupid, when we
        could spend all day exploring a patch of
        grass in an open field, digging for bugs—

                              BOY

          I remember.

Celly waits for him to continue, but he doesn't. Instead, Boy
packs his trombone in its case, locking it away.

                             CELLY

               You recognize me, don't you? We're still

               those kids. Sure, we do fewer whipped-cream-

               eating contests. Less whispering in each

               other's ears. But it's still us.

Boy looks back at her before he walks out of the room.

                        CELLY (CONT'D)

          It will always be us.

                    ————————

Zap and Lucinda ended just before Christmas. Two months ago. At least,
that was the word around school. They'd never been official—just rumors
here and there—but Zap was free now. The girls talked about it in the
locker room after gym class. I stayed in the corner, fighting to get my jeans
over my legs, which were still damp from the shower. *Heard she dumped
him*, someone said. *She wouldn't even tell him why.*

   Zap's last class of the day was band. He plays the trombone. This is a
new addition, a school requirement I think he secretly enjoys. Once, I saw
sheet music sticking out of his backpack: a cover of a pop song for trombone. I imagined Zap sitting in his bedroom with a foldable music stand,
lips vibrating against a frigid mouthpiece.

That day, I lingered in the music hallway, a textbook in my arms, neck craned like I was searching for someone. I wasn't. Through the window of the practice room, Zap disassembled the trombone into a long, padded case, wiping out the mouthpiece with a clean white rag. I took a few deep breaths and clicked open the door, holding the textbook in front of me like an excuse.

"Hey," I said. "You seen Emma?"

"Emma?" Zap asked. He folded the rag into the bell of his instrument. My heart, a tambourine.

"Yeah," I said.

"Emma Kazinsky? Nah. She doesn't have class here."

"Oh." I held the book up like an answer. It didn't matter. Zap clipped his sheet music into a binder and picked up his trombone case by the handle, making for the door on the other side of the room. I sat timidly on the edge of a piano bench, the book limp next to my leg. The practice room smelled like brass and polish.

"How've you been?" I asked. The words came out too fast.

"Fine. You?"

It was so stupid, this half-formed plan I'd concocted.

"I heard what happened," I said.

Zap already had one hand on the door, twenty feet away from me.

"I just wanted to make sure you're okay," I said.

He tilted his head to the side and squinted a little. He did this when he was angry and trying not to show it.

"Thanks," he said.

He pushed open the door.

"Have a good one," Zap said, like a host at a restaurant.

The bell of his trombone case banged against the wall as he left.

Don't you remember! I wanted to call after him. *Don't you remember before we were old!* The practice room was massive, empty but for the drums lined up against the wall, covered in tarps to keep the dust away. I ran my fingers over the ivory piano keys—too filled with shame, explosive and familiar, to make any sort of noise.

———

We went to Hangman's on a dare. The summer before high school started. Louis Travelli had called Zap a pussy, so he had to go, had to light three candles and say some chant. I knew he didn't want to do it alone. I was better than Zap at things like this: horror movies, going places we weren't supposed to.

Hangman's Hut is only half a house. The right side is burned down—a mess of fallen rafters and bare concrete beams. The house was built in the early 1900s. The Hangman family probably lived there during the 1930s. They based this estimate on the bones: the entire family's bones are now in the downtown science museum, where you can look at replicas in a special room if you ask.

I went in first, but only to prove I was brave. Zap glanced over his shoulder and hiked up his backpack straps. He wore a blue shirt that read "I LOVE BACON." I told him it was dumb, it wasn't even funny, but secretly I liked the way it made his brown skin look even darker. Already, the girls at school liked him. He had such light-blue eyes. His eyes looked French; I always thought so, even though French isn't really a way to look.

"God, this is creepy," Zap said from the splintered doorway of Hangman's Hut. He kicked aside a pile of crumpled brown leaves. They'd fallen from the tree in the yard and blown into the house through the nonexistent roof.

"Come on," I said. "Don't be a pussy."

"My mom says that's a derogatory word," he said.

"Are you telling me not to say it?"

"No. I don't give a shit."

"Don't say 'shit.' "

He smiled, this huge grin. Zap's teeth overlap each other in the front, leaving a hole the shape of a sesame seed. Everyone's always telling him he's got something between his teeth.

"Come on," I said.

He followed me hesitantly into the ruins. We walked beneath collapsing beams, until we were in the remnants of a kitchen. Broken bits of china lay in the rubble, so small you could only make out a fraction of a blue floral design. A flash of gold enamel. We ventured farther, the September sky unfolding above us. The corners of the room were filled with crushed beer cans and cigarette butts. Sun-faded bags of potato chips.

"So where'd they die?" Zap asked.

"The part of the house that burned down," I said. "Idiot."

Zap crossed his legs and sat in the middle of the floor, opening his backpack and pulling out the candles.

"You know, you're pretty funny, Jay," he said. I sat across from him, and we lined the candles up in a straight line. "Like, you act all mean and brave, marching in here like you don't even care, when I know that's not how you actually are."

"Shut up," I said.

"See what I mean?" he said. "Lucky I know you so well, or I would probably hate you."

He chuckled. I tried to laugh along, but something had stuck behind my throat. Lodged there. Expanded.

Zap used a stick to draw a penis in the dirt, complete with hanging balls. We both cracked up, and the tension fizzled away. Bright afternoon light poured down on us. Dry Colorado wind rippled. We were too childish to be starting high school, but we had no desire to deal with the fact.

This was around the time Zap started noticing everything with Ma: the bruises blossoming across my thighs, the cracked lips. The way my hands trembled constantly, searching for something to grasp. Zap had started watching me carefully, thinking I didn't notice. I tried to tell him that I always provoked her, and this was just how things went. My fault; it was always my fault. I didn't need pity. Still, he watched me like you'd watch a wild animal.

"We should have come here at night," Zap said.

"For the stars?"

"Nah, the moon. It's a waning gibbous tonight. A little vertical development in the clouds."

"What the fuck does that mean?" I said.

"It's supposed to be a nice night. We could see a lot, way out here."

"Do you talk to everyone like that?" I asked. "Like, 'vertical development'?"

"No," he said. "Just you."

"Why?"

"Because you're a freak, too," he said. "One day we'll move away together, me and you. We'll find a colony of more freaks and we'll never come back to this town. New York, maybe. We'll go to New York."

And that was it. I don't remember the rest of the afternoon. We set up the candles and read the chant and nothing happened. We crushed a bunch of beer cans. Lit a pile of leaves on fire. I remember the rest in bits and pieces—how the smoke twirled up into that incessant Colorado blue.

But I can tell you that this was one of the best days of my life. There's no one reason. It was just so free. I could exist in that house with Zap, no matter how haunted. I could be as rude as I wanted, as angry as I wanted, and he could be geeky, and it was all fine because we knew each other, we wanted to spend our days with each other. We were boundless, radiating.

A constellation, taking form.

Russ

Of Lee Whitley's defining traits, Russ remembers his eyebrows most accurately. Arched little worms, resting prudently on the ridge of Lee's forehead. Manicured. Russ asked Lee about this once—Do you pluck every morning? There's not a single stray—and Lee didn't speak to him for hours. They drove in muted hostility, so tense that Russ went home and took three shots of tequila just to rid himself of the abandonment. Those eyebrows, sharp and careful.

———

Day two: they bring in the ex-boyfriend.

Lucinda Hayes broke her neck. Cracked it on the edge of the carousel. At first, Russ wondered—is it possible she just went for a walk, slipped, and fell? But Detective Williams pointed to the gory close-up of the girl's face, whitish blue and smeared crimson. A bruised gash spread pulpy across her temple, the source of the trickling blood. Lucinda Hayes was smacked with something, Detective Williams said, probably something small and hard, like a brick or a rock. Honestly, it looks like she just landed wrong: if it weren't for the edge of the carousel after the force of the blow, which broke her neck on impact, she might have walked away with a few stitches and a nasty bruise.

The snow covered up any footprints, the snow washed away any finger-prints. No sign of the murder weapon, or Lucinda's cell phone.

Now, the ex-boyfriend is here. He is one of the few high-school students they've successfully reached. Most parents have refused voluntary questioning at the sight of Detective Williams's wide-brimmed hat on their doorstep. My baby did nothing wrong! I'd like to talk to my lawyer first. The kids they did speak with knew little about Lucinda beyond her place at the top of the social ladder. Detective Williams had gone from house to house last night like a political campaigner but given up on most.

The ex-boyfriend has come in voluntarily, escorted by his foreign, leggy mother. The kid looks like your typical high-school piece of shit, Russ thinks. He has swagger like a soccer player—too cool for football. His wide shoulders aren't quite sturdy yet, still growing, and he flicks a swoop of brown hair back every few minutes with a spastic jerk of his head.

Edouard Arnaud, the lieutenant says, coming up behind Russ at the coffee machine. I mean, the victim seems like a nice enough girl, but could she have picked a douchier boyfriend?

Ex-boyfriend, Russ corrects. They broke up months ago.

Russ watches the boy. Edouard Arnaud looks smaller than he should—flattened by the situation. He waits in the reception area with his mother, who holds his hand. The teenager grasps hard, fingers laced through fingers. Lifeboat. Russ cannot remember the last time he gripped someone that tightly.

———

They'd go to this cliff, Russ and Lee, to nap between shifts. Ten years before Lee's arrest. It was a fake cliff—Russ liked that about it. It looked more dangerous than it was, stretching out over the manmade reservoir, terrifying until you looked over the edge and saw that it only dropped to another plateau. That was how things went, wasn't it? A series of plateaus. You just kept sliding down, safe, safe, safe. But eventually you'd hit the water.

Lee would stretch across the back, and Russ would recline in the passenger's seat with his feet on the dashboard. They'd patrol assigned streets, sipping black coffee. Lee's thin, feminine fingers tapped rhythms against the steering wheel.

In Russ's memories, Lee's face is always slightly blurred, like when you wake up from a dream with only the vague essence of someone. Lee was unassuming. The long, pointed nose. Pasty skin, covered in acne, though Lee was older than Russ—by the time Russ met him, Lee was already married to Cynthia, twenty-six to Russ's twenty-one.

This was before Ines, of course. They made a habit of recounting Russ's one-night stands. These were usually girls from the surrounding towns that branched off the highway beneath the shadow of the mountains, who came down to Broomsville for a night out at Dixie's Tavern. Back then, Russ drank beer, beer, beer, because he so intimately understood the creeping heaviness of a beer drunk as its lethargic inebriation poked at the edges of your consciousness. The next day, hidden behind a Styrofoam cup, Russ would tell Lee about the night. What about her nipples? Lee would ask, thirsty for detail. Brown or pink?

Usually, fabrication. Often, Russ would make up some story just to see Lee's smile curl around those crooked teeth, an affirmation, aging Russ. Pink, Russ said, with little hairs around the edges, and Lee laughed so hard the coffee came out his nose. Fuck! He wrung out his hands, dripping with scalding coffee, and Russ had to grab the wheel, steering them down I-25 in a hungover stupor while Lee wiped his lap with a wad of Dunkin' Donuts napkins.

Lee was sensitive; he'd get worked up about the smallest, unpredictable things. Once, a drunk driver called him a faggot, and Lee rammed the guy's head into his own car window so hard the glass splintered.

They rarely talked about Cynthia. Back then, Russ didn't think he'd ever get married, or even fall in love, because what was the point? He didn't want to be Lee. Stuck in a deteriorating life, saying your wife's name like you've coughed up phlegm and you're glancing around, panicked, for somewhere to spit it out.

Lee did spit her out, eventually. It was like he spit her out, then looked at the lump of her, that slimy but inconsequential mess he'd made. Only after everything had fallen apart would Russ wonder about their marriage in the years before he'd come along, the magnet urge that had driven Lee and Cynthia to bed together, to the altar.

After his arrest, Lee bought a used car with cash and took off straight from the dealership, past the foothills, over the snow-capped mountains, and across the state, maybe on to somewhere warmer. Good-bye to no one. And then, it was over: ten years of companionship, of sunrises at their favorite spot in the mountains.

A series of plateaus. You keep sliding down, and eventually, you hit the water. You look around at the black and endless expanse, and you swim, because you've known no other landscape. You're sure that on the other side of the reservoir there's another mountain waiting, with other cliffs. Russ hopes Lee is on one of them, stretched lazily across some new back seat, ball cap pulled down to block out the early, peeking sun.

———

While Detective Williams interviews the ex-boyfriend, the news vans multiply—the local channels that span across the Front Range and even a van from CNN. A reporter with glossy hair speaks reverently into a microphone.

They've already gotten hundreds of calls from terrified neighbors and overbearing parents: We have to make sure our children are safe! One anonymous phone call from a man with a drawling redneck accent, claiming conspiracy, the same conspiracy that had overtaken Denver International Airport. New-Age Nazi-ism, he said—a fresh holocaust coming for anyone who doesn't love God, a concentration camp beneath Terminal B. Lucinda was a warning, he said, just the locusts or the frogs. Afterwards, the officers had laughed together at the man's expense, but not with their usual fervor. This time, uneasy.

Detective Williams went to the Whitleys' house last night, too. Cameron was already asleep, and Cynthia had refused to wake him up. There had been no hope for that one from the start.

Come back when you have a warrant, she'd said. Or at least probable cause.

They have neither of those things, for anyone. The news vans pull up and spike their antennas. The television in the corner threatens them all with images of themselves, their own building, their own shiny bald heads as they walk in and out of it. No comment, no comment.

———

Russ and Ines met again a few weeks after that summer day in the park.

It was a narcotics call. The Broomsville police had been chasing these guys for months. They were notorious, Ivan's friends: they dealt in shelled-out houses, places so far beyond repair that no desperate Broomsville real estate agent would go near.

This was the north side of town, where tiny, peeling structures housed sardine-packed families. Broken grills and sun-faded plastic chairs littered lawns. Mexico City, Russ's cop friends called it, snickering from air-conditioned cars. Russ laughed along, vaguely recognizing his own participation in this active coward's ignorance. Of course, he knew there was more to this neighborhood, so different from the manicured suburbs, but he did not know the shape of these differences, how they tasted, how they felt.

Russ had followed the squad into a building on Fulcrum Street. Outside, families were grilling meat and drinking Pacifico. Children ran through the sprinklers, shrieking in Spanish.

Ivan's friends wore Walmart shoes with low-sagging shorts, tattoos crawling up their necks like skin disease. But Ivan himself was clean-shaven and straight-backed in a blue linen shirt. Marco, the only man Ivan was personally close to, had a tattoo scrawled beneath his chin that read "DAHLIA," the name like an all-caps slit in his throat. Though Marco had never been formally involved with the drug ring, the squad still parked outside his house sometimes to keep watch.

In all his years as a police officer, Russ had arrested only a handful of people. He was always shocked and a bit disgusted by the satisfaction: a surging release as the metal pieces found their places. That clink. He'd memorized the Mirandas as a child, playing with a toy cop car on the back porch, his father watching from behind the sliding glass door. Russ had a lisp as a kid. You have the wight to wemain siwent.

After Ivan and his friends had been tackled and shoved violently into cars, the lieutenant sent Russ back into the house to collect the Junk. The house was dilapidated, the roof nearly caved in. Uncooked pasta spilled across the grimy kitchen counter. It smelled like rotting fruit.

There were two bedrooms. The first held only a mattress, half covered with stained navy sheets. The closets were empty. So were the vents. The second room didn't have a bed, just a rocking chair by the window. It was missing three slats in the frame. And in the rocking chair: Ines.

She wore a pair of basketball shorts and a men's tank top. Her hair was stuck to her cheeks; the room was stifling and covered in peeling wallpaper. An old, ailing floral print. She didn't see Russ. Not at first. She had her elbows on the windowsill, chin cupped in her palm, watching, paralyzed, as they drove her brother away.

Ines looked up at the sound of Russ, her face round and greasy, a splotchy red with panic. And in her eyes, recognition: man from park. Márquez. The heart's memory eliminates the bad and magnifies the good.

Only later, when Ines had made her statement—she didn't know

anything about the drugs in that house, where she had been living only
a few weeks, having just arrived to visit her brother, with a valid Border
Crossing Card and B-2 tourist visa—when the social worker had given her
a new shirt (a black T-shirt from the gas station, with Colorado's flag em-
blazoned next to a proud American eagle, because Ines's suitcase was being
processed as evidence), after Russ had driven her to the station, just the
two of them in the car, and as she watched Broomsville flick by in blurs of
summer green, Ines had said, I didn't know police could be nice, and Russ
said, They usually aren't, but it doesn't matter; are you thirsty? He bought
two cans of Coke at a 7-Eleven. When Ines unbraided her hair beneath
the bright station-house lights and unleashed it in clumps that reeked of
smoke—then, Ines looked beautiful. Like the girl he'd met in the park, sun-
glazed, with a hint of flirt. They sipped their Cokes in the stifling car and
Russ decided: he would invite her home. She wouldn't have to go back to
that house, covered in Junk. No funny business, he promised. Funny business. Ines would tease him, always.

Russ had stuck the page from *Love in the Time of Cholera* on his refrigerator, held down with a magnet that doubled as a beer opener, a souvenir
from his sister's vacation to Key West. That night, they drank whiskey in
mugs at the kitchen table and Ines slept on Russ's couch, which had never
been professionally cleaned, but was comfortable enough.

───────────

When Russ told the guys on the force that Ines was staying over—he did
not specify the couch—they slow-clapped and whistled. Russ assured them
that Ivan had been coerced, paid for menial tasks, caught in the wrong
place at the wrong time. Detective Williams slapped Russ's back, sarcastic
but proud. You finally did it, he said. Finally got yourself a girl. Better lock
that one in, quick.

Those first months, Russ cooked for Ines every night. She loved the old carpet, how it squished between her toes. They cooked steak with brussels sprouts, or salmon and potatoes, and Russ bought bottles of Merlot, fourteen dollars each. They sipped from shiny new glasses on the couch and they talked. Ines was so pretty when she spoke, that lilting accent, lingering on the E. Her English was nearly perfect, though she often dropped the word "the" or added extra plurals. Can you please pass the chickens? She was from Guadalajara, a huge city of Gothic cathedrals, gray spindles stretching toward the sky. More than a million people, she said. She and her family had lived in Zapopan, a suburb of the city, six of them in the apartment above their father's dental practice. She and her sisters cooked every night. Pozole—a stew with hominy and pork. Ines had gone to Universidad Autónoma de Guadalajara, and she had been teaching high-school English when Mamá had convinced her to follow Ivan to the States, because one of her father's clients—a regular root-canal patient—worked at the consulate. Her sisters would come too, eventually. Russ never asked what she'd studied. How she'd gotten here. What she missed.

Once, Russ found Ines on the kitchen floor, covered in sourdough yeast, crying for her brother. Russ scooped Ines up and carried her to bed. She had gone slack, but not because Russ had comforted her. She was simply exhausted, and Russ was there. Still, he held her. Ines fell asleep, and Russ stroked the soft belly of her earlobe, rolling it across the surface of his thumb, that little patch of peach-fuzz flesh.

Some nights, when they'd gotten tipsy, Ines would ask about Ivan, who was adjusting slowly to life in prison. Is there anything you can do for him? she'd ask, too casual. And Russ wondered if Ines stayed not for him—though they laughed often and spoke kindly to one another—but for her brother.

Yes, he'd say. I'll keep an eye on Ivan. I'll make sure they don't send him back home. A few months later, Ines's tourist visa would run up, and Russ knew she would not go back to Guadalajara, not with Ivan locked in a cold cement cell.

Despite it all, they got along well.

On those Merlot nights, Ines would fall asleep in Russ's lap, and he'd stroke her hair like he'd seen people do. So soft. She'd bought a new bottle of shampoo. She didn't smell like smoke anymore. Now, eucalyptus.

———

They went to San Diego, because California seemed like the next-best thing to Mexico. Ines leaned against the passenger's-side window and hummed along to the radio, while Russ adjusted the AC. They drove all sixteen hours in one day, stopping only four times for fast food and the bathroom. Ines listened intently to the radio ads, asking Russ about words she didn't know. Liquidate? Neoprene? Indigestion?

They stayed in a Marriott Rewards hotel. Ines bought a one-piece swimsuit because she didn't want to wear a bikini. They drank daiquiris by the hotel pool, and Ines tilted her head up. Sun breathed hot across her cheeks.

Art museums. Public parks. Three-star dinners. At a street fair, Ines made Russ try mango doused in Tajín, and Russ doubled over coughing. Ines doubled over laughing. One night, they went salsa dancing; Ines tried to teach him the steps at a crowded nightclub with overpriced drinks and sweaty, tan bicep men. Russ stepped on her feet, but Ines didn't care. She spun around in a red skirt and shook her hips at him and Russ felt wanted. Young and desired. When the club closed down they stumbled home, Russ shirtless because of all the sweat, Ines fanning her neck with one hand as she held her hair up with the other.

They took a shower when they got back, and, wrapped in a clean white hotel robe, Ines pulled Russ on top of her.

Tell me about the people you've loved, she said.

I haven't loved anyone before, Russ said, and he was certain, momentarily, that this was the truth.

———

They drove back to Broomsville, where the air was vacuum-sucked dry. That night, they did a load of laundry, and Ines did not go to the couch. She padded up the stairs, her small hand in Russ's.

Russ's sheets were nearly ten years old. He didn't realize this until he was swollen inside her, Ines lying flat on her stomach, face buried in the pillow.

Can you breathe? Russ asked.

Yes, she said. Muffled. Russ pressed a hand to her ribcage, feeling for oxygen. Afterwards, he mopped the sheets with a Kleenex and said, Will you marry me? California hung between them, like a dream or a fruit. Pulpy and ripe. Ines rolled over. She watched the ceiling, black hair splayed across the rumpled pillow like someone underwater.

Yes, she said. All right.

———

A man should always keep his word, Russ's father used to say. Your word is your dignity.

So when Detective Williams pulls Russ aside after the briefing to ask about his brother-in-law—Ivan Santos, ex-con and neighborhood idol—Russ puts on his bravest face. I know he's family, Detective Williams says, so if anyone asks, you've been put on temporary probation. But we need all hands on deck here. And hey, between me and you—could Ivan have done this?

I think so, yes, Russ tells Detective Williams, sinister and noble. I think Ivan could have killed this girl.

As Russ says it, his father's voice rings loud in his ears, confirming the valiance of this shaky proclamation—if your word is your dignity, then Russ is a hero. Besides, he has never promised Ines anything except to be her wedded husband, to have and to hold, for better or for worse, in sickness and in health. Russ knows that if it were to come down to it—if he had to choose someone to protect—it would not be Ivan.

Take care of my boy, will you? Lee Whitley had asked, the day he left for good.

Okay, Russ had said.

Okay.

This was Russ's word. He had no choice but to keep it.

Cameron

Back when Beth DeCasio said that Cameron was the sort of kid who would bring a gun to school, they sent him to the school social worker.

"My name is Janine," she said, with a gaze that did not feel. "I'm going to ask you a few simple questions, okay?"

"Okay."

"Have you ever thought about hurting yourself?"

When Cameron first heard about Andrea Yates, he ran a bath.

The ceramic surface of the tub was slippery. Cameron lowered himself in carefully, one hand on each edge. Rested his spine against the metal faucet and slid down, like a person getting into bed after a long day stomping through loud, slushy streets.

Cameron sank until he could feel the wall of bathwater against his eardrums, rising, a tide that sloshed gently toward his brain. He tilted his head back. Hair spread around him in slow motion. He could have danced, he thought. Underwater, it would have looked all right. He sank farther, until the only parts of his body exposed to oxygen were his eyes and his nose, which felt very close to the webbed cracks in the ceiling.

When he went under, it was a pleasant hum he heard, a pressurized sound that was not uncomfortable. He opened his eyes. The cracks in the ceiling were gone. So was the stained shower curtain, and so was the mirror, and even his toothbrush, crusty next to the sink. Muted by this veil of water. He closed his eyes again, reveling in the peace of it.

Cameron thought how it wouldn't be so bad, dying like this—aware of your own insides.

"Have you ever thought about hurting yourself?"

"No," Cameron had said to Janine.

She scribbled in her spiral notebook.

———

"It looks nice."

Mr. O stood over Cameron's shoulder, studying the unfinished portrait. The lion's left eye was looking much better. Cameron had finished the lashes, and they carried the same texture as the whiskers. The lion was Cameron's portrait project for art class. He thought lions were both intimidating and graceful, and this was an underrated combination of things to be.

"Try for more shadows around the eye," Mr. O said. "See that blended area? Your darks need to be darker."

Cameron thought his darks were plenty dark.

"Come with me," Mr. O said. "Bring your stuff."

As Cameron followed the art teacher past the industrial paper cutter, backpack slung over his shoulder, lion and charcoals in hand, the class fluttered and murmured.

"That's the kid?"

"Yeah, him. Creepy, right?"

"Sick little fucker."

Mr. O's office was a converted supply closet that he had covered in student art and furnished with a stool and easel. A single lightbulb hung from the ceiling. Bits of pink eraser littered the linoleum floor, and acrylic paint spread in dripped patterns across every surface. Cameron suspected Mr. O spent nights here, working on his own projects. He'd seen a painting, once, propped against the wall. A pair of hurting blue eyes set against cotton skin.

"I'm worried about you."

"I'm fine."

"I heard the gossip, Cam. Kids can be so mean."

A smash came from the other side of the door. They'd just finished a unit on ceramics. His classmates whooped.

"You miss her?" Mr. O asked.

Once, Mr. O told Cameron to try photography. He hadn't explained why, but Cameron deduced: photography was about capturing moments other people had missed.

Photography never worked for Lucinda. She couldn't be reduced to a single second. Drawing was different—lines were intentional and they spanned in range the way she did, light to dark to heavy to soft to smudged and everything in between. He thought this described Lucinda much more naturally than a snapshot.

"Yeah," Cameron said.

Mr. O patted him on the shoulder, hesitated, and cracked open the metal door.

"You can work in here today," Mr. O said, and the crinkles around the corners of his eyes looked very kind.

———

Mr. O fell in love with Mom last year, when they started a unit on painting.

"They usually don't allow it until junior year," Mr. O had said. "But they're making an exception."

"What kind of painting?" Cameron had asked.

"Realism," Mr. O had said. "Acrylics."

When Mr. O made the announcement in class, everyone groaned, even the popular girls who were always smiling at Mr. O, blinking fast and passing notes about him.

"Calm down," Mr. O said. "We'll be working together. I've been commissioned to finish a painting for a gallery in Denver. We can teach each other."

Cameron decided to paint a barn swallow, with a red neck and blue body. He found a picture on the internet, printed it, and traced it onto canvas. The bird was perched on a lone branch.

The following week, Mr. O showed up at Cameron's house for tea. He and Mom had met at parent-teacher conferences. *So you're responsible for this talented kid?* Mr. O had said, paint-splattered hands shoved in the pockets of his corduroys.

Mom and Mr. O sat on the old couch in the living room, drinking Mom's favorite ginger tea. Cameron went for a walk, meandering aimlessly to the foot of the mountains. He debated going up to Pine Ridge Point, but it wasn't that sort of night, even though he felt awfully sad. It was a specific melancholy, the sort of sadness you felt when you were in the process of losing something: you had to watch it go with the knowledge that you couldn't stop its leaving.

When Cameron came home, the house smelled like acetone and turpentine. Mom sang while she did the dishes.

A few days later, Mr. O showed the class his painting.

"It's called *The Calla Lily*," he said, propping it up at the whiteboard.

Mr. O had painted the calla lily in melting shades of yellow, the petals tinged a blushing red. The inside of the calla lily was done with a smaller brush, in quiet strokes you had to focus hard on. The anther and the ovary peeked out from behind the petals, and Mr. O had left blank spots in all the right places—the flower had holes, but they were intentional. Spaces that didn't need covering, empty parts that made it look more whole. The flower was familiar to Cameron, like a song you had heard as a child and couldn't remember the words to.

Mr. O had studied Mom. He'd understood all her edges, the places where she blended into the background, the places where she popped—he'd taken the sound of Mom laughing to herself at late-night television—and he had turned these things into colors and strokes and put them in the shape of a calla lily.

Cameron guessed Mr. O was around the same age as Mom, but he looked ten years younger. He had black hair with gray bits that poked out around his ears and the sort of wrinkles people got in their thirties. He had a slim, lean build, and he smoked cigarettes against the back fence of the school every day at three o'clock.

Mr. O's parents had emigrated from Japan when he was only five. He'd taught himself English by watching sitcoms. He used to have a wife, but she moved to New York to be a ceramics designer. He told Cameron and Mom this very casually, at the bakery after the winter art show, as they dipped three forks into one piece of cheesecake.

"People change," he said, and that was that.

Sometimes at night, after Mr. O had come and gone, Mom would sit on the porch steps, her body folded in half, hugging herself and watching the dim world exist. Cameron wanted to tell Mr. O about loss—the hissing sound it made, like air drained from a tire, how that sound could continue forever if you let it—but maybe Mr. O already knew.

––––––

Cameron tried to work on his art project. He tried to fall into the spaces between charcoal strokes, but today was Thursday. Lucinda had ballet on Thursdays. Cameron had followed her, once, and watched from the Chinese restaurant across the street as Lucinda did pliés and jetés in a tight black leotard. Her hair was pinned up in a bun. Even though Cameron couldn't see from so far away, he was sure the strands in front were curling wild against Lucinda's forehead.

Cameron left his stick of charcoal next to the easel and wiped his hands on his jeans. His fingers left charcoal tracks across the denim. Cameron's hands were usually steady. Artist's hands. His hands had a sense for the way things moved, and he could confidently replicate that movement. Cameron's hands were his favorite part of his own body because they spoke in all the ways his mouth could not.

Now, they shook as they reached into his backpack.

Even though Cameron knew Mr. O was probably only nice to him because he was in love with Mom, he had a lot of faith in the easiness of Mr. O's eyes and the way he gave instructions in class—*You have to understand the emotional undercurrents of your work if you want genuine results.*

For this reason, and because he did not know what else to do, Cameron dug to the bottom of his backpack and pulled out Lucinda's purple diary.

Mr. O had seen Cameron's drawings of Lucinda. Cameron had brought them in that September, when Mr. O was deciding about the advanced figure-drawing class. *You have an eye for realism*, Mr. O said. He'd never seen a ninth-grade student with Cameron's abilities, he said, and—*Wow, Cam*—the portraits were lifelike and clear. *Majestic.* Cameron had exactly replicated her face with his fingertips, drawing her exterior lines and smudging them around to give her a life and texture Mr. O said he wasn't sure she possessed in actuality. Cameron respected him for this.

When the bell rang, Cameron wrapped Lucinda's diary in his oversized green sweat shirt and left the bundle on the stool, next to the lion with half-drawn eyes—an apology to Mr. O with a signature at the bottom.

———

Cameron was stumbling out of the art classroom, breathing hard, when Ronnie grabbed his shoulder. He whirled Cameron around forcefully. Ronnie had PE in the wrestling gym while Cameron had art class, and now he smelled like dirty socks.

"Dude," Ronnie said. "What's your deal?"

Ronnie glanced pointedly past Cameron, in the direction of Mr. O's office. Curious.

"What's going on with you?" Ronnie said. "Seriously. People keep talking. Asking me what you did, if you really were obsessed with Lucinda. Are you some kind of creep or something?"

Crowds of kids jostled with their backpacks and squeaked their shoes. Cameron tried to Untangle—*in, two, three, out, two, three*—but Ronnie tightened the straps of his own backpack and a pen clattered to the floor. Ronnie did not move to pick it up, only drew a reddened hand across his clammy forehead.

"Fine." Ronnie pushed past Cameron, knocking him in the shoulder. "Don't answer. When people ask, I'll just tell them yes, you are a fucking freak."

After one more suspicious glance toward Mr. O's office, Ronnie disappeared into the swarm of stares. Cameron picked up the pen that had fallen out of Ronnie's backpack. A Bic, with no cap on the end. It dripped at the head, where ink bled down metal. Cameron would keep it in the Collection of Pens, where he had two other Bics belonging to Ronnie Weinberg.

Cameron kept the Collection of Pens in an old shoebox at the top of his closet. When he felt bottled up, he would line up the pens in chronological order of acquisition and imagine how certain hands looked holding certain pens. It was like curating a museum of things he knew about other people, and the Bics and gel pens made him feel like those people and their hands were right there with him.

Last summer, Ronnie and Cameron went to the park. It was misting outside, the sort of rain that came down in drops so tiny you couldn't catch them in an open palm. Ronnie kept a Bic pen in his pocket (white, chewed at the end). He twirled it compulsively as they walked. He wore plaid shorts that fell below his naked hips. A few wiry sprouts of black hair curled just above the button—Ronnie never wore underwear.

"My mom's been such a bitch lately," Ronnie said. "Menopause or something. That girl shit makes me want to kill myself. Can you imagine? Bleeding out your pisshole every month."

Cameron didn't think it was their pissholes they bled from. Mom had explained it once, but any discussion of female anatomy was dangerous around Ronnie, who truly didn't care whether Cameron talked or not.

They sat on the swings, popping open cans of Mountain Dew with cracks, bubbles, hisses of cool steam. Ronnie pulled out his cell phone, squinting as he typed a text message. Ronnie had his own cell phone, one of the first kids at school to be so lucky. A green Razr flip phone, sleek and sophisticated. Cameron didn't like to be around people who texted without his own piece of plastic to shield him. *We already have a phone at home*, Mom said. *We don't need anything fancy.* She finally bought a cell phone for emergencies, but the battery was never charged.

"This playground sucks," Ronnie said, putting the phone back in his pocket. "Do you remember when we were kids and we had to play on this shit? It looks so sad. God, though, I could get used to scheduled naps and arts and crafts again."

Cameron faked a laugh. He looked at the mountains. They loomed on the outskirts of town, persistent shadows that stood and watched. The mountains probably found it all amusing, these families in their beige houses lined up on the street like stationary soldiers. The mountains made Cameron feel so scrubby.

"And Beth DeCasio! During art class, do you remember? She'd paint those watercolor pictures of horses that looked like Satan. Swear to God, if I could get my hands on one of those now, I'd worship it like the fucking devil. Beth got hot this summer, didn't she?"

"I guess."

"Her tits look like water balloons. You could just pop 'em."

Ronnie had bitten his fingernails down to ten circular bumps, red at the edges and brown underneath. Now, he used them to scratch off a flaking piece of scalp.

"How would you fuck her?" Ronnie asked.

"What do you mean?"

Cameron had never thought about fucking Beth DeCasio. Not that she wasn't pretty. Beth DeCasio was very pretty, with her shiny black hair and tight tank tops and the way she walked in small skirts.

"You know," Ronnie said. "Like, doggie style? Rough? Passionate? Sensual?"

Last year, Mom found the porn magazine in the top drawer of Cameron's dresser. It was the three-year-old issue of *Playboy* Ronnie had stolen from his dad. The issue with Rayna Rae in the center, legs spread—Cameron spent hours wondering about the pink between her legs, so slippery and rubbery, something you'd want to touch just to see how it would feel.

Cameron came home from school to the magazine, open on the coffee table and covered in sticky notes dictating the portions Mom disapproved of. *You can't expect women to look like this. You see the shape here? She paid thousands of dollars for those breasts.* They had a long talk about *changing bodies* and *the objectification of women* and Cameron couldn't remember the rest of the conversation. He hadn't looked at Mom once throughout the entirety of the talk, because this was the most shameful and miserable and embarrassing moment of his life. When it was over, Mom didn't hug him or kiss him on the forehead. She took one step toward him, hesitated, and turned around, murmuring something about *dinner in twenty minutes* to mask the fact that Mom and Cameron were changing.

She was a woman. He was a man. This would always exist between them. She could lecture him all she wanted—about fake breasts and loving people gently, differently—but all this aside, neither of them had any control over what kind of man Cameron turned out to be.

Cameron had just watched internet porn for the first time, and it made him want to cry. Those shiny women—their springy bodies that went *smack, smack, smack.* He watched with a tingling and urgent fascination. It wasn't love, he knew, because love was not supposed to hurt anyone, but it felt somehow related. It rose like love, it swelled. Sex. Mystery of mysteries. The biggest hurt.

"Doggie style," Cameron answered.

"My mom reads *Cosmo*," Ronnie said. "There's some seriously kinky shit in there. I mean, you gotta see it; I'll bring it to school tomorrow. This one article talks about how you should freeze fruit and run it down a girl's body—like, can you imagine a frozen fucking banana . . .?"

There was an oak tree on the right side of the fence that separated the playground from the Thorntons' yard. Even from the distance of the swing set, the bark curved in a way Cameron wanted to remember, burying its roots in the ground and snaking up like vertebrae climbing toward the base of a neck. The oak looked hundreds of years old, out of place in the painted metal playground, grinning and jeering at him, crying and pleading with him, touching Cameron in places he had not been touched before.

"Let's be real though," Ronnie said. "Beth wouldn't fuck either of us, would she?"

The wet wind pushed the branches to the left, blowing damp green leaves onto the Thorntons' lawn.

Ronnie bit the end of the Bic, and ink bled blue all the way down his chin.

Jade

"You're late," Aunt Nellie says.

"Sorry." I don't sound very convincing.

"You hear about that girl?" Aunt Nellie says. She stands behind the concierge desk, hands on her hips. Her eternal post. I swear, Aunt Nellie will die behind that desk someday, with a handful of Life Savers Mints stuffed in her uniform pocket.

"What?"

"The dead girl."

"Yeah, of course I have. Everyone's talking about it."

"You think he did it? That neighbor boy of hers?"

"No," I say. "I don't think he did."

"Well, you're one of the few. Anyway, you're late, and the guest for Room 208 is waiting to check in. Hop to it."

After cleaning Room 208 (where someone has crushed a trail of M&Ms into the carpet), I take my break behind the kitchen dumpsters.

Melissa, the housekeeping manager, only lets you take breaks if you're a smoker. This seems backwards to me, but I own a single pack of Virginia Slims for this purpose. I forgot them today. I wind through the kitchen and mime a smoking signal: Melissa wears a hairnet as she unpacks grocery-store croissants from the freezer, preparing for the morning's continental breakfast. She nods permission. Sometimes she'll join me outside, and I'll light one up just for show, but I always end up coughing my brains out. Last time, I nearly puked in the rot-lined dumpster after Melissa had gone in for a room-service call.

I've stashed a Coke in my apron pocket to get me through the last two hours of this shift. Tonight feels particularly desolate. Cars whoosh by on the highway across from the hotel; garbage wind wafts over me. When I came outside, the sun was still glowing amber over the foothills. Now, I can barely see its forehead. I crack open the can of Coke and lean against the wall.

Halfway through the can, I notice that I have company.

Querida stands a few feet away, shimmering in the kitchen light that filters through the open door. I clear my throat, announcing myself in the shadows.

"Ah," she says. "You scared me."

"Sorry," I stammer.

Querida's jeans tent over her calves in an outdated bell bottom. Her waist bulges a bit beneath a zip-up sweat shirt. She has an accent—I've never heard her speak before. Spanish, maybe.

"Is it okay if I smoke here?" she says, though she's already flicking a lighter. She tosses a tangle of long black hair over her shoulder and inhales, shoulders slumping as smoke fills her lungs.

"Do you want one?" she says, passing me the pack.

"No, thanks," I say, and take a sip of flat soda.

WHAT YOU WANT TO SAY BUT CAN'T WITHOUT BEING A DICK

A Screenplay by Jade Dixon-Burns

EXT. HOTEL—NIGHT

Celly stands by the dumpsters behind the building, the highway just feet away. Cars whoosh by, a noise like a sea. Celly takes a drag of a cigarette and exhales the smoke coolly. WOMAN (28, beautiful) stands beside her.

                         CELLY
        Will you tell me how it feels?

                         WOMAN
        I'm sorry?

Celly blows a thin line of smoke away from Woman, then turns to face her.

                         CELLY
        To be loved like that. How it feels. I can't
        imagine.

———————

"I am sorry?"

"What?"

"Did you say something?" Querida exhales a plume of smoke from the pursed corner of her mouth.

"No, I—"

"You asked how it feels."

"Oh," I say. "I mean, how does it feel to be loved like that? Like you and that guy upstairs?"

I can't believe I've actually asked her such an idiotic question, this pretty woman in casual jeans, cloaked in her misty aura. Lust. Querida takes another drag; I wish I'd accepted a cigarette. I feel like a child, swirling around the last sip of flat Coke in a can.

"Wow," she says, with a laugh. "This is a question."

"Sorry," I say. "I didn't mean to—"

"No," she says. "It is okay. If I am being very honest, I have not thought enough about it. I'll let you know later, okay?"

She drops her cigarette on the filthy pavement and stamps out the flame. Pulls her sweat shirt tight and retreats back into her sparkling heart-pound world.

"What'd you bring me today?" Howie asks.

Howie wears a peeling visor and an Ann Arbor sweat shirt he found last January. He leans against his shopping cart, legs crossed, jiggling one bare foot. The first time I saw Howie's feet, I nearly vomited—they're swollen. Cracked. So black with grime you can barely distinguish his toes.

"Sorry," I say to Howie. "Slim pickings."

I hand him a block of cheddar cheese, the cheap kind that comes by the prepackaged pound. It's practically plastic, the sort of cheese the patrons of the Hilton Ranch won't miss. Howie is well acquainted with the lost, back-end contents of the Hilton Ranch's walk-in refrigerator: the half tub of olives I brought last Thursday, the still-frozen breakfast croissants from the Thursday before.

Howie pulls his cheek to the side with one swollen finger, using his molars to bite into the naked hunk of cheese. Like a sneer. Saliva leaks from the corner of his mouth into his crusty beard.

"Why do you eat like that?"

"Doesn't hurt as much. You wouldn't know. All that money your grandma paid for your teeth could feed me for a year, little Celly."

Howie thinks my name is Celeste—*call me Celly*. I am an orphan living with my ailing grandmother in the hills (my parents were killed in a tragic car accident). I am nineteen, and engaged to be married to the love of my life. I justify these stories with canned artichokes—like if I leave some offering, I'm allowed to lie.

"Come sit," he says.

"That's okay."

I sat on Howie's blanket once, last winter. After a few minutes, he reached one nubby finger beneath my ski jacket and into the waistband of my jeans.

"You hear about that girl?" he says.

"Yeah."

"Pretty girl, she was," he says. "I saw her picture in the paper. They came talking to me, but I don't know nothing about her. Pretty girl, she was; pretty girl, I told them. But you know, Celly, my little Celly-girl, she's got nothing on you." Howie's gaze travels from my neck to my boots. His eyelids droop.

This awful habit: trying to see myself through other people's eyes. This is probably why I visit Howie on Thursdays, adding half a mile to my commute home from the Hilton Ranch. Around the back end of the suburb, past the small patch of forest, is the library, Howie's shield from wind and snow. I park Ma's car down the street even though half the time Howie's eyes are shut and when they're open it's impossible to know what he sees.

"How's your Ed-*ward*?" Howie asks. He licks his lips with a glazed, lazy hunger.

"Actually," I say, "I have big news. Edouard and I are leaving in a few months. We're moving to Paris together before the wedding."

"Paris, eh?" he says. "Paris, Paris, Par-eee. That's great for you, Celly; that's great for you, my Celly-girl."

I wish I wasn't such a good goddamn liar. I swear, for the rest of my life I'll remember how Howie looks now: huddled in the shadow of his shopping cart, gnawing the block of cheese I stole from the Hilton Ranch, swaying back and forth, lost in some fantasy.

Maybe he's picturing me, in love, in front of the Eiffel Tower. Maybe this makes him both happy and jealous. This might be what I came for.

Then I see it: a painting. It rests between Howie's shopping cart and the graffitied wall of the library. The bottom is browned and muddy from snow. But even then, her ankles—a ballerina. She's lacing up her shoes. It's Lucinda's Degas, the same image she printed out and taped to the front of her notebook. Not hers, of course. Its long-lost twin.

"Where'd you get that?" I ask, but he's nodding off, out of it. "Howie, where did you get that painting?"

"Found it," he says, and his chin lolls against his chest. His eyes sink closed.

The surrounding night feels all-encompassing, so thick it could swallow me. For the first time, I wonder if I've spoken with him—Lucinda's killer, whoever he is. If I've sat across from him and had normal conversations, both of us ignorant to the dark in each other. Cameron. Howie. Zap. Anyone. Me, and my stupid spell. I think of the man from *Modern Witchcraft*, hanging from the ceiling in a house of locked doors. Lucinda, holding her Degas notebook. *You don't even know him; he's not crazy.* And Cameron, standing on her lawn just minutes before she was smacked so hard that she fell and cracked her neck. And of course, Chapter Two: "Signs from the Dead."

The Image.

A chilly wind slithers between Howie and me. I blow on my hands to warm them. I don't bother to say good-bye, because Howie is gone, burrowed deep in his demented mind. I slide back into Ma's freezing car. The simple rumble of its engine is a relief, company. And me? I am glass. A bristle. A stutter.

———

They're at the dinner table. Terry has three cans of beer in front of him, which means the meal has already progressed into argument. Amy sits on the couch, curled up with a plate in her lap, earbuds in and bopping her head to her Discman, which is probably playing Kelly Clarkson. The house smells vaguely like Indian food.

"Look who it is," Ma says from the head of the table. Her lips are stained purple with wine. She sips from a mug with a snowman on it. Presumably, the wineglasses are dirty. "Glad you decided to join us."

"I was working at the hotel," I say. "Like I do every Thursday."

Ma is drunk. She runs her fingers through her frizzy, dyed hair, preening for an audience. When Ma is drunk, she stares at her own reflection in the kitchen window, puckering her lips, batting her eyelashes. Ready for her debut.

Terry tilts his beer can to examine its contents. This is his way of avoiding confrontation: Pick at the lint on your shirt. Scratch at a spot on the table. If no one notices you're alive, maybe you aren't, and maybe that's for the best.

Ma hates when I call him Terry. But there's no reason to call him "Dad," even though he is my biological father. He's home at nine every night and gone by six the next morning, always wearing some version of the same short-sleeved button-down, floating through the house like a ghost or an old Labrador.

When things get bad with Ma, Terry slinks up the stairs. He fakes yawns. His eyes rove over the bruises on our arms—*Goodnight, girls,* he says, and instead of looking at us he fiddles with the glossy fountain pens in his shirt pocket.

"You missed it," Amy says, pulling out an earbud and twisting it around her pointer finger. She looks smug. "The neighbors have been calling all night. Apparently they have a lead. They're arresting someone at Jefferson High."

"Who?"

"I don't know, but Zap has been in for questioning."

"What?" I ask. "They're arresting Zap?"

Amy shrugs and puts the earbud back in. Ma takes a gulp of wine, twirling a strand of hair with long plastic nails. The smell of Howie's clothing is still in my nose, mingling with hours-old Indian takeout.

"Your food's in the fridge," Terry says.

"You can heat it up yourself," Ma adds.

"I'm not hungry."

Upstairs, I leave my lights off.

The bottle is on the top shelf of my closet, underneath a baby blanket Ma is too sentimental to touch. I've only got about three inches left, because half the bottle was payment to Howie for buying. I don't like the taste of rum, but I don't drink for the taste. And I don't drink much. It's only for nights like tonight. I twist off the top and take as much as I can, trying to usher it past my tongue, straight down my throat. It runs south. Moments like these, I morph into the spitting image of Ma; my hands just like hers, clutching the neck of a bottle. These are the moments I feel sorry for her.

I slump against the closet door and wait to feel better. Guilt isn't something I feel often. It's a pointless emotion—completely unproductive. I hate the way guilt festers, then absorbs.

I try to remember the Cameron I saw at the cafeteria table today, so lonely. Or the Cameron from the principal's office yesterday, pressing his hair down over his forehead, fragile and nervous. Both of these images end in that of Zap, cuffs rattling on his wrists, hands behind his back.

Guilt reminds me: Cameron was a shadow shaped like a boy the night Lucinda died. She pried her bedroom window open and Cameron stayed, motionless, as Lucinda climbed to the roof of the porch. She jumped, landing on her hands and feet, crouched, a few feet from where he stood.

Wherever she is now, Lucinda knows this. The Image. She's asking me something. But she should know by now—girls like me don't answer to girls like Lucinda Hayes.

———

This is how it feels to be a stutter.

You're walking down the street and the night hasn't settled yet. It doesn't know what it wants to be. You've lived on this street your entire life. Your family hates you because you're an asshole. You genuinely enjoy being an asshole. This is why you have no friends except the homeless guy who lives behind the library.

People like Howie push you too deep into yourself. You sink this way often, and there are things you can do to temporarily soothe your mind: turn on new music, cut your bangs in the bathtub, pick at old scabs. But you'll still itch. You itch, constantly, because even when you think you might be happy, these truths bubble up to prove you wrong. You're fat. You're angry. In a different world, you could be blond or kind or friendly, or all of the above. When you slept you could look like a porcelain doll. But this is not a different world, this is your world, and you have to find a way to deal with such irony.

You walk past the Hayeses', the Thorntons', the Hansens'. The night is clear. The neighborhood smells clean. The rum churns, hot against your ribs. Dashboard Confessional is blasting in your headphones, and you're wishing you could live inside the aching lyrics, inside the guitar's shriek, that violent voice box.

You want to know what Cameron sees when he walks down this street under the forgiving cover of night. What he finds so fascinating. You want to know how he can stand in one spot for so long, with the explicit knowledge that his wanting will never be returned. How he stands with his wanting on the lawn for hours, and how he retreats home with it, unable to stash it away.

Your tiny consolation: Magic can't be real. This can't be your fault.

Your feet are so heavy on pavement, you take up too much space.

You want to hear the ocean, because you never have before.

Russ

Though it has been six years now, the particulars of Broomsville still remind Russ of Lee Whitley. The cigar shop on Main Street where they bought Fat Boys to smoke on the porch. The park, where they took Cameron on weekends, Cynthia pushing the stroller while Russ and Lee lugged a cooler of beer and hamburger meat. They spent time with Cynthia, of course, but more often it was just the two of them—even when their shifts didn't overlap, Russ and Lee often joined one another on duty. A tagalong, unpaid backup reinforcement. Both thankful for the easy company.

Nowhere holds more memories than the cliff, but Dixie's Tavern takes a close second place. The sticky tables. The broken jukebox in the corner, hills of ash in browning glass trays. The stink of the place, like old fermentation—things left to decay.

Tonight, Russ slides onto a stool at the edge of the bar. He folds his coat and gloves in a ball in his lap.

What can I get you? Tommy asks.

Tommy has worked at Dixie's Tavern for nineteen years—Russ used to come with his friends in high school. Tommy, just a few years out of high school himself then, would serve them mixed drinks he later told Russ were half water. Russ and his friends would stay out until two, three o'clock in the morning, exhilarated. They'd drive home late, mildly intoxicated, their heads hanging out the window like lazy dogs—whooping to the gas stations and the oil rigs, whooping to the wide pastures and the mountains, remote and distant in the night.

I'll take a double whiskey, Russ says.

Ivan lingers by the pool table, alone. On the corner is a bottle of decaffeinated green tea, its label advertising peace and serenity. Tommy charges Ivan two dollars a game, and Ivan brings his own chalked pool cue. He spends hours this way, maneuvering polished wood across the fake green lawn of a table.

You gonna play your brother-in-law? Tommy asks.

Not tonight, Russ says. He downs his drink and places the glass on the table for a refill.

You want another? Tommy asks. The neon sign behind Tommy's head reads "BEER" in capital letters. Russ should have a beer instead, but the idea of all that liquid sloshing around in his stomach just makes him angry, so he orders another double.

The third drink tastes like less than the second, and the fourth just tastes like the inside of Russ's mouth, chemical and numb.

The first September they were married, Russ came home to foreign smells in the kitchen. Ines danced in socks to Lupillo Rivera playing on the computer in the corner of the room. Something was frying on the stove, and something else was boiling. Ines had hung red, white, and green streamers in the hallway.

Mexican Independence Day, she said. We are celebrating this year. Guadalajara has the biggest celebration in the country, did you know?

Okay, Russ said. He retreated to the living room, where he watched a rerun of *Law & Order* until she finished cooking.

Ines had set the table with colorful paper napkins. A ceramic dish steamed in the middle. Birria de borrego, she told him. That's spiced lamb, and queso fundido on the right. When Russ took a bite, it burned the top of his mouth. Everything was too spicy.

Good? she asked.

Yeah, he said.

Back home they'd have fireworks, she told him.

Cool, Russ said, and he eyed the NASCAR race on the TV in the living room, whose volume was turned all the way up.

Ines carefully watched his plate, which had gone mostly untouched. She rubbed a spot on her neck and looked up at the ceiling, the expression on her face like a cracked windshield. For the rest of the meal, she didn't look him in the eye. She smacked Russ's hand away when he tried to help with dishes. When Ines had finished cleaning, she came to Russ in the den.

Ines switched off the television and stood in front of it. Fire in her eyes. Russ had never seen Ines angry—he was almost afraid. She came at him quickly, and he did not put his arms up in defense because he wasn't sure if she would kiss him or hit him.

The latter: she slapped him across the face. A sting. Russ's cheek burned where her palm had struck.

After that night, Ines never cooked Mexican food for him again. Russ would come home late from work to the smells of rice and spiced meat, but Ines always hid the evidence, ingredients for a grilled-cheese sandwich laid out on the counter beside an empty plate. Punishment. Russ thinks about this night often—if he had handled it correctly, asked questions, shown even one morsel of honest interest, how different their marriage could have looked. Instead, Ines cradles these things to her chest—recipes, stories, songs, memories—unwilling to share with Russ. Stupid American man.

Ines's anger is there, in the white bread on the counter. Russ wonders where this anger goes when he is not around. He wonders what else she conquers.

———

A few weeks before Ivan got out of prison, Ines looked up from the breakfast table. A rare Saturday morning off duty—eggs and bacon. Ines read a novel while Russ skimmed the newspaper.

He gets out soon, she said to Russ.

Who?

Ivan. He gets out in two weeks.

Oh, Russ said, though he had been dreading the date for months. Ines watched him, expectant.

I'll make sure the right people know, Russ said.

Ines smiled and picked up the book again.

Ivan had overstayed his visa a year and a half by the time he'd gotten to prison. Now, it was three and a half. Russ wasn't clear on the procedure for checking papers—for deportation after prison—but he knew Immigration and Customs Enforcement was strict about narcotics. Russ's father had been close with an officer who made the move from patrol to agency with ICE, and Russ had spoken with this man briefly at department barbecues. Anyway, everyone loved Russ's father. That Monday, Russ found the right office, knocked on the right door.

Hey, he'd said to the stranger hunched at the desk. I need to ask for a favor.

Within ten minutes, Ivan had not been granted citizenship or a green card or even an application—only a promise that he wouldn't be checked for any of these things upon his release. When he told Ines that night, she flung her arms around him and they danced together, hips pressed to hips in a sway that felt genuinely joyous, if not like romance.

The night Ivan got out of prison, Ines threw a dinner party. She blew up balloons and tied them to the mailbox. She hung a homemade poster in the front hall: "WELCOME HOME, IVAN!"

Russ grilled steak on the back patio while Ines, Ivan, and Marco gathered in the kitchen, laughing over one, two, then three beers. Marco had visited Ivan weekly, delivering books like Machiavelli's *The Prince* and Leopoldo Zea's *The Latin-American Mind.* Marco had studied hard and taken out loans, and now he was in school to become a physician's assistant.

By the time the steak had browned at the edges, all three were drunk and arguing happily in machine-gun Spanish. Russ dumped his beer in a potted tomato plant. Through the window, Ines glowed in the light of her brother, home at last.

When the food was ready, they gathered around the linen-set table, and Russ held Ivan's hand for grace.

You're all great dinner company compared to the inmates, Ivan said, as he cut a civilized bite of steak. Though, I will say, I had a lot of time to think. I learned a lot from the other inmates, bad company as they were. I learned a lot about evil.

Russ swallowed.

I learned that evil does not exist, Ivan continued. There are only different ways people try to be good. Very few people in this world do things with evil as the intention.

So, Russ said to Ivan, you're saying you dealt narcotics in an effort to be good?

The words just came out, in the voice of the men he'd worked with for years, that hypermasculine tone Russ could adopt without trying or thinking. Ines's back straightened. She and Marco exchanged a look. A hideous pause.

I didn't mean it like that, Russ tried, but Ivan had pushed his plate away.

Ivan lifted his beer to his lips and downed it in one chug, a trickle running down his chin. This was the last drink Russ would ever see him touch.

Here is what I am saying, Ivan said. I don't believe in evil, not the way you and your cop friends define it. You are an ignorant bunch of middle-class schoolboys, and it is terrifying that you exist in the hundreds, the thousands, all refusing to turn around and see the world for what it is. You're so busy chasing us outsiders, you never stop to look behind you and realize that half the people you're putting away are better people than you, with far less evil intentions. I don't think you're a bad man, Officer Russell Fletcher, and that's what bothers me most about you. You're just another one of the power-tripping minions, and somehow, I've let a fucking puppet like you marry my sister.

Ivan stood, and the table wobbled. The vase of flowers Ines had bought earlier toppled, and muckish green water leaked across the tablecloth.

We should go, Marco said. Thank you for dinner, Russ.

It wasn't Ivan's anger that scared Russ as Marco pulled a stumbling, drunken Ivan out the door by the wrist. Not even the hulking size of the man. It was those words, the ease and surety of Ivan's proclamation: You are a puppet. You are everything that is wrong.

You're not scared of him, are you? Ines asked, in bed that night. She'd cried in the shower, and Russ had pretended not to hear. Her eucalyptus hair spread wet across Russ's chest as Ines drew circles on his shoulder with her pointer finger.

No, I'm not, Russ said, and he pulled her close.

Ivan never apologized, though he has not tasted a single drink since. Despite this reformation, Russ knows that Ivan is dangerous—who could be unafraid of a man who does not believe in evil?

———————

Now, at the bar, Ivan's arms stretch the length of the pool cue, his starchy shirt tight. He bites his lip in concentration.

Russ slaps a twenty on the table and stands. He sways. Steps forward.

Finally coming over to say hello? Ivan says. Too polite. The heat of him on Russ's mouth: Warm breath. Gold tooth.

Tell me what you did, Russ says.

I told your friends and I'll tell you again, Ivan says. I don't know anything about that poor girl.

I asked you a question, Russ says. What the fuck did you do?

The words slur as they leave Russ's mouth. Ivan smiles in a pitying way. Russ could hit him.

Russ, Ivan says. Come on, my brother. Take a look at yourself.

Russ deflates. Looks at himself: a very small man. The entire room spins, a playground carousel.

———————

Now, late at night. Ines is passed out in the guest room, a paper cup of microwaveable noodles topped on the nightstand. She sleeps with her hands clasped below her cheekbone. Above her is the one photograph Russ bought from the drugstore, a landscape, a feeble attempt to make the room look more alive for when his parents stopped by. The mountains look very small on the wall, Ines a slumbering giant beneath.

She stirs only when Russ moves to shut the door.

Russ? she whispers, a little girl waking in the night.

Her makeup has dried beneath her eyes. The television in the corner is playing the news.

The detective came by, Ines says. He asked me questions. He was with the lieutenant. I hoped you would be here. I answered all of their questions and I sent them away.

I'm sorry, Russ says, whiskey-full and dizzy. I had to run an errand. Did they ask about me?

No, Ines says. But they asked about my tutoring with Lucinda. And about Ivan. How could you think my brother killed her? Russ, how?

I don't know what I think, Russ says as the alcohol creeps back up his throat.

Ivan is good, Ines says, and she starts to cry. My brother is good.

Ines sits up, hair flattened on one side from the pillow. She rubs her face. Adjusts the strap of her tank top, which has fallen down her arm. She pulls her knees to her chest and stares past Russ, even though there is nothing behind him but the chilly upstairs hallway. The linen has left a crease across Ines's cheek.

Once, Russ stopped by after school. He stood outside the room where Ines tutored and watched her through the rectangular window. Ines and Lucinda bent over a textbook. When Ines laughed, she looked so full and round—this turned Russ on. He imagined another man standing here, another man watching his wife through the window and wishing he could have her. Lee. Yeah, Lee. Russ went into the men's restroom, where someone had carved a swastika into the stall door with a pen, and jacked off into the toilet.

Standing in the guest room, Russ becomes aware of his own stench, the slow, sludgy fade of his drunk. He smells like Ivan's cologne, the kind you buy from the back of a pickup truck in a department-store parking lot.

Come to bed, Russ says.

When he goes to rouse Ines, she flinches, her doughy arm tense at his touch. Russ leaves her there, cursing his job and how old and how dumb he's gotten.

As Russ brushes his teeth, he watches himself in the mirror. His skin doubles at the chin. Small, watery eyes. He has worn his moustache the same way for sixteen years, since someone told him it made him look intimidating. Tonight, the moustache feels like an affront to his face. Intrusive. Everything sags. He sucks the water from the plastic bristles of his toothbrush and shuts off the lights.

Cameron

Cameron had one real friend in the whole world—Ronnie didn't count. No, his only true friend was the night janitor at the elementary school.

When Cameron played his game of Statue Nights, he wandered down cemetery streets. Quiet, like this small town was an island in the middle of an unchartable ocean.

Cameron liked the way the janitor slouched in his jumpsuit beneath the streetlamp, on the back left side of the school. The janitor smoked a cigarette every hour, on the hour. It must be nice, Cameron thought, to know that comfort was waiting for you—you just had to live through so many more minutes.

They had a secret language, Cameron and the night janitor.

Nights when Cameron felt good, he would nod once from the other side of Elm Street. The janitor always nodded back. On nights when he felt Tangled, Cameron would not nod—he would only stand there, so heavy inside himself. This was enough for the janitor, who would remove his foot from the school's exterior, where he leaned like a cool kid from an old movie. The janitor would shake out his long, hulking limbs. He'd shrug, as if to say: *So?*

These nights, Cameron felt less alone, even if your one true friend couldn't really be made across a yawning midnight street.

———

Cameron started with the underside of her jaw.

This was the darkest part of Lucinda's face. The underside of the jaw blending into the neck blending into the collarbone blending into the chest—a continuous spectrum. The light in his bedroom was bad. A frigid dusk. A fly, somehow alive in the cold, slapped its little body across the ceiling. Buzz and thud and buzz and thud. Cameron couldn't concentrate.

The memorial service was tomorrow, and Mom was ironing his dress shirt in the laundry room. She'd bought the stupid thing for a seventh-grade choir concert, and Cameron had worn it to every formal occasion since. The sleeves were too short. The buttons barely closed around his wrists, and the fabric scratched his skin. But it didn't matter—the service tomorrow was just a memorial. It was at Maplewood Memorial Chapel and Funeral Home, but Lucinda's body wouldn't be there. Her body was probably in a morgue, on a metal table in the basement of some hospital, and people were probably peering down at her over surgical masks.

Cameron started again with her chin. It was too wide, but that was okay, because if you drew someone's chin too wide, it could still look like them. He moved up toward her lips. His hand was quaking, and his hand never quaked. The edge looked wrong. Once Cameron had looked at it wrong, he realized with a horrifying lurch that he would never look at it right again, because it was on that table now. Her jaw and her lips were there, peeling off their bones, decomposing—unless, maybe, they used some sort of preservation fluid.

Untangle.

He was trying to draw her cheekbones, but these were not right either,

and he couldn't remember where her freckles went, so he counted them—
one, two, three, four—but they were in all the wrong places and she was
beginning to look cross-eyed and he couldn't place the corners of her easy
eyes or the peaks of her mountain cheeks and when he pictured her face, he
could see only the unpainted wall of Jade's skin. When he looked down, the
picture he had drawn was not Lucinda and it was not Jade, and February
fifteenth had happened, somehow. For all of them.

Cameron imagined himself holding a gun, pressing his index finger to
the cool metal trigger.

Untangle.

He imagined himself holding a gun, pressing his index finger to the
cool metal trigger, pressing the barrel to the back of Lucinda's shiny yellow
hair.

Untangle.

He imagined himself holding a gun, .22, pressing his index finger to the
cool metal of the trigger, pressing the barrel to the back of Lucinda's shiny
yellow hair; *No*, she was saying, *please don't*, and a *whack*. He imagined
himself looking down at Lucinda on the carousel—his own dirty sneakers,
the left shoelace was untied—looking back at her contorted form, watching
blood ooze from the gash on her head like a sick sort of halo.

———

Lucinda first asked Cameron for help on a sunny Saturday, a whole year and
a half ago. Last August. The neighborhood was roped off with orange traffic
cones—people set up food stands on their driveways. The incoming eighth-
grade girls wore bikini tops and denim shorts. The boys walked around
shirtless, tan from a summer of chlorine and SPF 15.

Cameron wore his baggy sweat shirt. *Take that thing off*, Mom told him
as she scooped a piece of banana bread onto Mr. Thornton's plate. Baby
Ollie, newborn then, slept in a car seat by Mr. Thornton's feet. Mom had

microwaved the banana bread so the neighbors would think it was fresh. *You must be boiling.*

Cameron trudged to his bedroom and changed into a plain white undershirt. It made his arms look like two sets of disjointed bones poking from oversized sleeves. No matter how Cameron twisted in the mirror, he was a mess of angles—jutting elbows and corners that didn't look natural. Like one of those paper skeletons teachers hung in classrooms around Halloween.

Something crashed down the hall. It sounded like broken glass.

When Cameron followed the sound to Mom's bedroom—to the back, Mom's marble bathroom—Lucinda Hayes stood in front of the vanity. A smashed perfume bottle lay on the floor, and the smell of Mom on a good night leaked down the cracks in the tile.

Lucinda wore a yellow bikini top and a pair of ripped denim shorts. White strings dangled from the pockets' seams. Tiny, translucent hairs spread up toward her belly button, and then, the flat expanse of her stomach: it stretched before Cameron, a boundless plain. The tan line on the soft inner skin of her breasts, where another swimsuit had protected her from the sun—it was two shades whiter, naked and goose-bumped. The plastic straps of the bikini top created red tracks that traveled across her collarbone and over her shoulders.

"I'm so sorry," Lucinda said in the bathroom, standing over the broken perfume bottle. "I didn't mean to break it. I was just looking."

"It's okay," Cameron said, pulling Mom's bath towel off the hook next to the shower curtain. He kneeled down to collect the bits of broken glass in his cupped palm. Lucinda watched from her spot next to the toilet.

Cameron knew Lucinda was pretty, but he'd never seen her squint like this. She squinted at him and she did not seem annoyed or disgusted. She squinted at him like she would squint at anyone else, and this in combination with the small smile that folded across her mouth made Cameron very certain: she was kind. So while Cameron desperately wanted to know why Lucinda was in his mother's bathroom, he would not ask. Later, when Cameron stood on Lucinda's lawn and watched her through the window, he would think: no reason at all. Fate. The world had simply pushed Lucinda toward him.

"So?" Lucinda said.

"I—I'm sorry?"

"Do you want me to buy you a new one? Or your mom, I guess?"

"No," Cameron said. "It's fine."

Lucinda pulled aside the curtain at the bathroom window and peered out, rubbing her hands together nervously, a fruit fly. Her fingers were tan and tapered, thin, but not too bony.

"Can I stay here for a minute?" she said.

"Sure."

Cameron was conscious of his skeleton body's every bone. He wished he were handsome, so he wouldn't need to fill this pause.

"Do you ever wonder?" Lucinda said. "What actually goes on in all these houses?"

"Yeah," Cameron said.

Lucinda shook her head—maybe she thought Cameron was weird, or the kind of kid who would bring a gun to school like Beth had said, but he couldn't tell, and he didn't want to know anyway.

"Believe me, I wonder all the time," she said.

A sliver of crystal had lodged itself in Cameron's left pointer finger, but he didn't care. The bikini top clung to Lucinda's ribcage. He wanted to document her in charcoal, if only to save the specifics: blond hair stuck to her neck with sweat, lashes curled over eyelids. It started in Cameron's sternum and blossomed there, a fondness that split open and gushed out. This gentle wave.

Lucinda opened the curtain. Closed it again. She ran a hand through her hair and let her head fall back onto the crux of her spine.

She began to tremble.

Cameron hadn't seen many people cry. Only Mom, and probably a girl at school once or twice. But he rarely caught the start of it—the build, the peak, the inevitable quake of a sob.

"Are you okay?" Cameron asked. He didn't understand how they'd gotten from the window to a moment where she was crying, but when Lucinda lifted her head to the mirror—Cameron standing behind her like a ghost that accidentally came back to life—he knew.

Lucinda's eyes were a forest, and she was calling from its depths, asking for help.

"I'm sorry," she said, peeking out the window again. She shook her head, a memory cleared, and adjusted her bikini top. Fresh skin. "About the perfume bottle, I mean."

When she pushed past him, Cameron caught a whiff of Mom's perfume in her hair. Lucinda had dabbed it on her wrists, or maybe her collarbone. Gold and gardenias.

Only in Cameron's smallest moments could he admit that this day in Mom's bathroom was the first, and last, time they'd spoken. That the rest of their conversations took place through fleeting glances—in gym class, when Lucinda ran laps twenty feet ahead of him, glancing back every few minutes to make sure Cameron was still there. She would pant onto his neck, even from twenty, fifty feet away, both of their legs burning, lungs screaming for them to stop. He could tell from the way she turned away, red-faced and shy, that he had whispered to her. It was a bizarre sort of conversation Lucinda and Cameron had, but it thrummed and it throbbed.

———

Cameron found the gun one summer when Mom was at work. He'd been hunting around the house for new exhibits to add to his Collection of Photos—pictures of Mom before Cameron was born, when her ballerina neck was still long and graceful.

The gun was under Mom's bed, in a polished oak box with a latch that didn't lock. Cameron's head turned hot and swollen.

He didn't touch it. He didn't dare.

He tried to forget.

When Mom left for work the next morning, Cameron wrapped the gun in a cotton T-shirt and shoved it to the bottom of his backpack. He hiked to the field behind Ronnie's house—a vast, open space with wheatgrass that grew too high and mosquitoes that swarmed in clouds.

When Cameron was sure no one had followed, he set his backpack on a log. The Rockies were fresh and bitter. He unrolled the T-shirt and examined all the foreign parts—the sight, the barrel, the grip, the cylinder. He'd looked it all up online, fascinated by how the thing worked.

The Tree had the general proportions of a man. Six feet of bare bark, then the extending branches, a billion arms swaying to a beat Cameron could not hear. There was a hole in the trunk. A bird nest. They rustled about in there, hopping on tiny legs across a bed of twigs. The gun was heavy and unnatural in his hand.

Cameron squinted an eye, like they did in the movies. He didn't look like an actor, one toothpick arm raised to point at the chest of the tree. No, he looked like his small self, standing alone at the edge of a forest with a gun he didn't know how to use, listening to the pecking of beaks against wood and wind against grass and his own bones trying to understand themselves inside his awful skin.

He closed his eyes and shot. In Cameron's head, the Tree was living, breathing, a fully grown man. The noise cracked against the sky, and Cameron's whole body tingled with the force of the bullet's expulsion.

He shot again. And again. Three bullets lodged in the left armpit of the Tree. The birds flew out in a frenzy, all desperate wings and frantic squawking.

They flapped up through the branches, feathered bodies growing smaller, surrendering to open air. Cameron imagined how stupid he must look from the birds' perspective—a lanky boy in an oversized sweat shirt, cupping a .22 in wavering hands. The weight of what he'd done hit in waves of self-disgust. Cameron was so scared. Just that year, his hands had grown bigger than Mom's. The knuckles were dry. The lines on his palm mapped out a road he could not read. They looked like someone else's hands. Like Dad's.

Cameron wrapped the gun in the T-shirt again. He sat in the dirt with the bundle in his lap and listened to the field around, because that was all he could bear to do.

———————

The iron sizzled in the next room over as Mom glided it across Cameron's dress shirt. When Mom shifted her weight, her ankles popped and cracked, a Morse code message he couldn't understand. Possibly the talus, possibly the subtalar joint. It was the saddest sound Cameron had ever heard.

Lucinda stared up at Cameron from the floor, all terrible angles and inaccurate shading. A beg. Cameron wanted to cry, but he didn't know how, so he pressed his cheek right up to the picture of the unidentifiable girl on the floor, thinking there was nothing worse than loving someone and mixing up their earlobes with someone else's.

Russ

Russ can't sleep. Ines is in the guest room and twice, Russ shudders awake: we've got a body. He throws the covers off and goes to the kitchen in his boxer shorts. Russ leans over the sink with his weight in his elbows. He had hoped to see the moon—to stare at the moon and ask it something—but instead he sees the clouds. Outside has lost its snowy touch. All drudgery. The white has melted in patches and a base layer of mud pokes out beneath, visible through the glaze of the night.

Russ tugs on a pair of pants and backs the car out of the driveway. Ambles with headlights off toward Fulcrum Street.

Ivan rents an upstairs bedroom in a house where two elderly women have begun the slow process of dying. Ivan buys their groceries and cooks their meals. At night, he spoons medicine into their quivering mouths.

Two in the morning and Russ parks outside, lights off.

Ivan is standing at the old women's kitchen window, behind a set of frilly drapes pulled partially open. His hands are in his pockets—baggy black sweat pants—and his shape is illuminated by the overhead kitchen lights. He stands very still. Straight and tall.

At first, Russ thinks Ivan is staring at his own reflection, examining himself. But from the street, he can see Ivan's view out the window: it points directly into the living room of Ivan's backyard neighbors, where an elderly couple has fallen asleep in the glow of the forgotten television, hands clasped together on the couch.

Ivan stands in the kitchen, watching them sleep, and Russ sits in his car, watching Ivan. Russ wonders if maybe Ivan too—so strong, so sure of himself—feels like a millisecond in the middle of an infinite, stretching night. Puny, fleeting. Lost to the dark.

———

Ines took Russ to church. Just once. They'd already been married a year, and Ines had suddenly asked him to join. Okay, he said, and he dug out his old scratchy brown suit. Delighted and surprised by her desire to share.

Ivan was delivering the sermon.

Ivan's Sunday speeches had changed the churchgoing community. Ivan's religion diverted from the devout Catholicism that many of the community members had known in their home countries. It took the basic principles they knew, but allowed more. Greater. Deeper. A combination of philosophy and religion, a devotion that had no strict boundaries, yet no less intensity, a formal introduction into American philosophy, all under the discerning gaze of God. Ines explained that Ivan had become a symbol, a beacon of hope: You can change. You can educate yourself, you can ask questions. You do not have to be a stranger inside your body, even in this cruel country.

So Russ went. They sat in the second row of plastic chairs: the church was a converted trailer, just a long box with cheap carpet, folding chairs, and a simple wooden cross. Russ fanned himself while Ines made her rounds, hugging all the stooped old women, guiding them gently over to Russ for introductions. *Hóla*, Russ knows to say. *Cómo está usted?*

Russ knew how to greet in the formal. During long nights on duty, he'd listen to the British accent on his Rosetta Stone. How are you? *Cómo está? Muy bien, gracias.* Very well, thank you.

When the service started, Ines shut her eyes and sang all the songs by heart. Between, she glanced sideways at Russ, nervous and expectant. Squeezed his hand. Russ sang along without really making any sound, and the few times Ines opened her eyes, Russ tried to look exultant. They talked about divine love and divine providence, and when Russ had sweated entirely through his suit—later, he'd have to peel the fabric off his thighs—Ivan took the podium.

We are here today to talk about the nature of evil, Ivan said, first in Spanish, then in English. How might we distinguish evil from God's inherent goodness?

At the altar, Ivan gestured with oversized hands, and Russ recognized the desperation in his gaze. Ivan was not a man seized by the fervor of religion. Ivan was a man who had written a sermon on a sheet of notebook paper, memorized it, practiced in front of the mirror. Timed to perfection, the whole thing, down to the gospel smile and the feverish "Amen." Every tilt of the head, every impassioned squeeze of the eyelids, every time Ivan clapped his hands together in praise—all of it, a show. Beautifully performed.

Afterwards, Russ joined the snaking line to speak to his brother-in-law.

My brother, Ivan said to Russ when they reached the front. Did you enjoy the service?

Very much, Russ said.

I hope you'll come back soon, Ivan said. God is ready to hear of your sins.

———

To entertain each other, Russ and Lee played never-ending games of gin rummy on the middle console, using Lee's old, tattered deck. Between shifts, they watched movies in the break room at the station house, sprawled on the stained, fraying futon. Lee's favorite movie was *Pulp Fiction*. 1994. Cameron young, just starting school, and Cynthia had been all over Lee about taking on more responsibility around the house. I should just become a hit man, Lee said. Put all this training to good use. He'd pat his gun affectionately. But despite all their talk, neither Russ nor Lee had ever used their guns. As long as Russ knew him, Lee never shot a single living thing.

It wasn't for lack of trying. Days off, they donned Russ's father's hunting gear, gifted to Russ for his twenty-seventh birthday; Russ had managed to utter a halfhearted thank-you. Russ's father had been trying to teach him to hunt since he was seven years old, but Russ could never do it, could never pull the trigger at the right moment. Could never want to. Still, he'd gone with his father, at least twice every summer. The sergeant never spoke on the car ride home.

With Lee, it was different. They would traipse into the woods at the base of the foothills, a designated hunting area, clothed in camouflage and orange neon. Russ had never understood this combination—one color meant to conceal, the other meant to alert, layered on top of one another. They'd change in the backseat of the car so Cynthia didn't suspect (she was wary of guns, especially for recreational use). Once, Lee fell out of the backseat and into the unpaved parking lot, trying to get his legs through pant holes without flashing the entire highway. It wasn't lying to Cynthia, not really, since they never actually hunted a single thing. It was more about the ordeal—the walk through the woods with their guns strapped awkwardly to camouflage pants, listening for the rustle of animals in bushes and hearing only themselves, that panting, aging breath.

They'd stop at this rock for lunch. Hasty, white-bread sandwiches.

Once, Lee laid flat against it, breathing hard. You ever think how old you're getting? he asked.

Sure, Russ said.

Sometimes I think it's going to be the end of me, Lee said. Time. It's going to be the end of all of us, isn't it?

Russ remembers the swell of air around them, how the wind picked up and announced itself in every branch of every tree. A warning. It whipped a plastic sandwich bag out of sight, and when Lee bounded after it, Russ almost called out: Don't go! That time, Lee came back. He crumpled the bag in his pocket and they stomped around in the woods until it was time to go home, or Cynthia would worry.

Back in the one-room church, Ivan stared right through him. Those glassy eyes. Unsettling smile. Ivan pulled him close for a threat of a hand-shake. At that moment, Russ was certain that Ivan—and maybe Jesus him-self—knew every one of his shameful sinner's secrets.

———

Russ slips into the house just before sunrise. At some point, Ines climbed back into their bed. Russ kisses the crown of her head and changes quickly into a pair of athletic pants. Plain white sweat shirt. A hat, to keep his ears warm. He laces his shoes quietly by the door and sneaks back out into the rising morning.

It's five o'clock when Russ starts down Pine Ridge Drive. The morning is brisk and frosty, but most of the snow has melted, and Russ can hear his own footsteps, slapping methodically on the pavement. He passes sleeping neighbors; Russ has lived here for years, but in this neighborhood, he is the Cop, and no one gets too close. He jogs past Lee's house—Cynthia and Cameron's now—without slowing. When Russ runs, theirs is like any other house on any other block. A small victory.

Russ considers: someone out there knows what happened to Lucinda Hayes. It's likely that he passed the killer's house just moments ago, that he is passing it now, that the killer snores into a cotton pillowcase while Russ runs right by. Russ thinks of Cameron's old bedroom, with its twin bed and sky-blue walls, and he wonders about genetics. About the inevitability of your own heritage, of badness passed down reluctantly from father to son.

Around him, the mourning neighborhood is sound asleep. The sun is bald and orange on the horizon, and when Russ gets to the edge of the suburb, he picks up speed.

Soon, he is at the base of the mountains, his heart rate is at least 140, and the peaks tower over him like wild, hungry beasts. It is this moment in which Russ understands himself best. In which he could easily say, My name is Russ Fletcher, I am a man living a certain sort of life, and I am happy. This gasping moment is free of obligation, of expectation and that bruised yellow past. It is only Russ and his beating man's heart, Russ and the cloud of his breath as it unfurls white in the cold morning, Russ and the burn, burn of his legs. The needle-prick attention of his mind, as it focuses on blazing extremities. Running, Russ is okay. Running, he moves forward.

Day

Three

FRIDAY

FEBRUARY 18, 2005

Jade

We are on a beach. Sun glares bright from all sides. Lucinda and I lie flat on our backs, bellies cast toward the sky. We are bundled in winter clothes: me in my army parka, Lucinda in her yellow down jacket and sparkly tights. A seagull screams.

Lucinda is speaking, but the wind and waves are too loud. Horizontal, she is very beautiful. Angelic—I see what they mean. We lie like lovers sharing a pillow, but her seashell mouth is opening and closing, opening and closing, her chest is heaving, tears are falling sideways over the bridge of her sloping nose. *I can't hear you!* I try to say, but my mouth is stuck shut. Shoulders glued to the ground. *I can't hear you!* She's screaming now, but no sound comes out, arms wild as they reach for me. Lucinda begs and cries and pleads and all of it is lost in the ocean's seaweed jumble.

———

Five in the morning. I wake up shaking. Outside, it's still night, the world suppressed.

The book is beneath my dresser, a magnetic force. I keep it there so Amy doesn't find it. She'd tell Ma, who'd probably check me into rehab or Jesus camp.

When half an hour goes by and the lumps of clothes start to look like faces and small animals, I flick on the nightstand light and lug the book onto my mattress. I navigate by feel to Chapter Two: "Signs from the Dead."

"When you receive a sign from the dead, you must ask: What is the deceased trying to tell me? Is there anything I can do to ease their transition into the spirit world? When the deceased communicate with the living, they are bestowing a task: you must seek out their unfinished business."

I slam the book shut. Pad to the bathroom with my hands as guides and start the shower running cold. I step in with my pajama shirt still on and try to rinse the dream away from my vulnerable unconscious.

Only here, in the shower, with my clothes still on—only here will I let myself remember the day of the ritual. The Thorntons' driveway, Lucinda in her flip-flops, how I waited until Ma and Terry were settled in front of the TV. I snuck up to my room, desperate with the realization that the Thorntons had been calling me less, that soon they'd stop entirely and I'd have to get another job, all because of Lucinda and the perfect gold braid down her back. I imagined that hundred dollars clamped in Lucinda's fist, her face all dimples and eyelashes.

I assembled everything in my room. You're supposed to be comfortable when you perform a ritual—a lot of people do it naked. But I refuse to be naked. Ever. So I put on an old swimsuit, a faded, stretched Hawaiian-print one-piece.

First, I covered a spatula with brown construction paper. The wand.

Next, I constructed the altar, sloppy and quick, using a few tealight candles from the dollar store—the kind that don't burn for more than twenty minutes.

In the middle of the altar, I propped up my favorite photo: Zap and me on the first day of second grade. We're standing on his front porch, squinting into the sun, and Zap has one pudgy hand raised above his brow. Now, we both have coiffed Sharpie moustaches drawn expertly beneath our noses.

I like this photo because we don't look happy. We're both frozen in motion, stuck there. Years later, from the floor of my bedroom, it's like Zap will move his hand from his face to hike up his backpack straps, and I will yell at Ma about how I hate having my picture taken. This photo is the middle of something. I can always pick it up and dip a toe back in, testing the temperature of my own memory.

I carefully followed the rest of the steps. The pentacle necklace, which I bought at a garage sale, went in the middle of the altar. I sprinkled salt from the kitchen table shaker (a ceramic cow). Clockwise, three times. Repeat with the thyme from Ma's spice cabinet. I arranged the candles an inch apart and sprinkled "holy water" from a Dixie cup.

They don't tell you what to do once the circle is made.

So I sat cross-legged in the middle of the carpet, candles flickering around me, hoping I had remembered to lock my bedroom door. Manufactured TV laughter echoed up the stairs, and faint pop music pulsed from Amy's room. I tried to meditate on one thought, and I tried to make that thought something useful. I wanted to pray that I'd be nicer to people, that this year wouldn't suck as much dick as the last. But I got lost in the circles of my own head and ended up where I always did: thinking about that night with Zap and Lucinda, trying to forget her sweet dough hands.

That's how it happened, I guess. In that sweaty circle, I prayed to some unspecified force that Lucinda Hayes would simply disappear.

I wanted her gone.

Even though I'd gotten this all from a book, and there's no such thing as real-life death spells, and I never believed it would work, I didn't, I swear I didn't—when I opened my eyes, it was there. Fear. Singular and inexplicable.

I didn't properly disassemble the circle. I jumped out instead, childishly scared, and flicked on my bedroom lights. The scene looked almost casual in the glow of the overhead lamp. As I blew out the candles, wax dripped into herbs and everything seeped into the carpet, thyme and salt and hot wax all tangled in singed plastic fibers. I kicked down the altar. Shoved everything into a black garbage bag, which I stuck under my bed and immediately tried to forget.

This sick sinking overcame me, like I'd proven to myself what Zap had already said: You are a disposable girl. Temporary. A mess of skin and lard over thinning, brittle bones.

———

Two hours after the dream, I'm eating cornflakes cross-legged on the couch, listening to Ma and Amy fight about Amy's eye makeup. *Just a little darker on the top lids*, Ma is saying, and Amy's saying, *Do you* want *me to look like a slut?* Mornings like these, I'm thankful that I am not Amy. Amy is Ma's Barbie doll, a mannequin for Ma's regret about her worry lines and all those cigarettes she smokes.

Miracle is, no matter how Ma dresses me, I'll never look how she wants. In fact, she has never even tried.

———

It has been like this for as long as I can remember: Ma sipping wine from three o'clock onwards. Me and Amy tiptoeing around upstairs, daring to come close only when Ma calls for us, a predator luring in her prey.

When we were little, it was only me. Now, reliably, it's only me. But when Amy was in the second grade, she gained weight—the usual little-girl pudge around the middle. And for those few years, it was her, too.

It was always worse after we'd been at Lex and Lucinda's house. The place turned Ma into a raging, spitting monster: the Hayes girls and their golden hair, the Hayes girls and their Popsicle-stick thighs, the Hayes girls and the Lysol house they inhabited, with hospital corners and dimness settings for the dining-room chandelier. Ma would pick us up, chatting amiably with Missy Hayes in the front hall as we tied our shoes. She'd bring us home—back to the kitchen floor covered in Saltine crumbs from her own midnight snack, to the triangles of hardened microwaveable pizza, to the half-full glasses of wine she'd left on the counter for days, rotting sticky. Ma would look down at us, her flabby little offspring, the both of us round and bucktoothed—even Amy, with her pretty red hair.

Ma would pour herself an afternoon glass, stewing and fuming while Amy and I huddled upstairs, awaiting the shrill screech of her call. *Girls!* she'd finally yell. *Get down here!*

One Saturday, Lex Hayes won the third-grade gymnastics tournament. The judges released the scores, and Lucinda clapped and hollered while Mrs. Hayes filmed, both of them teary when Lex came down from the podium with a heavy plastic medal around her neck. They were so proud. Amy and Lex jumped around and hugged, like winning a third-grade gymnastics tournament was equivalent to an Olympic gold.

When Ma called up the stairs that day, Amy was tense under the blankets in my bed, still wearing her expensive, rhinestoned leotard, hair pulled into a rock-solid hairspray bun. Clumpy mascara lashes. *Girls!* Ma shrieked.

"Stay," I told Amy, and I locked the door behind me before easing down the stairs, a doomed boxer walking into the ring.

"Where's your sister?" Ma asked. She'd polished off half the bottle of Barefoot Chardonnay, and she swirled the stem of the wineglass along the grainy faux-marble counter.

"Upstairs," I said.

"Go get her."

"She's tired."

When Ma stood up, I took a few criminal steps backwards. Instinct. Of course Ma noticed: she wasn't quick, but she was strong, and since I'd locked Amy in my bedroom, there was nowhere to go. Amy's door didn't shut all the way, and the bathroom didn't have a lock. So when Ma said, *Stop right there*, I did.

She sidled right up to me, wineglass in hand. Dragged one long plastic nail down my cheek, so hard she'd leave a scratch that would stay all night but disappear by morning. Ma pinched my chin between her thumb and her finger like a vet inspecting a sick dog's teeth.

"Lost," she murmured, breath foul and reeking. "You're a lost cause."

Ma swigged and gulped. Drained the glass.

"Your sister, though. Your sister, with that pretty red hair. Get her down here."

"No," I said, as I closed my eyes—

Ma socked me in the stomach so hard I doubled over, her fist a freight train. As I gasped, winded, Ma pushed past me and started up the stairs.

I don't remember the next part. Only the aftermath: somehow, with the air knocked from my insides, I jolted after Ma up the stairs, hooked my hands onto her shirt, and yanked her backwards.

The wineglass went down first. It rolled down each carpeted step in slow motion, shattering at the foot of the stairs. A slice of glass embedded itself between my heel and the floor, but I did not have time to feel pain— only to jump aside as Ma came tumbling past me.

She looked like a rag doll, a small, shrieking bundle of thrift-store de-signer clothes, as she flipped, neck over head over waist over legs, all the way down the stairs.

"Stay!" I screamed to Amy, who had come running at the sound. She stood at the edge of the landing, sparkly leotard tucked up against her right butt cheek in a wedgie. "Stay right there."

But Amy didn't need to be cautious, or afraid: Ma was lying seven steps down, with a bruised collarbone and a broken wrist, looking up at me with shocked and furious eyes. Like I was the devil incarnate. And for the first time, I wondered if maybe I was—if maybe this was the only worldly gift I'd been given.

———

Now, Amy stomps in on high heels and turns on the TV. She sits in the armchair across from me and gnaws on a Pop-Tart. Crumbs of frosting stick in her lip gloss.

"The investigation continues as the sweep of the crime scene wraps up," a shiny reporter says. "In a statement from the Broomsville police chief, we've learned they have substantial leads. He revealed nothing further."

A photo of Lucinda appears. The same photo they've been showing since she died—the yearbook picture.

"Change it," I say.

"No," Amy whines.

I grab the remote, flick one channel up.

People hanging from rafters. A documentary about the Salem witch trials. *It's February 1692, and more than two hundred people have been accused of practicing the Devil's magic.*

Two more channels up, a Spanish-language soap opera. One busty woman screams at another.

"You killed her!" she shrieks. "You killed her!"

I click the TV off. A dusty quiet.

"What the hell?" Amy says. "I wanted to watch that."

I don't even bother bringing my backpack. I stomp out of the house and slam the front door behind me.

It's clear I've been called upon to finish Lucinda Hayes's business. Maybe this is punishment for the ritual, or maybe it's because I've seen what I have. But there's only one person who might know what happened to her. Cameron. And I know a place where honesty comes easy.

The sun is cold today, the wind a whip. I tilt my head to the sky and give Lucinda Hayes a double-handed middle finger.

Cameron

Cameron buttoned his funeral shirt in the bathroom mirror. He tried not to be afraid, but he did not like crowds, especially not crowds of kids from school, and especially not when they would all watch him.

They'd gotten three hang-up phone calls last night. One caller growled, in a whisper, *If the police don't get you, Cameron Whitley, I will.* Mr. O had called twice, but when Mom knocked on Cameron's door he had pretended to be asleep. He would not talk to Mr. O about the diary. There was nothing to be said. Mom and Mr. O murmured to each other over the phone, but Cameron couldn't catch Mom's side of the conversation.

Cameron wet a comb and ran it through his hair. He looked like Dad did in the mornings—when Dad got out of the shower and brewed coffee with a towel around his waist, his hair all mussed and bristly.

———

It was like this:

Cameron and Dad loved all the same things. They liked sunsets at

Pine Ridge Point, they ate breakfast before they brushed their teeth. Mini-Wheats and orange juice. They both watched Mom practice ballet, sitting together behind the banister on the basement stairs: Mom was the most graceful thing in the world.

For most of Cameron's childhood, Cameron and Dad would retreat to the living room after dinner. No TV. Cameron would draw in the sketchpad on his lap, and Dad would sip whiskey in the armchair, appreciative. Silence was their practiced language, and these nights—as Mom did the dishes, or the laundry, or read a book in bed—Cameron and Dad were the same. Father, son. A thick tree trunk and its rustling little leaves.

After Dad left for good, Cameron wondered where his own muted wanting would find its breaking point.

———

The girl from the principal's office was waiting in front of Cameron's house.

She wore a white summer dress—the kind you'd buy in the kids' section of a department store—and a camouflage army jacket. Her legs were bare, though it was barely thirty degrees.

"Remember me?" she said. "Jade. Like the rock."

"Yeah." Cameron squinted. "What are you doing here?"

"We're ditching this morning."

"Why?"

Cameron had never ditched school.

"A sign from the dead," she said. "Come on. We only have a half day anyway."

Jefferson High was bussing the ninth-grade class to Maplewood Memorial as soon as the eleven forty-five lunch period began. Mom had looked concerned when Cameron left the house—*Are you sure you want to go to school today? You could stay home. We could go to the service together,* she'd said. *I'm fine*, Cameron had told her, *I want to go to school*, and he'd zipped up his jacket.

Now, Jade was standing in Cameron's driveway. It took effort not to stare at her chest, which bulged from the seams of her white dress and merged with the acne sprinkled across her collar. She'd painted the skin above her eyes a powdery blue, and it smudged across her temples, down her cheeks. A small chin faded into her neck. Chapped lips. A bruise snaked from her thigh to her knee in an unnatural purple triangle, like a watercolor mountain done by someone who had never seen a mountain.

"I should go to school," Cameron said.

"You don't want to do that. Let's just say, you should probably listen to me."

Cameron tried to understand what she meant.

"I know, Cameron."

"You know what?"

"I know," she said, and with an ominous raise of her eyebrows—a threat—she turned in the direction of Willow Square and marched ahead. Cameron could not let her go, not without even a sliver of answer. It occurred to him that this had been Jade's intention, but still, he followed.

———

Cameron stumbled along behind Jade, passing all the closed boutiques and the pub where Mom bought craft beer. The Willow Square fountain was turned off for the winter, a drained sink. No one had been assigned the job of taking down the Christmas lights strung across the square, and as February progressed they burned out one by one.

He followed until Jade finally stopped—Cameron's mouth was dry from walking, and he was trying hard not to panic about the facts of the situation. Lucinda was dead, and Cameron was not in school, and soon he would have to go to her memorial service. He would have to sit and watch everyone grieve, alone with his own missing.

They had stopped at a building next to an ice-cream shop. The place was derelict, a giant fluorescent cross resurrected where a drugstore logo should have been.

"Is this a church?" Cameron asked.

Cameron's family used to go to church. He would sit between Mom and Dad and wonder how long he could hold his breath without dying. The world record for breath-holding was twenty-two minutes, but Cameron never came close. And anyway, they stopped going to church after everything with Dad because Mom couldn't sit there and hear about sin.

"Well, it used to be a Rite Aid," Jade said. "But now it's the Church of the Pure Heart. It's not open until August, and they don't work in here on Fridays. Come on."

Cameron stood like an idiot, anxious, wishing he had gone to school or at least stayed home with Mom, while Jade wedged her fingers between the automatic glass doors. In a matter of seconds, she had tugged open a space big enough for both of them to squeeze inside and disappeared into the dust.

The church smelled like sawdust and peeled-up floors. They were in the entrance to an industrial-sized chapel—the ground was bare and the pews were scattered in awkward, temporary arrangements. The place had no windows, just frames where glass would someday be. Wind howled through.

"I'm going home," Cameron said.

"You can't. I still haven't told you what I know."

Cameron realized, as Jade skipped down the aisle, that he wanted to run. When she sat on the altar's steps, a pair of panties flashed, black lace hugging the pale block of Jade's upper thigh. Cameron would not run, partly due to Jade's knowledge of something mysterious—the things she could know were all terrifying—and partly for the simple reason that she, unlike anyone else, had looked directly at him. She had looked right at Cameron and still, she wanted him to stay.

So he walked to where Jade sat, beneath a gigantic wooden cross propped lazily against the far wall. Cameron could still picture the drugstore that had existed here before: rows of shampoo and body wash, a clearance sale on razors and peanuts. A few empty shelves had been broken into dusty piles of wood and stacked against the wall, and the gaping room echoed, bulb-less fluorescent lights a taunt from above. A price tag was stuck to his shoe: $14.99.

"This place is so great, isn't it?" Jade said. "It's one of those perfectly abandoned places where you can go to think or wallow or whatever. Everyone has a place like that, right? A place where they feel like they can be anyone, say anything?"

"Yeah," Cameron said, brushing plaster off a small ledge to sit next to her.

"Where is it for you?"

"Nowhere."

"Come on. If you tell me that, I'll tell you why I brought you here."

"Okay," Cameron said. A pause. "It's this cliff in the mountains. Over the reservoir. It's very calm."

"All right," Jade said. "Fine. I saw you the other night. The night Lucinda died. I can see you from my bedroom window, standing out there. Watching her. I don't care and I'm not going to tell. But I have to ask. Why her? Of all the girls in the world, why Lucinda Hayes?"

The beginning of Tangled enveloped Cameron—a hissing, furious cloud.

———

Cameron had not chosen Lucinda. She was simply brighter than anyone else. And Cameron's Collections—Lucinda had planted them, and they'd grown and made him better. He liked her tan body and her ski-jump nose.

And Lucinda had that pull. Like she'd unraveled his intestines, tied them to her bedpost, and was tugging him back there, constantly, inch by painstaking inch.

Lucinda kept a figurine balanced carefully on her nightstand, and Cameron had loved to watch them together. A ballerina in a purple tutu, with one leg stretched in an arabesque—a term Cameron knew from Mom. The ballerina wore a pink V-necked leotard, her blond hair pulled into a tight ceramic bun. She had pinprick red lips and was no bigger than Cameron's hand, palm to pinky, if he flexed. Lucinda would sit with the figurine before she went to sleep, like she was daring the ballerina to move.

Cameron loved to watch them during his Statue Nights. The little dancer stood guard over Lucinda as she slept, a toy version of the girl—graceful, slender, so controlled. The easy elegance of this *pas de deux*.

———

"Hey," Jade was saying. "Yo. Dude."

Cameron was lying on the ground. His winter coat was covered in dust and his head ached. It must have hit the floor. Jade kneeled beside him, blurry in the light of the single stained-glass window: a shepherd leading his herd up a shaggy grass hill.

"I'm sorry," she said. "Jesus. I didn't mean to upset you. Are you okay? Do you need, like, a hospital or something?"

Cameron sat up, dizzy. The flat ceiling of the chapel above him did not look holy.

"No; we have to go," he said. "The funeral."

"We still have an hour," Jade said. "Come on. Let's get you out of here."

———

The man at Tasty's Ice Cream eyed Jade's bare legs and her boots, which were covered in sawdust and plaster. Cameron ordered a small mint chocolate chip cup and pulled a crumpled five from the bottom of his backpack. *I got it*, he told Jade, because he'd never been to ice cream with a girl before and it seemed like the right thing to do. But the total came out to $5.95, so Jade dug through the pockets of her camouflage jacket for change, which she counted in her cupped palm.

There was a bench outside, between the ice-cream store and the church. They sat in the cold. Jade stuck out her tongue and licked the dripping sugar from her spoon. The ice cream was too sweet. Cameron put the cup down on the bench and tried not to think about it melting in his stomach.

"Are you okay?" Jade said. "I mean, you were only out for a second. But I'm really sorry."

"I'm fine," Cameron told her. "It happens sometimes."

"I just thought maybe that place would help you talk. Always does for me."

Cameron snuck a glance at Jade's pink plastic Hello Kitty watch. Thirty minutes still. *You have to go*, Mom had told him last night when she'd laid his dress pants out on his desk chair. *People will ask questions otherwise.* And this, more than anything, filled Cameron with impossible dread.

"Tell me about your dad," Jade said.

"Please," Cameron said. "I don't want to talk about the police."

"Am I being insensitive?"

"Yes."

"Well, I hate the police, too. Especially here. It's fucked, the whole system. How your dad walked like that, how technically he was innocent, when everyone knew he almost killed that girl."

"Please," Cameron said.

"Do you think he did it?" Jade asked.

"Yeah," Cameron told her.

"And you still love him, right?" No one had ever posed this question before, and it made Cameron's trapped little heart want to shrink deeper in its cage.

"I don't know."

"It's okay, you know," Jade said. "I mean, it's okay to love someone who does something bad. Just because you do something bad doesn't mean you're not a good person. Look at it this way: wouldn't you rather be a good person who does one awful thing than a bad person who does a bunch of good ones?"

Cameron thought of Lucinda then. How he'd twist the corner of his comforter into a lump shaped slightly like a torso and wrap his body around it. Just tight enough to feel the contours. He'd convince himself, in the soft blue of his bedroom, that the comforter was warm, and the cotton pressing against him was not his blanket. Instead, lavender pajama pants. And under those pajama pants was skin, hot, wet skin, skin that folded in all the right places, that smelled like vanilla lotion, the sort of skin you could see only when you'd knocked down some unspoken barrier. Boy—man—in each push he came closer to the yellow curls of hair he imagined spooling across the pillow like fine strands of yarn.

Jade angled her body on the bench to face him, bare legs pointed toward the street, abdomen pudged over the waistline of her dress. Cameron felt bad for her then, sitting in her combat boots with no real battle to fight. The acne on her forehead looked on the verge of bursting, dozens of pustules clustered around her hair. A filmy line of chocolate had surrounded her mouth, like his grandma's lipstick when she talked too much.

He watched as Jade dragged the plastic spoon across the paper bottom of the cup. They sat like that. At 11:31, Jade said, *We should go*, and Cameron said, *Yes*, and they threw their ice-cream cups in the trash can on the curb.

———

Cameron remembered when baby Ollie was born last summer, and this was mostly why he knew he was not bad like Dad. The Thorntons had just moved to Broomsville—Mom baked a pan of ziti and said, *Let's welcome the little one to the neighborhood.*

Mom chatted with Eve Thornton at the counter while Cameron examined the baby, lying on her blanket on the living-room floor. The baby was only six days old, just a bundle of pink, with a scrunched nose and wispy hair matted to her smooth, round head, and wasn't it crazy that everyone started out this way? Pudding hands. Blank and soft and tucked tight against themselves. *Do you want to hold her?* Mrs. Thornton had asked, and Cameron had said, *No, that's okay.* But she looked sick, Mrs. Thornton, with a greenish-pale tint to her face and permanent droops under her eyes, like a cartoon of someone who hadn't slept in months, so Cameron said, *All right.* They led him to a rocking chair beneath a painting of a sunflower.

Cameron hadn't wanted to hold the baby. He knew what could go wrong. He could drop her. He could shake her. He could squeeze too hard.

He could want to hurt her.

Hold your arms like this, Mrs. Thornton said, and Cameron cupped his palms around his elbows. They lowered the baby into his arms.

It was then that Cameron knew he was not bad. Cameron had overheard Mom talking on the phone after Dad had gone, telling someone how Dad had never liked to hold Cameron as a baby. *Never a good sign.* All these years after Dad left, Cameron held baby Ollie, and the result was a small but necessary reassurance. He loved Ollie's extremities—the tiny legs and the tiny arms. Technically, he knew Ollie's body was similar to his own, only smaller in scale. She had baby veins and a baby liver and a baby femur and a baby cranium and even a baby heart. Baby toes that would grow and someday be shoved into socks and shoes, that would dance ballet and touch other toes beneath blankets. All these were in Cameron's care, beating so calmly and so normally that Cameron wanted to kiss the baby—but he knew it was against the rules. So he swayed his arms instead, side to side. He knew where Ollie had come from. *When two people love each other very much*, Mom had said. He wanted to love someone very much, or at least well enough to make this little creature that smelled like musk and wool and baby powder. He wanted the weight in his arms.

Tuesdays after that, Cameron watched Lucinda and Ollie Thornton as they existed together in the clear-window house. It made him both sad and excited, lonely and hungry, these two fragile anatomies through glass.

Russ

Russ always wanted to carry a gun because his father had carried a gun.

A gun makes you a man, his father used to say.

Russ has few memories from childhood. His father was a cop, and his mother was a receptionist at a doctor's office. Now, they live in a nursing home, and Russ's sister lives in California—she had wanted to be a painter, but became a receptionist at a doctor's office, too. When Russ hit adulthood, his family had separated, but not in any messy, painful way. Continents shifting lethargically away from each other. No real tragedy. Russ does have a few fond memories: fishing trips in their old sedan, Russ's sister reading a book in the back seat, mother so white and nibbling on potato chips, father focused on yellow highway lines. Russ, blank canvas of a boy. This moment, so unexpectedly golden.

Often, Russ wonders why that particular memory stuck out above the rest: his father patting a fat police belt, Russ staring up from belly-button height.

A gun gives you the power. A gun shows 'em who's boss.

Russ is standing by the water fountain near the front doors of the station house when a teenage boy walks in. The receptionist is away from her desk, so Russ stands a bit taller.

Can I help you? Russ asks. He runs his fingers over his moustache. Russ likes how he looks when he touches his moustache. He has practiced this stroke in the mirror.

We're looking for the detective, the father says. The boy looks nervous—he bites his thumb, and the skin around the gnawed nail glistens. Russ had acne as a teenager, but never that bad. The boy is cystic. Craters will scab and scar across his cheeks.

Have a seat, Russ says. I'll see if the detective is free. What's your name?

Ronnie, the kid says. Ronnie Weinberg.

What brings you here? Russ asks.

I came to tell you about something I saw, Ronnie says, as he and his father shuffle to the plastic seats at the edge of the waiting room. Ronnie sighs, and his father pats him on the back, urging him on. And then he says: I think I know who killed Lucinda.

———

Four months before the arrest, Russ and Lee sat on Lee's front porch. Late spring. Sudden warmth had spilled over Broomsville a few days before, welcome, promising. Inside, Cameron watched cartoons while Cynthia cleaned up dinner. Boxed mashed potatoes sprinkled with Hamburger Helper.

Lee hadn't meant to tell Russ about having sex with Hilary Jameson. It came out after the third beer, a blurted brag.

Where did you even meet her? Russ asked.

The pharmacy, Lee said. She works behind the counter.

The pharmacy downtown?

Yeah, Lee said. We talked. You know, when I went to pick up Cynthia's anxiety meds. Anyway, we flirted for a while. She finally slipped me her number, stapled to the bag like a prescription slip. I called her up, and we saw each other a few times, nothing serious, but then last night—

So you're cheating on Cynthia, Russ said.

The words surprised them both. They watched the street like maybe it would change, reveal something remarkable about itself. Nothing happened. The rosebushes Cynthia had planted years before were still dead. There was nothing beyond the smooth white sidewalk, clean because the snow had dried and the rain would never come. And the feeling in Russ's chest: a tight constriction, pulsing weight. Stricken.

You're cheating, Russ said again.

The bottle whistled past Russ's ear, shattering against the siding of the house. Upstairs, Cynthia's voice. The Heineken bottle lay in shards by Russ's work boots and Lee put an elbow over his eyes. He shielded himself, arms in a triangle around his face, like a child counting through a game of Hide and Seek.

I'm sorry, Lee said, face still buried in the crook of his arm. Just keep it between us, okay? I trust you.

Russ left without saying good-bye to Cynthia or Cameron. Fitting. Walking home, he wondered if it was warranted, this wretched, mammoth trust. What had he done to deserve it? Through the following months, Russ would nod uncertainly when Cynthia asked about the drinks at Dixie's Tavern that had never happened, or the overtime shift Lee hadn't worked. Russ felt he owed Cynthia the truth, as a human, a friend, a near part of her crumbling family. But he was enthralled by these words—I trust you—so he lied for Lee, even as Lee's absence made Russ's own world six shades darker. On the nights that Lee was supposedly at Russ's house, or on a weekend fishing trip, Russ himself would sit on his couch and think, What am I, without this scheming, cheater friend of mine? The television, no consolation.

Later, Russ met Hilary Jameson. She was Broomsville pretty. She wore tight jeans low on her hips, flared and slightly too long. The bottoms were ripped and dirty from catching beneath her shoes. Brunette. Wide-set eyes. Her hair was straight, her teeth were straight, but something was missing.

Shape. Color. She had a tattoo, the first thing Russ noticed about her. Miniature blue hearts followed one another up her neck, like regretful little ducks.

When Russ met Hilary Jameson, he was embarrassed for Cynthia. Cynthia: supple thighs and aging curves, a mane of wild gray hair she never thought about. And then there was Hilary, with perky breasts and a clean-shaved pussy, which Russ imagined she spread with her fingers like a porn star.

Russ hates to think about Lee now, because he should have known that night, as he kicked bits of jagged green glass into an empty planter at the edge of the porch. He should have paid more attention to the way Lee cowered as the bottle hit the house, as if his own hand had not just thrown it. A prophecy.

After that night on the porch, Lee became two people at once. One: a man with a family and an entry-level job in law enforcement. Lee supplemented this colossal disappointment with Hilary Jameson, hurried and messy, in the car on the side of the road. Two: a man with a friend who would do anything to protect him, blindly and without question. Two: a man capable of hurting someone. Two: No one's hero.

Despite all this, Russ so gravely misses him.

———

Every Tuesday night, Ines goes to Bible study. She comes home late, so gloomy she'll hardly speak. You shouldn't think so much about sin, Russ advises. It'll tear you up for no reason at all.

Thursdays, she's better. Thursdays, Ines kisses the crook of Russ's neck when his alarm goes off in the morning. *Get up, sleepyhead.* By Friday, Ines melts back into herself. Quiet Ines is inevitable. Ines, his solemn wife, unreadable as the walls of their perpetually unfinished home.

Russ doesn't ask Ines about her life in Guadalajara, and she doesn't offer it up. She had followed Ivan to Broomsville a year after he'd come, because Mamá had urged and Ivan told her it was good here. America was fine, all fine. He didn't tell Ines about the drugs—an occasional break from his under-the-table work at the church, basic tasks for some extra cash—until she arrived, alone, with a copy of Lorca's *Canciones* tucked in her pocket and a bundle of handwritten letters from the rest of the family. An emissary.

Russ didn't ask for these things, and he doesn't want any more. He cannot picture this Ines, and it seems she doesn't want him to. Russ's Ines lives in Broomsville, Colorado. His Ines knits so intensively she's filled the upstairs linen closet with lumpy blankets and sweaters and socks. Russ does not need to know about exotic fruits or the inimitable temperature of a Mexico sun—the unspoken world of old Ines, a woman not forgotten, only folded and stored away. Russ and Ines are all right like this. They are skating.

The day Russ realized Ines was unhappy, he went to the run-down mall on the outskirts of town. Bought her a diamond necklace he couldn't afford.

Russ almost begged her then—Tell me about home. Tell me how you got here. All the stories Russ had heard through work about the border— none of them specifically belonging to Ines, whose journey he had never heard. A plane, a train, a car, a bus? He wanted to ask her why, why would she leave what she'd known? Perhaps it was her brother. The amount of time Ines spent worrying about Ivan made Russ think that maybe, yes—it was Ivan, the reason she'd been imprisoned in this country. In this house.

But Russ knew what happened when you bared your insides to someone else. He had been there—maybe was still there—in the squad car with Lee, sharing the things that thrashed and squirmed. Unprotected. He wouldn't make that mistake again. So Russ gave Ines the necklace and said, I want to make you happy; I'll keep trying. Ines clasped the diamond around her neck. Smiled.

She did not look like someone who needed saving. So sturdy. A building with locked doors. I love you, she told him, but her voice sounded too high-pitched and very far away, like she'd yelled it from some unreachable height.

———————

On a Saturday in October, just weeks before her tourist visa ran out, Russ and Ines married. They took the squad car to town hall. Russ turned on the sirens because it made Ines laugh; she pressed her face to the window and watched cars pull to the side. Russ imagined that Ines felt American then, and maybe she'd write home to Guadalajara and tell her family how lucky she was, and how happy, because sometimes all it took to be lucky and happy was the easy matter of driving faster than everyone else.

Ines wore a white sundress, but it was a cold October so she zipped one of Russ's sweat shirts over it. The sweat shirt had holes in the sleeves where Ines had poked her thumbs.

They filled out the paperwork at the clerk's desk, and when she stood next to Russ, Ines looked like a little girl, or one of the high-school students she tutored. Pink on her lips, a white flower in her hair. They signed the papers. Ines leaned over, kissed Russ on the cheek. Her smile. Not dazzling, but rare.

The party was in the park where they'd met, just a few months earlier. They spread boxes of pizza beneath a metal awning in the wind. Detective Williams showed up, and so did the rest of the patrol guys—all but Lee, gone four years by then. They brought beer and laughed like men, debating whether Bush would send troops to Iraq. Ivan sent a letter from prison, with a drawing of a bouquet of lilies, the only one to give a semblance of a gift.

In the park, everyone toasted to Russ and Ines. To a long and happy life together. Detective Williams nudged Russ in the ribs and said, You better make her happy tonight.

Is this how it's supposed to feel? Russ asked himself, but he refused to linger on an answer. He knew, that windy day in the grass, that his love with Ines did not quiver, not on either side. They had taken the vows you were supposed to take, and that was love, or some subset of it. So he drank champagne and watched the leaves rush toward winter. When everyone chanted Kiss, kiss, kiss, they did. Ines was sour from the brut. Russ held Ines's waist for the camera, thinking how later they would have sex and Ines would climb on top of him, as she'd been doing since their trip to San Diego. Hands clamped tight around his neck. She would roll away when he had finished and say good night, and just like that, they would be married. He would love her, as best he could.

On his wedding night, Russ thought of Lee Whitley in the way you think of someone dead. Fondly, too fondly, until absence takes this fondness and multiplies it, stretching until it becomes something invasive. Until it swallows you whole.

Cameron

Cameron stood outside Maplewood Memorial and wondered how many bodies it held that did not belong to Lucinda. How many blue, unbending thumbs. How many jellied hearts.

"Come on," Jade said, and she pulled him forward by the elbow, her palm sweaty from the walk across town. In the parking lot, Cameron's classmates were solemn as they stepped off the school bus. They moved in parasitic groups, crying in clumps, the girls tugging at black dresses, at their hair. There was only one bus—most parents had kept their children home and were now walking with hands on shoulders across the parking lot. Cameron counted three police cars.

"See you later," Jade said, with an inappropriately exaggerated wink. She bolted ahead, toward the big glass doors.

Cameron joined the clusters of his classmates, feeling like he'd crash-landed in some faraway and lonesome place.

Things People Said at Lucinda's Funeral:

"You look great. I mean, terrible circumstances, but did you do something with your hair?"

"A bit early to be having the memorial, isn't it? Just a few days. I think the family wanted to get it over with."

"That photo is beautiful. Such a pretty girl."

"And the little sister, it's so sad. She's only in the seventh grade. Having to go through something like this at such a young age—I can't even imagine."

"They're saying it was someone in the neighborhood, no motive yet—"

"Timmy Williams is all over the case; I heard they've got a new suspect—the ex-boyfriend, what's his name, the Arnauds' kid? They let him go."

"Broke her neck—heard she died immediately. At least she didn't suffer, you know?"

"I'm glad to hear business is going well. I knew the new lease would bring in more customers; you picked that perfect location right on Willow Square."

———

The funeral was a movie Cameron had not meant to see.

He took a pew in the middle of the crowd and watched the town of Broomsville file in around him. It was a spectacle, electric. The girls from school cried in circles, holding hands. Parents watched with eagle eyes, gloating at the fact of their own children's aliveness, masks of sorrow placed expertly over their relief. A woman near the podium shrieked and keened, and there was a bubble near the corner of the room where the governor sat, his police escorts hovering along the wall.

There was so much chaos, Cameron pretended he was not there but in the yellow house on the lane, where Lucinda was very much alive—sitting on the wooden swing that hung from the Valencia orange tree. Gleaming and sunlit.

But for now: Funeral. Mourners. Family sad up front. A line of people snaked up the aisle to offer condolences to the Hayeses, and Lucinda's father shook their hands, murmuring quiet thanks. Lex wore a lavender dress and kicked her knobbly legs back and forth. Lucinda's mother stared straight ahead. She sat on her hands. No one tried to speak to her.

Lucinda's friends took up the next two rows of pews—Beth, Kaylee, and Ana were huddled together. The soccer girls, with thick, lean thighs, and the boys' basketball team all stared at their laps, standing intermittently to sign the neon poster boards that lined every wall. Notes written in bubbly handwriting.

And the flowers. There were hundreds of flowers, toppling over each other in stuffed vases around the room. Flowers were draped across people's legs because there wasn't space to set them down, and everything smelled like pollen and antiseptic. A poster-sized photo of Lucinda had been propped on an easel—a basket of ballet shoes sat beneath, signed with notes to Lucinda in Sharpie, like ritual offerings. One girl stroked Lucinda's pixelated photo face, sobbing hysterically while her less aggrieved friends hovered around the periphery, solemn and teary.

"Cameron," Mr. O said. He slid into the pew next to Cameron, bringing the scent of cigarettes and the spearmint gum he chewed to cover it up. He peeled off his winter coat and draped it across his lap. "How are you holding up?"

"I'm okay," Cameron said.

"Look," Mr. O said. "I know you've been avoiding me, but we need to talk about yesterday."

Mr. O took Mom out dancing once, to a dingy restaurant that offered free salsa classes on Tuesdays. Mom put on a red dress—tight at the top, like a river at the bottom—and a pair of high heels. *Haven't worn these in years.* Her feet puffed out of the shoes like baking bread straining to break free from a pan. Mom's chest was wrinkly, sun-spotted skin sagging over her breastbone and drooping under the cut of the dress where cleavage should have been. *Well, look at you*, Mr. O had said at the door.

"Cameron, I'm not going to say anything to your mother, okay? I'm still thinking of a way to get it to the police without implicating either of us." Mr. O leaned close. "But I need you to tell me how you got that diary. I read some of it and I'm going to turn it in, but before I do, I need to make sure you weren't involved in Lucinda's death."

"I don't know."

"You don't know if you were involved?"

"I don't know how I got the diary. And I didn't read any of it. You have to believe me."

The Thorntons' toddler was wailing in the pew behind them, shrill and unrelenting—both parents tried desperately to calm her. Cameron stared at Ronnie, sandwiched between his parents' backs, flakes of dandruff snowing across his wiry shoulders and down his crinkly black shirt. There was a vase of orchids next to Lucinda's photo; the petals blossomed up from a single stem, then arched back toward the ground in surrender. And the eye of the flower (the stamen, which held the ovaries and the ovule, where the pollen was produced)—looked like a human skull made of silk.

"Cameron, please," Mr. O said. "I need you to talk to me about this, I can't— Hello."

Mom slid into the pew on the other side of Cameron. She wore her favorite black dress, the dress she wore on Christmas when she cooked salmon with orange peels and they drank sparkling grape juice from wineglasses. This made Cameron sad, because now that dress would remind them both of Lucinda's funeral, and it really was her favorite.

"I shouldn't have let you go to school today," Mom said, putting her knuckles up to Cameron's forehead as if to check for fever. "This is a madhouse. I can't believe I let you come here by yourself."

Mom pulled three copies of the Holy Bible from the bench pocket. As they flipped through the pages, Cameron thought of the term "three peas in a pod," but remembered that wasn't the saying, the saying was "two peas in a pod," and this made him lonely, so he pretended to be extremely interested in Deuteronomy.

———

Cameron had started working in Mr. O's office three months earlier, when Beth DeCasio began referring to Cameron as "American Psycho." Beth cut off a lock of her own hair and pinned it to Cameron's easel, while Ana Sanchez and Kaylee Walker giggled at the next table over.

That day, Mr. O walked by just as Cameron discovered the horrible thing. Mr. O picked up the lock of hair, dangled it in the air, examined it in warm art-classroom light. When he strode over to Beth's table, the whole class hushed. Beth picked at her crimson-painted nails.

"Does this belong to you, Ms. DeCasio?" Mr. O said.

It was common knowledge: Beth and all her friends had crushes on Mr. O. When he leaned over the girls to critique their paintings, they blushed and crossed their arms over growing chests.

"I think I'll keep it," Mr. O said. "Could make a fine addition to an experimental sculpture I'm working on. I'll make sure Principal Barnes sees the finished product."

The girls didn't talk in class for the rest of the day, and Mr. O helped Cameron pack up his things and move to the closet office, where the sound of the ninth-grade class was muffled through a thick aluminum door.

"Tell me if they bother you again," Mr. O said.

Before he left Cameron to that delectable solitude, Mr. O stopped with his hand on the doorknob. Someone laughed, loud, but Cameron doubted it was Beth.

"Oh, and tell your mother I say hello."

For the rest of the semester, Cameron drew and erased and drew again in peace.

People Cameron did not expect to see at Lucinda's funeral:

1. The night janitor. He sat with a veiled woman in a back pew, wearing
    an itchy-looking suit. As people walked past, they glared and whis-
    pered. Rumors had spread about the man who found the body.

    When the janitor noticed Cameron watching, his eyes were
    strong but friendly. Cameron's stomach rolled, and he turned around
    fast. Mom was saying something he couldn't hear—the familiarity of
    the janitor's gaze made Cameron dizzy. Curious and faint. He dared
    himself to turn around again; he would do it after ten seconds, nine,
    then three, two, one.

    The janitor was smiling at Cameron, coy, one hand lifted into a
    barely perceptible wave.

Cameron had never tried to recreate Hum. That would cheapen it—he'd
never be able to make the strokes look so organic. The pastel trunk of the
Valencia orange tree. The green-shuttered windows. The road that barely
brushed the side of the canvas: you knew that road was long, but you
couldn't see how long, and the sight of it disappearing into a minuscule
point had been branded in Cameron's mind like a pinky promise.

Hum was beautiful in all its physicality, but the best part was the house.
You couldn't quite tell where the back of the house ended, and the lines were
just blurry enough that you couldn't count the windows.

Cameron looked around at all the crying people, how they bent and
how they broke, and he thought, *I am sorry for your loss*. He did not feel it

himself, their grief, because he knew where Lucinda had gone, and the air there was easier.

Cameron could not remember the night Lucinda died, but he hoped that whoever had sent Lucinda to Hum had done it with the best of intentions. He tried to be happy for her, that beautiful girl.

So he did not grieve because he missed her (though he missed her, he really missed her). He grieved because she would not contribute to the balance of things—at least, not in the space he occupied. Whether or not she had loved him before, she would not love him now, in that careful, tender way of hers, and he was overcome with the loss. There was one less person in his corner of the world, one less person to see the colors of snowy afternoons on Pine Ridge Point. All that foggy gray.

———

Cameron was in Lucinda's bedroom once. Over a year ago, near the beginning of his Collection of Statue Nights. Cameron had pushed this night so deep inside him he was never sure if it had actually happened. Sometimes he was ashamed, and sometimes it scared him, so he remembered this night only in his quietest moments.

He had gone into Mom's closet for a pair of nail clippers and come across Dad's shoes. Beat-up leather loafers. He imagined Dad standing in them, lanky and self-assured. The shoes repulsed him. He remembered Dad, sitting on the edge of the bed. Dad, pulling on his socks and slipping his feet into them. Dad, thundering down the stairs. Kissing the top of Cameron's head, and Mom's cheek. *I won't be home tonight.* Mom, putting a bowl of chicken nuggets with ketchup in front of Cameron at the kitchen table. *Daddy will be back soon.*

Cameron had climbed out the window and sprinted to Lucinda's house.

On this night, Cameron felt so horribly inside himself—swimming in his own DNA. Half of him was Dad: he couldn't escape it. He could only

hope he'd inherited Dad's good half, the parts that liked baseball and sang
opera in the shower and went on long runs early in the morning.

It was late. The Hayeses had gone to bed, both Lex's and Lucinda's
rooms enveloped in dark. Cameron could see straight into Lucinda's window—the ball of her sleeping form, breathing steadily beneath her comforter. The splay of her yellow hair on the pillow.

He unlaced his shoes on the bottom step of the back porch. The wood
was wet, ice frozen in patches across the deck. He considered it. Stepped
outside of himself and analyzed. He hated what he saw: a scrawny teenage
boy standing barefoot outside a snowy back door, innocent but enamored.
Cameron didn't stop himself. He couldn't.

The glass door slid open, squeaking as he shut it behind him. The
Hayeses' kitchen was dim but familiar, all shadows and their resulting ge-
ometries.

Cameron took the stairs one at a time, waiting a full thirty seconds
between each. *Toe, ball, heel. Pause. Toe, ball, heel. Pause.* He imagined that
he was a fish breathing water, because he assumed that was much more
fluid than a human breathing air. It took him eight minutes to get to the
top of the stairs, but when he did, Lucinda's bedroom door was cracked
open.

From the other side of the door came the swell and sway of her breathing, a delicate rhythm that reminded him with such peaceful clarity that he
was alive. *I am, I am, I am*, she told him with this inhale and exhale and
inhale and exhale. *I am alive, and so are you, and isn't this a paralyzing thing?*

Cameron inched the door open.

Lucinda's bedroom smelled like vanilla perfume and sleep. A good
dream. She was an infant, swaddled in her quilt—checkered violet, with
cream-colored lace around the edges.

In sleep, Lucinda was flawless and clean, a lump of breathing blankets—he did not dare to touch her because she was so precise and so tender.
He wanted to cup the curve of her, to feel all of her lines, to press his tongue
to the sweet spot between her neck and collarbone. He wanted to merge
them together with sweat. He wanted to be the air that escaped effortlessly

from her lungs, the swatch of quilt clenched in her fist, he wanted to crawl into a corner of her and live there where no one could find him.

He hoped that everyone could feel a love like this, at least once in their lives. Every single person deserved it. He pictured all the families in all the houses down the block, the red-shingled roofs spanning out toward the mountains, all the people in this sad little town, the good ones, the bad ones, the lonely ones: he wished he could give them this.

He became another one of Lucinda's bedposts, solid and erect.

Cameron did not know how much time passed, but he did not leave until the sky was flushed pink, the color of her cheeks in the early morning—the symmetry of the two made him so sure that this was okay, that what he did was okay, that their love was complex, but God, wasn't it exquisite?

Jade

When people die, they become angel caricatures of themselves. Lucinda practically failed out of English class last year—now she's a star student, role model to all her peers. I can't even muster a hesitant sadness. Only a misplaced jealousy. The fact is: Everyone dies. Good people die and bad people die, some earlier than others.

Everyone writes about Lucinda in metallic marker on hefty slabs of poster board. Long, rambling epitaphs from everyone at school, signed next to lopsided hearts.

We had the pleasure of getting to know you over the past two years as you babysat our little Ollie. We will be sure to tell our daughter, as she grows older, the impact you had on her early years. Lucinda, it is our belief that your light and beauty will shine in our little girl forever.
—Chris, Eve, Ollie, and Puddles Thornton

I LOVE YOU LUC! I'm going to miss you so much. You're in a better place now, sweet angel.

—Ana Sanchez

Lucinda, you have been my best friend since the fourth grade. Really, my best friend. When I moved from California, you were so nice to me, even when I was the new kid and I had, like, really weird teeth. And when I broke my toe on the bottom of the swimming pool on vacation and you ran into the hotel and you couldn't find my mom, you made the hotel concierge carry me out of the pool, remember? I'm going to miss our sleepovers and our pillow fights. I still have that blue shirt of yours, the one you let me borrow for the dance, and I'm never going to wear it because it still smells like you. I love you. Okay. I have to go now.

—Beth DeCasio

Dear Lucinda—it was such a pleasure to have you in class this year. I know chemistry was never your strong suit, but you worked hard and you excelled. It breaks my heart to think of all the potential the world lost this week. I speak on behalf of the entire faculty at Jefferson High School when I say you were an incredible contribution to our student body and you will be terribly missed.

—Mrs. Hawthorne

I wonder what they'll do with the poster boards once all this is over. I doubt Lucinda's family will want them. I wonder if the man who takes out the garbage will look at these scribbled notes and think what a great girl Lucinda Hayes must have been. How humble. How beautiful. How smart. How kind.

———

No one remembers her how I do.

The annual neighborhood barbecue, the summer before sophomore year. It was a few weeks after everything went to shit with Zap, just before the ritual. I'd started showering in a baggy T-shirt so I didn't have to look at myself. I didn't blame Lucinda—not at first, anyway.

Ma told me to wear a swimsuit to the barbecue, but I refused to stoop to such frivolity. The girls on my block used the sprinklers as an excuse to get naked while the creepy dads watched. It worked. Kids ran around with sticky Popsicle mouths, but everyone watched Beth and Lucinda. Flat, tan stomachs dripping sprinkler water. Lucinda's hair was brown at the ends, stuck in messy clumps to her bare shoulders. They seemed proud of their firm, bony bodies, bald under the gaze of the sun.

Amy ran around in a bright-pink one-piece with Lex. Lex looked so young that day, two purple barrettes pulling her hair from her face like a drawn curtain. Lex has never been as pretty as Lucinda. Her hair is cut to her chin. Where Lucinda has the right amount of freckles, Lex has too many. Her nose is bigger, beakier, and her stomach tubs out like a baby's.

I stayed in my room until Ma made me come down. She had done her hair up big and was sipping a Jack and Coke on the driveway, even though it was barely noon. I sat on the porch with a warm Sprite and observed as Lucinda and Beth pushed their tiny tits together in front of the Hansens' beverage table. Mr. Hansen stared down at their bikini tops. He heaved a jug of vodka from the cooler by his feet, and sloshed it into plastic cups. They giggled. Pressed their faces close together. I wanted to tell them to put their bodies away—that nobody cared to see them naked—but this was clearly not the case.

They wobbled away from the table, sipping and scrunching their noses at the bitter alcohol, until Beth spotted me. Pointed.

"Look who it is," Beth said. She tottered halfway up the driveway. "I forgot. You're completely above all this. You're not even wearing a swimsuit."

"Fuck off," I said.

"Do you even own a swimsuit?" Beth said.

Beth didn't bother me. I'd taken much worse from her (fake love letters addressed to me, dildos stuffed in my locker). Beth didn't scare me, with mascara running in pools beneath her eyes.

"Go fuck yourself, Beth."

"Why don't you?" Beth snapped. "It's not like you'll get it anywhere else."

She laughed loudly. Nudged Lucinda for support.

This is how I will always remember her.

Lucinda stood there, vacant, radiant and timeless in her yellow swimsuit, blond hair curling wet against her skin, toes painted white in those plastic flip-flops, not caring—not even knowing—what she'd taken from me.

It was worse than anything intentional. Girls like Beth, I could handle. But Lucinda was indifferent, so caught up in her bright, easy world, that contempt for her filled me like it never had before. How she stood, glittering and oblivious. It ignited me.

I saw you, I wanted to tell her. I saw your toothpick legs wrapped tight around him, I saw the way your back arched, I saw how the two of you thrashed and moved, a pair of undulating eels in shadow. I saw how he touched you. Hungry. Piggish. You can have him, I wanted to say.

But I couldn't, because Lucinda was somewhere else. She stood in the August sun, one hip jutted out, completely removed from Beth's taunts and my submission, her pretty head tilted charmingly to the right.

Lucinda Hayes didn't recognize my goddamn face. She was unaware. The world is special for girls like her. It was this that burned me.

———

The funeral is almost over. Ma and Amy press tissues to their faces, and makeup seeps into the paper. The minister goes on about Lucinda's "light," how she will "never be forgotten," how during a "tragedy like this" we must "support and appreciate the ones we love." The old man in front of me is asleep, the Hansens are holding each other, and Jimmy Kessler wraps a piece of chewed gum around a Q-tip, which he pokes into a crack in the pew.

Hey, I would say to Zap, if this were a different world. *Are you okay?*

Zap wouldn't need to say anything back. When we were little, we played a game called Telepathy. We'd freak out our parents by reading each other's minds; I could tell you what he was thinking in less than three guesses. In reality, we'd invented this complicated system: words in sets of threes, a countless number of them, which we memorized and dictated to one another. *Are you okay?* I would say. The answer would be either *Rottweiler*, *bagel*, or *Gandalf*. By the third try, I'd undoubtedly get it right.

Zap sits a few rows in front of me, wedged between his parents. He watches the photo of Lucinda on the altar like he hopes it will start moving, like if he stares long enough, she will jump out of her glossy frame and into the pew next to him.

His glasses are folded in his lap. Hair flat in the back. It's not that I wish he wanted me again, as a best friend or anything else. That's not it at all. I guess I hate that he looks like a wilted, airless version of himself—all for someone that isn't me.

The blatant narcissism of this thought nearly makes me laugh out loud. How self-indulgent. I stop myself, only to realize that the funeral is over.

People stand. They mill around, hugging one another, gossiping in hushed voices about the possibility of a town curfew if the police don't catch the killer. Amy beelines for her friends from school. She pointedly ignores Lex: Maybe she doesn't know what to say. Or maybe all Amy's fuss about Lucinda is just a sign of her melodrama. Her own liar grief.

I don't know what to do with myself, so I uncoil my headphones and place them over my ears. The sound of the memorial chapel is muffled, filtered through pieces of plastic and foam. I don't turn on any music. I'm thankful for the barrier between my ears and the scene around me, so I sit while everyone chats, trickles out.

That's when I see her: Querida. She clings to the arm of a man who is not Madly. A black veil covers her face, but I recognize the sway of her hair, the slight bulge of hip beneath her form-fitting black dress. Part of me wants to walk over, say hello. But how do you categorize your knowledge of someone like that? Someone you've only watched, who you've asked a dumb question once, someone you wish you could magic yourself into? The answer: you don't. So when Ma sends Amy over to collect me, I put on my jacket and follow them out, headphones still on.

A few paces ahead: Cameron and his mother. He hasn't looked away from his own feet.

When we get outside, the wind is brutal. Two police officers are getting out of a squad car. They're both burly, just how you'd imagine cops would look, with broad shoulders and beer bellies. One has a moustache—the kind of moustache you grow as a joke—and the other twirls a toothpick between his jaws. They walk toward us. No—toward Cameron.

———

They arrested Cameron's dad on Labor Day. Fifth grade. I was at Zap's house, watching a *SpongeBob* marathon and eating butter mixed with brown sugar, when Terry rang the doorbell.

Ma had sent him to bring me home. *You could have just called*, Mrs. Arnaud said. Terry was small and twitchy on the front porch, wringing doughy hands. *You haven't heard?* he asked. *Our cop neighbor was just arrested. Jade, it's time to come home.*

Ma sat on the couch in the living room, drinking cold tea from earlier that morning. With the phone pressed between her ear and her shoulder, she picked through a container of leftover Chinese food.

"Lee Whitley," she said into the phone. "You know, the police officer who lives around the corner? Next to the Hansens?"

Faint babbling from the other end.

"The police department just released a statement. It's awful, just so awful. He pulled her over on the highway, claimed she was speeding. Poor girl was only twenty-three. Dragged her into a ditch on the side of the road and beat her nearly to death. She's alive, but still in the hospital."

A string of lo mein slipped from between her chopsticks.

"Yeah, they're sure it was him. I know, I know. He was always so nice, wasn't he? And his wife. Sweet woman, very timid. They have that boy, too; he's two years below Jay in school. Skinny little thing. Never looks you in the eye."

That was just the start of it.

The town talked for weeks. No one tried to hide it from the kids. Me and Amy weren't allowed to walk past the Whitleys' house, not while Cameron's dad was awaiting trial. We had to take the long way around the backyard to get to school. I broke this rule whenever possible, dragging my feet across the sidewalk by their house, trying to get a peek into the Whitleys' living room, to see where the bad man ate dinner and brushed his teeth. The Whitleys kept their curtains shut.

I'd steal glances at the headlines before Terry whisked them away every morning.

"WHITLEY TO STAND TRIAL; VICTIM WON'T TESTIFY"

"BROOMSVILLE POLICE DEPARTMENT DENIES ALLEGED ASSAULT"

Lee Whitley never looked particularly threatening. He was slight, like Cameron, with duck feet and a scraggly beard that never looked full. He had pale skin and light eyes, somewhere between green and brown. Perpetually sweaty. Not intimidating. I'd see him in his cop car some days after work, just sitting in the Whitleys' driveway, sipping coffee from a Styrofoam cup with his feet on the dashboard.

The headlines escalated as the trial progressed.

"EVIDENCE FOR ASSAULT CASE DISAPPEARS FROM POLICE HOLDING"

"BROOMSVILLE POLICE LIEUTENANT TESTIFIES FOR DEFENSE"

"WHITLEY PRONOUNCED NOT GUILTY"

"His friends got him off," Ma said, swirling white wine at the kitchen table with the windows open. "Sick. It's just sick."

"RELEASED POLICE OFFICER FLEES, LEAVING WIFE AND YOUNG SON BEHIND"

The victim was a skinny brunette with a trail of hearts tattooed down the side of her neck. Hilary Jameson. She moved away after Cameron's dad disappeared. Once they were both gone, everyone stopped talking about it. A few weeks later, I walked past the Whitleys' house—the curtains were still closed, but someone had planted a single tulip in a pot on the front porch. It was a violent shade of purple, the color of a bruise.

———

WHAT YOU WANT TO SAY BUT CAN'T WITHOUT BEING A DICK
A Screenplay by Jade Dixon-Burns

INT. CHURCH—DAY

Celly and Friend sit in a church, surrounded by construction. Above them: a lopsided crucifix. Friend eyes Celly as she fidgets with an earring, impressed by her no-bullshit demeanor.

                    CELLY

      Do you ever wonder why some people have
      beautiful faces and others don't?

                    FRIEND

      Genetics?

His words echo through the cavernous space. Celly looks up.
Leans in.

                         CELLY
                      (whispered)
          I have this idea. Maybe ugly people exist so
          we can understand the human brain a little
          better. If everyone was pretty, no one would
          need to talk.
                        (beat)
          I've seen your drawings, stashed away in the
          art room.

Friend averts his eyes.

                         CELLY (CONT'D)
          You make people prettier than they actually
          are. The way you smudge the pencil. The way
          you shape their faces.

                         FRIEND
          I draw people exactly how I see them.

                         CELLY
          But isn't that a lie, if it's not actually
          how they look?

                         FRIEND
          Art can't be a lie.

                         CELLY
          That sounds pretty pretentious.

                    FRIEND

It's all about perception. What I see is

automatically my truth, simply because I've

seen it. I've interpreted it that way.

                    CELLY

            (in spite of herself)

Fair.

Celly picks at her black nail polish.

                  CELLY (CONT'D)

What do you see when you look at me?

He watches her.

                    FRIEND

    A knife. An idealist. A rock. Soft flesh.

Russ

Cynthia used to be a ballerina. She told Russ about the big auditions she'd gone to in New York City. Showed him her old shoes, broken and streaked black from marley floors, sweat-stained ribbons tangled around invisible ankles. Put them on, Russ said, a joke. Cynthia laced them up her bare ankles and stood on her toes, using the arm of the couch for balance. She wore a pair of matronly khaki shorts and an old, faded polo shirt. Beaded earrings.

Lee came in from the kitchen and walked awkwardly to his wife. Russ, so small at the other end of the couch. Lee pressed his hands to Cynthia's stomach, and she leaned into him. Lee's smell: roll-on deodorant, hours-ago coffee. Wrapped around his balancing-act wife, Lee kissed the veins that bulged out the side of her neck.

Chapped lips, wrinkled skin.

A wound, gaping.

———

In the parking lot outside Lucinda Hayes's funeral, Detective Williams plays a game on his flip phone.

Of course, Russ isn't supposed to be here. But Detective Williams had nodded schemingly at Russ on his way out of the building, gesturing for him to follow like he was bestowing Russ with some cosmic honor. Russ almost reminded the detective that his brother-in-law was a suspect, but he kept his mouth shut and followed anyway. He found it interesting, detective work, in a temporary and provisional way: you could sit down for two hours and be fascinated by this, then you could go back to your everyday world. Your house and its stained carpet. You didn't have to live inside this.

There's a catch, Detective Williams says, distracted from his game of Tetris by the slow exodus of mourners from the funeral home.

And what's that? Russ asks.

We can't call him a suspect, Detective Williams says, but we still have to look productive. Make a bit of a stink. The chief has made it clear, we have to look like we're doing something.

It's a funeral, Russ says.

It's over, Detective Williams says, gesturing to the people as they file out.

Ines is inside with the other mourners, wearing a black cotton dress she bought at a garage sale. She did her hair all curly and nice, bunched at the nape of her neck. Russ sighs. Regrets it. He is bigger on the inhale.

———

Russ has not seen Cynthia in years. Only a glimpse, a few summers ago, as she pushed a bright-red cart through the Target on Elm Street. Cynthia browsed the cereal aisle, flipping boxes upside down to look for price tags. Russ had the perverse urge to approach her, but instead he bought shaving cream and a box of Oreos for Ines. Double Stuf.

He drove home. Stopped at the light on Elm Street, Russ thought of Cynthia's hands—how delicate they'd looked as she pulled her beat-up purse farther up her shoulder and placed an off-brand jar of pasta sauce in the cart. Had they always been so fragile? You'd think Russ would remember a detail like this. But after so many nights around tables—eating and drinking, Russ sliding accidentally into the lava core of Lee and Cynthia's marriage—Russ can still recall her smell. Hand-sewn bags of lavender and rice, which she'd heat in the microwave and rest across the hump of her neck.

Now, Cynthia walks out of Maplewood Memorial. She wears an oversized ski coat. Pastel purple, browned at the sleeves from years of wear, with a collage of ski tickets dangling from the zipper. How does Cynthia look: a wilted daisy.

And it's too late. Russ has seen the boy. Cameron is in that awful crux, the period of teenage disaster you never believe you'll grow out of. He's too long, sandy hair hanging in greasy clumps. Oily skin, that curved beak of a nose. Greenish-hazel eyes, too close together. Russ looks away, but already his heart fights some battle—to hate or protect, to hold or to hurt? How does Cameron look: just like his father.

———

When Cynthia was eight months pregnant with Cameron, Russ and Lee went out to Dixie's Tavern. A freezing night, between Christmas and New Year's.

I told Cynthia I was on duty tonight, Lee said, after they'd ordered two beers with a plate of hot wings to share.

She wouldn't approve? Russ joked, clinking his frosty glass against Lee's. A cloud of foam dribbled down the side and onto the sticky table.

She's pregnant, Lee said. No one is allowed to have fun.

At Dixie's Tavern, Lee wore a hooded blue sweat shirt with the Denver Broncos logo blaring off the chest, a fuming, angry horse. Lee was swallowed up by the hoodie, a men's medium; beneath it, Russ imagined the waistband of Lee's pants, bunched up at the hips, fabric pulled in by a thick leather belt set at its tightest notch. Lee had shaved that day, and his jaw was smooth. No stubble. Just a few pimples around his mouth and two razor-edged cuts at the chin where Lee had nicked himself. Russ imagined blood flowering through a single square of toilet paper, pressed tight to Lee's jaw-skin.

Lee picked a steaming-hot wing from the top of the basket and held it carefully with his pointer fingers and thumbs, like a full husked corn still on the cob. He ripped into it, pungent orange sauce gathering on his lips as he carefully pulled meat from bones with crooked teeth.

Soon, those greasy orange fingers would be gripped in a baby's choke-hold grasp. Russ didn't know whether to laugh or to tell Lee to wipe himself clean. He handed Lee a napkin across the table.

Four weeks left, right? Russ said, picking up a drumstick.

Four weeks, Lee repeated.

You nervous? Russ asked.

You kidding? Lee said. You try having a kid. Nervous is the wrong word—I've got four weeks to get my shit together.

You'll be fine, Russ said. He gulped at his beer, choked, coughed. Took a bone off the plate and licked it white-clean.

That night in the shower, Russ looked down to find his hairy arms bent in the shape of a cradle, wishing for a miracle, squirming life—something of Lee's he could nurture and grow.

———

There he is, Detective Williams says, and Russ physically starts. He has forgotten his surroundings: car, parking lot, funeral.

Detective Williams is watching the doors. Ugly, hungry gaze. All wolf.

We got him, Detective Williams says. You ready?

They get out of the car and Russ stays a few steps behind Detective Williams, who swaggers toward the entrance of the funeral home, so confident that Russ wonders if Detective Williams looks this way always. When he pulls on navy socks in the morning. When he's on hold with the credit-card company. When he's eaten too many French fries.

Detective Williams makes his deliberate way through the crowd. The people stare and whisper, Russ trailing hesitantly behind.

Excuse me, sir, Detective Williams says, as the crowd mutters in the sun. We'd like you to come with us to the station. We've got a few questions for you.

What? Cynthia asks, panic like a sheet flung over her face. Are you arresting him?

No arrest, ma'am. Just a few questions.

Her gaze a spotlight.

Russ, please, Cynthia begs, come on. This is ridiculous.

Russ thinks of Cynthia's feet, muscles straining in pink silk ballet shoes. The veins in her neck, Lee's noodle arms. He steps back from the scene and that's when he sees her: Ines, his lovely wife. She stands next to Ivan, one hand folded over her mouth. Ines is watching, but not like a foal. Instead, bystander to wreckage. Her breath curls in the cold.

Russ is only feet away, but he has never felt further from Ines. Detective Williams has not singled out Ivan, and this should make Ines happy. Appreciative. But they could very well be strangers, Ines a disgusted witness to such injustice—a scene outside a funeral, tragedy within a tragedy.

Once, Russ was sick with the flu, and Ines tucked him into bed and put an empty bucket on the floor just in case. She held a cool washcloth on his forehead, and when he'd closed his eyes for long enough, she began to sing. A lullaby in Spanish. He understood then, as he begged his own eyelids not to flutter: her past was a thing she doled out like dog treats, holding it close to her chest to ensure it would not be taken away.

Detective Williams escorts the bewildered suspect to the car. Russ starts the engine. As they pull away, Russ looks at Ines one last time.

She is no foal. She is a woman and Russ is a man, and that is all. That is all they can do.

———————

Russ tried to tell Cynthia about Hilary Jameson. Two months before Lee's arrest.

Lee had run to the gas station for another six-pack, and Cynthia was weeding in the garden. She wore a floppy straw hat and overalls. Eight-year-old Cameron sat at the patio table, coloring in a cartoon book—he had an entire box of crayons, but he used only yellow. He shaded so hard with the yellow crayon that it was just a nub, Cameron's chubby fingers nearly touching the paper as they jammed it with wax. Why don't you try purple? Russ suggested. Purple is a nice color. The boy didn't answer. Only pressed the yellow crayon harder.

In the garden by the back fence, Cynthia held a fistful of greenery.

Come see, she said to Russ, and he carried his unsweetened iced tea over to the patch of blooming vegetables.

We're getting rid of the poisons, Cynthia said, as she wiped her forehead with a leather-gloved wrist.

The poisons?

See the roots? Cynthia tugged a small plant from the soil. When she squatted, both her knees cracked.

I see them, Russ told her.

There's no science to it, Cynthia said. But I think you can tell which weeds are poisoning this garden by how deep the roots go.

They peered into the shallow hole the plant had left. A sluggish earthworm curled around a pebble, squeezing and oozing through its subterranean home. Cynthia squinted up at Russ, her sun-sweating face so close that Russ could see fresh mint leaves caught in her teeth.

He tried to imagine Lee and Cynthia having sex on top of Cynthia's hand-sewn quilt. Russ's stomach dropped, and with it a pleasurable feeling that had nothing to do with Cynthia's proximity and everything to do with guilt. He wanted her very far away. It was a longing Russ felt, but not for Cynthia; too sharp. The sort of longing that dug into you, penetrated hard.

See this? She held up the plant and a chunk of soil landed on the front of her overalls like a wine stain.

The roots go deep, she said.

Russ should have told her then. He wanted to. All the time Lee had been spending with Hilary Jameson—Cynthia thought he'd been with Russ. And what about Russ, here? Russ, who spent most nights alone in the shadows of his too-big house, drinking just to keep himself company. He should have told Cynthia, should have shared the weight of this sudden alienation.

He tried to tell her, but what could he say: You poor woman. There's no science to it. You are lying with the poison. Your little boy watches as you hand glasses of whiskey to that poison, three fingers thick. You're sucking on the poison, you're letting it inside you, you're stroking its forehead afterwards, tender where tenderness is expected. Not deserved. You've given birth to its incarnation. Those roots—they're swollen fat.

More tea? Cynthia asked.

Yes, Russ said. Yes, please.

Only after she'd gone inside, leaving him in the vegetable garden beneath that valiant sun, only then did Russ mumble: Take care of yourself, okay?

Feeble.

Russ is a man prone to regret, and this fact has abused him in every moment since.

Jade

"Y"ou'll need to come to the station with us," the officer says. "We have a few questions for you."

The crowd erupts. People swarm in all directions, trying to get a better glimpse of the drama, and only when the mass shifts can I see: Cameron clings to his mother's arm as the officers take hold of the person to his right.

I'd recognize the sweater vest anywhere. He has a collection of four or five sweater vests that he wears throughout the school year, regardless of the season. He wears a black one now, coat folded over his arm, shoes speckled white with plaster.

I had Mr. O for art last year. He would always stand too close, looking over your shoulder, making comments like *It's just a paintbrush. Play around with it a little.* He was one of those teachers awkwardly invested in his job, personally offended when you didn't give a shit. The girls always fluttered and speculated—Mr. O was one of those young, attractive teachers. He dressed like a high-schooler, and he was always so friendly. There were rumors, of course, about his relationships with students, but they were always started by the meanest and stupidest girls. *Did you hear what Mr. O said about Lucinda's pottery project? "Gorgeous."* A series of giggles.

The scene is chaos. Cameron's mom is pleading with the officers.

"Please," she says. You can tell she's uncomfortable with the sound. "Please, you can't take him. Russ, come on, it's me. You can't just take him."

I catch snippets of conversation. *The art teacher; he was her art teacher—Years at Jefferson, I never thought he'd—So inappropriate for a funeral, they should have waited—Wanted to make a scene, makes them look productive—*

The two police officers march Mr. O away like a trophy. He keeps his head bowed to the ground, takes each step purposefully. His hair, peppered with gray, shines white in the sun.

Cameron's mother hugs him close, and they both watch, horrified, as the officers lead Mr. O into a squad car.

Sirens wail. Doors slam. People follow, and a few have their flip phones poised to take grainy photos. But most stand, dumbfounded, circling a drama that has now gone, leaving an empty, pulsing space in the middle of the crowd.

———

I've met that police officer before—with the moustache.

Howie used to live in Willow Square. In winter, he'd set up his sleeping bag in the drained, empty fountain and shake his cup of change at you. The city complained, and one day, when Howie and I were playing checkers on the steps of the fountain, the cops came to move him. There were two of them—one was the lieutenant, gruff and mean. Pile of dirt, he spat at Howie as he shooed me away. I retreated to a storefront as the other cop squatted down into Howie's line of sight. "Fletcher," his badge said. He helped Howie up by the arms, gathered Howie's things into his shopping cart while the lieutenant filled out a report on a clipboard, grumbling with annoyance under his breath.

As he arrests Mr. O, Officer Fletcher's gaze is somewhere else. When I follow his line of sight, I see her: Querida. Querida, in her black veil, gripping the arm of a man who could be her brother, tears streaming down her face as she shakes her head like *No, no, no.*

Querida notices me, but only for a second. She looks away quickly, panicked. But in that second, her dark eyes hold mine. So brief. Ashamed. I see myself very suddenly, too. It's like looking into a mirror as shower fog evaporates: I am the line connecting the dots.

It makes you wonder, doesn't it—how it's possible to be a secondary character in your own story.

———

The sun is blinding. Cars idle in the parking lot, silent witnesses.

"You had him last year, didn't you, Jay?" Ma says. "For art class, what was it, pottery?"

"Ceramics."

"Did he ever do anything to you?"

"What?"

"Did he ever touch you?"

"God, no, Ma. That's disgusting."

"He always creeped me out," Amy chimes in. "He stays for hours after school every day, just looking at paintings and stuff."

"I don't know, Amy . . . he is an *art* teacher."

"Watch it, Jade," Ma snaps, digging through her purse for the car keys.

People stand in small groups around the parking lot, gossiping. Everywhere I go, Mr. O's name.

"Jade!" someone says from behind.

Mrs. Arnaud holds up her long black skirt, hurrying over from the other side of the parking lot. Ma has already started the car, and Amy fixes her hair in the passenger's-side mirror.

"Jade." Mrs. Arnaud stops near the bumper of Ma's Subaru. She wears her hair in black mourner's lace like a 1940s widow, and it falls in pretty tendrils around her face. The Arnauds are technically two years younger than my parents, but it's like they're impervious to time, the way naturally good-looking people tend to be. They do things like running and hiking and biking. Mrs. Arnaud always looks like she's just returned from a tropical vacation.

Now, Mrs. Arnaud squints at me, using a tanned hand to shield her eyes from the sun.

"It's Edouard," she says. When I first met the Arnauds, they both had thick French accents, but in the years since they've become barely detectable. "He's a mess. He won't speak to anyone. We don't know what to do."

I wonder if she's somehow missed the memo—if the last year has shrunk into a short blip in her mind, a speed bump in my and Zap's friendship. If she even noticed at all.

"I know you haven't been over in a while," she says. "But maybe you could stop by this afternoon? I think he'd like to see you."

She's wrong, but I don't tell her that. I nod and fight the urge to pull her close, to rest my tired head on Mrs. Arnaud's shoulder, which I know will smell like Burberry perfume and brand-name laundry detergent.

WHAT YOU WANT TO SAY BUT CAN'T WITHOUT BEING A DICK

A Screenplay by Jade Dixon-Burns

EXT. FUNERAL HOME PARKING LOT—DAY

Celly and BOY'S MOTHER (43, glowing tan), stand side by side against the whiplash wind. Celly looks beautiful in a white summer dress.

                              CELLY

            You know him. Boy. Your son.

                          BOY'S MOTHER

            Yes, of course I do.

                              CELLY

            Can you tell me where he's gone?

                          BOY'S MOTHER

            I just told you, he's home.

Celly shifts her weight from one foot to the other.

                              CELLY

            That's not what I meant.

                            ———

We weren't friends at first. Zap had the three thirty slot for piano lessons, and I had the four o'clock. Our teacher was named Erin and she had three cats—they would sit on top of the piano during lessons, letting the sound reverberate across their furry stomachs.

Erin always ran late, so Ma would sit in the living room and make small talk with Mrs. Arnaud. They were new to town. Ma invited them over for dinner one day after piano lessons.

That summer, we rode bikes. Around the cul-de-sac, through the swamp on the outskirts of the neighborhood where the irrigation system had flooded a concave field. The town didn't have the funds to clean it out. We collected sticks and pretended they were fishing rods, dunking them in slimy water. We caught toads in buckets and hid them in Amy's room. One died in her closet. I was grounded for three weeks. We read easy novels in Zap's backyard hammock, picking aphids off the white rope.

I spent most of my days in Zap's clean, well-decorated house. The Arnauds had this grandfather clock they'd brought over from France, a family heirloom—I remember thinking how cool that was. How genuine. My family would never do such a thing. *Garbage*, Ma would say, with a pull of her cigarette.

Zap became obsessed with astronomy after the fifth-grade trip to the Denver Museum of Nature and Science. They had this giant planetarium, and the guide bombarded us with facts that Zap wrote down in the miniature notebook he kept in his back pocket. *There are fourteen known black holes in existence*, and *The Big Dipper is an asterism, not a constellation*, and *You can't hear a scream in outer space*. He typed all these facts up on his parents' computer, 16-point Verdana, and hung them on his bedroom wall, adding to the list every time he found something new or noteworthy. Soon, his room was covered in charts and diagrams, in pictures of astronauts in marshmallow suits bouncing across the surface of the moon. He was going to be an astronaut, he said, and even though it sucked because he'd be gone for years at a time, he promised he'd bring me back rocks from as many planets as he could, to add to my collection.

Our parents had dinner—usually at the Arnauds' house—while Zap and I disappeared upstairs. We played Pokémon cards. We watched the neighbors with binoculars. *They'll get married one day*, our parents used to joke.

Ninth grade, a week before Christmas, Louis Travelli nudged Zap as we walked down the hill toward my neighborhood. *Into fat girls, eh?* Louis said, kicking the bottom of Zap's backpack. Zap looked at me with this twisted face: anxiety to such an extreme, it could have been disgust. *I should go home*, Zap said, once Louis had gone. *I have a lot of work to do tonight.*

We didn't speak for days. It felt like when you accidentally jump into the deep end of a swimming pool: you expect concrete beneath your feet, but instead you flap, panicked, toes grazing water and water and water.

After Christmas break, the spell lifted. He called me one Saturday. *Let's make a fort*, he said. We gathered all the blankets and pillows in the house, rearranged the furniture in the living room. We pressed the couch against the wall, moved all the dining-room chairs to the front of the fireplace. We built a castle out of floral-print sheets and down comforters, lining the different rooms with Persian rugs. When it was finished, we climbed into the "master bedroom"—the largest quarter of the thing, roped off with cream-colored sheets, and we lay down side by side, gazing up at white cotton.

"People have been talking, you know," Zap said.

"About what?"

"About us. It's getting pretty annoying. Like Louis the other day. I keep telling them there's nothing going on, but they won't believe me."

I wondered if I was going to be sick. It wasn't a bad thing I felt then, as he folded his glasses and set them on his stomach. Zap's elbows were filling out, gaining the muscles and contours I'd come to recognize on grown men. I watched them, his elbows, in the hazy pink light of the fort, and I thought about how you could know someone really well, know everything about them—how they tuck in their sheets, messy in the morning. How their legs bleed when they run through tall grass in summer. You can know all these things, but you'll never know how it feels to be them: to inhabit their space, to exist in their skin, to grow into their elbows.

I'd seen movies. I'd watched people kiss. I knew how it was supposed to work, kissing, but it always seemed so unnatural to me: pressing parts of your two bodies together, feeling someone else's wetness against yours. Zap's mouth was very close to mine, and for the first time, the reality was palpable. Someone else's teeth were so close, someone else's tongue. I wanted it. His lips were full, in the dim light of the overhead lamp that filtered through the sheets. Our bodies were cast in this creamy glow, thick with some surging emotion I didn't recognize.

He felt it, too. When I think about what I've lost, it's not the end I drift back to. Instead, this: Zap's neck stretching closer to mine, the hollow space above his collarbone, and the seam of his red T-shirt nearly brushing the tip of my chin. He wanted it, too.

Zap sat up, so fast that the top of his head caught the sheet and it engulfed him like a hood. He was a ghost. A corner of the fort fell, leaving us gasping, feeling much older than we were supposed to.

I went home. We didn't speak for another two weeks. For a few months, our friendship went on as it had, but by the time summer came around, he stopped calling entirely. That's how it goes. People change, they grow up, I understand. But sometimes it's like I can still feel the heat of him, can still feel our young stupid hands reaching for one another, shaking with some sort of bewildered love.

Cameron

Cameron had lied. He had read Lucinda's diary, one page, before he gave it to Mr. O.

January 11th:

What is a window for
Except to watch
Through glass, sometimes
I can feel u
U terrify me

He couldn't read any more.

Lucinda had doodled five-pointed stars across the top of the page, but they were not careful—they were messy, ink smeared in the corners. Also, she dotted her "i"s with bubbly circles.

U terrify me. Cameron could not look at the words, could not think of glass, could not allow this thing to exist anywhere but with him. So he ripped the page from the diary and tucked it where he'd found it in the first place: the crack between his bed and the wall, where it fell to the dust. He tried desperately to forget.

Her handwriting was not elegant; it did not swirl. Lucinda's words didn't dance the way he'd hoped. They didn't dance at all.

———————

Mom's van pulled out of the Maplewood Memorial parking lot, and Cameron rolled down his window, even though the dashboard display read twenty-six degrees. The day should not have felt like this: so bright and unabashed, like it wasn't even sorry. The dry trees flicked by in blurs of naked brown, like they'd peeled off their layers and were learning how to breathe again. This was so unfair.

The quiet calm of the car was oppressive, interrupted only by Mom's crying. It was not the sort of crying you could hide. Cameron wanted to comfort her, but she was crying for Mr. O, and this was all Cameron's fault.

They inched forward. Cameron knew what was happening in all the other cars: *Mr. O,* parents were saying to each other, *Mr. O, the art teacher from Jefferson High; remember him from parent-teacher conferences?* Kids were sitting wide-eyed in the backseat, hoping this would get them out of homework.

When they pulled up to the house, Mom turned to Cameron.

"Go inside," she said.

Her eyes were small and red. She pulled a coffee-shop napkin from the cup holder and used it to wipe her nose.

"Where are you going?"

"I'm going down to the station. Cameron, I want you to go in the house. Do not leave until I'm home, don't answer the door, don't speak to anyone. Do you understand?"

"Yes," Cameron said as he slid his legs over the seat and onto solid ground.

"Cam?" Mom said before he could shut the door.

"Yes?"

"I know how you felt."

"What?"

"About Lucinda. I saw your drawings."

"Mom, I didn't—"

"I know you loved her, is what I'm trying to say. I know you loved her in your own Cameron way."

Mom's bony hands grasped the steering wheel.

"When I get home," she said, "I need you to tell me everything. I know it's hard, and you must miss her terribly, but sweetie, I need to know what you have done."

Mom motioned for him to shut the door, and before Cameron could tell her that he loved her and he wished she wouldn't be so hard on herself, the van was bumping out of the driveway and around the corner. Cameron let those words fall off him like snakeskin, rearranging themselves as they hit the ground: *What have you done?*

———

Cameron had been in Dad's closet twice before—both times after Dad had gone, when Cameron had been so Tangled he had lost all sense of time, curled up on cream carpet.

1. When Beth said Cameron was the kind of kid who would bring a gun to school, he came home and opened the chest under Mom's bed. He stared at the .22 handgun, wondering: Was it possible to lose control of your own body? Could your hands do things your head didn't want?

2. When he read that book on Mom's shelf, about the man who killed

someone while looking directly into the sun. Albert Camus, *The Stranger*.
Cameron dreamed of ultraviolet rays burning straight through his pupils.

Now, Cameron did not turn on any lights. Even though it was daytime,
the windows in the living room faced south, and the house was gloomy. He
slipped off his shoes by the front door, and locked it so he would hear Mom
coming home. Carefully, Cameron padded toward the den.

When Dad left, everyone said Mom should get rid of his stuff. Instead,
she'd left it encased in a tomb down the hall from her bedroom.

Cameron creaked open the door to the closet and all Dad's smells
gushed out. Whiskey. Aftershave. He liked Dad's leather shoes, with tissue
paper balled up in the toes to keep their shape. He liked how Dad's two
fancy suits stood, rigid on hangers. He liked the belts that hung from hooks
on the door, the different shades of brown, black, and suede. Even though
Cameron hated all these things in theory, he was so Tangled that their familiarity was comforting. He turned on the overhead light, stepped inside,
and shut the door behind him.

The relief was immediate. Here, he would not think about Mr. O,
chained to the bar in the room where they held bad guys. He would not
think about Mom, standing by the coffee machine at the station house,
pleading with Russ Fletcher to *let him go; he didn't do anything wrong.* Here,
it was just Cameron and Dad, playing the quiet games they always did.

Dad had kept his police uniform in the back corner of the closet when
he took it home for washing. It had a set of shelves all to itself, even though
it belonged to the Broomsville Police Department and had lived there most
of the time—one for the pants, one for the belt, and a rack for the jacket,
which he hung before he ironed it on the laundry-room table. These shelves
had been empty since the arrest, when the chief took Dad's uniform away
for good. Cameron pushed aside a rack of windbreakers and ran a hand
along the cold wood. On top of the shelf, where Dad used to keep his
badge, Cameron's hand ran over a folded sheet of paper.

Cameron picked it up. It was not dusty. He held it to the light.

Even in the fog of the closet, he recognized the corners of the paper;

they were serrated, made special for extra absorbency. It was a sheet of watercolor paper. Strathmore, eleven by fifteen inches. It had come from the pad beneath Cameron's bed, the pad filled with Lucinda's eyes and the sweet strands of her hair, done in charcoal so thin it could have been pencil.

Cameron sat, criss-cross-applesauce, on the carpet and unfolded the piece of paper.

Immediately, he wished he hadn't. He wished he hadn't come into Dad's closet, he wished he didn't live in this house, on this block, in this state with pointed mountains. He wished he had never seen Lucinda Hayes, that he had never loved her the way he did: with X-ray eyes and such an uncontrollable heart.

———

They came for Dad on a Monday.

Mom wore pink-striped pajama pants. Cameron remembered it from below. He looked up at Dad, whose own friends were clinking him into handcuffs and saying things like *Why, Lee? You didn't leave us any choice.* And Russ Fletcher—who used to come over for dinner and laugh so loud at everything Dad said—cowered in the corner. Cameron didn't watch the rest. Instead, he looked past the chaos from his spot at the kitchen table, at the painting Mom had hung above the window.

Later, he would learn the painting was a Van Gogh. He would learn that the version in the kitchen was a re-creation, digital paint on plastic canvas. The painting was called *A Lane Near Arles*, and it was done in 1888, the same year Van Gogh chopped off his ear. Cameron liked this fact, because even though Van Gogh must have been Tangled while he was painting, the piece was very calm. Van Gogh had spent December of 1888 in an insane asylum, and Cameron liked to think *A Lane Near Arles* was the view from Van Gogh's window as he tried to feel okay in his head.

The last Cameron saw of Dad: thin fingers clasped behind his back next to the kitchen sink, held in place by shiny metal handcuffs. Cameron knew these fingers—they clutched cigars on the back porch, they shook out the newspaper in the morning, they pulled navy uniform buttons through fraying loops. They tucked Cameron's racecar blanket over his little body before lights out. The smell of Johnson and Johnson, these fingers combing through wispy hair in the bathtub, these fingers gripping baseball bats, *See, swing from the right like this. Eye on the ball.* Those hands, resting in Dad's lap as they spent lullaby nights together in the living room, that companionable introversion. His father's fingers were interlaced within the restraints of the handcuffs, twisted back, palms facing out like some shameful plea.

Mom yelled. Officers yelled. Cameron sat at his dinner spot at the kitchen table and studied the painting. *A Lane Near Arles.* There was a yellow house next to a giant orange tree, on a winding road lined with Valencias. It was like a dream. He could live in this house, where things were not sad, where Mom didn't plead in her unsure voice—*Please, Russ, tell me what's going on.* Cameron felt like he'd been here before, to this house on this road, so pacified in the sun. Grandma Mary was there, he liked to think, along with all the good people who had once been in the world and had gone: they all found these smooth brushstrokes, this yellow calm.

The sirens outside screamed, red and blue into dusk.

They took Dad away.

When Mom came back into the kitchen, she didn't speak. She stirred the pot of mac and cheese on the stove with a metal spoon, her back bent like a branch. Water boiled.

Outside the window, a Calliope hummingbird stopped at the feeder Cameron had made from a water bottle. It was male—Cameron knew from the burnt-red feathers on its neck. They'd learned about hummingbirds in school; the Calliope was the smallest bird in North America, rare for Colorado. It flitted around, quick and light, like nothing bad had ever happened. At the bottom of one fact sheet Cameron read was a footnote: *The hummingbird is the creature that opens the heart.*

Of that night, he would remember the painting above the window, the calm yellow house where he could get some rest, and the creature lapping sugar water from a branch in the yard. He would remember Mom, weight in her elbows, hunched over the stove, trying not to sob, and he would think: This quiet place, this place I will take the ones I love?

I will call it Hum.

———

The day Dad actually left—after the arraignment, and the trial, and the *not guilty*—the walls started breathing.

It began in the kitchen. Cameron checked the stove, but the knob was twisted to "Off," and the teapot sat idly on the fake marble countertop. Cameron checked the fluorescents above the sink; he flicked them on, off, on, and off again. Nothing. He unplugged the refrigerator. The whir of the machine stopped, but he could still hear it: a barely discernible intake of breath.

Dad was a heavy nose-breather in sleep. Cameron used to lie awake between scratchy hotel sheets—on mountain trips, at weddings, the night before his grandmother's funeral—listening to oxygen fight its bitter way through his father's nose hairs.

Cameron knew Mom would be angry if the milk went bad, so he plugged the refrigerator back in and stood in his browning socks in the middle of the kitchen.

At first, it came from behind, and then from the hallway, and then from the direction of the living room, and Cameron felt so stupid spinning in circles, trying to catch something that didn't want to be caught.

He pictured Mom waking up at four in the afternoon to the sound of Dad's breath. Sleeping pills and crusty bowls would greet her from the nightstand. She would imagine his big, awful arms around her. She would miss him. Cameron could not bear the thought of Mom missing him.

"Stop." He said it with all the authority his child voice could muster.

But the walls did not listen. They only stood there, being walls, ignoring his little-boy pleas.

Dad's hammer was exactly where he'd left it: hanging from a nail in the garage, lodged between Cameron's old tricycle and Mom's dusty skis. Cameron pulled the hammer from the wall and stomped back into the kitchen.

The house was filled with the physical remnants of Dad. Crumpled socks in the laundry hamper, sweaty bottles of beer lining the door of the refrigerator. And, of course, his breath. Cameron was sure he was standing in Dad's lung cavity, the walls were his filthy ribcage, and oxygen was moving up through his windpipe, past his nasal cavity, and into the air of a house, a family, a life he did not deserve.

Someday, Cameron's windpipe and his nasal cavity and his lungs would be as big as Dad's. They'd be shaped the same.

"I hope they put him away. I hope he does his time," Mom had said, on the morning of the arraignment. Her voice had been shaky, a frog. "He deserves it, Cameron. Someday, I promise you'll understand."

Cameron didn't know which wall the sound was coming from, but he figured it didn't make much of a difference. He started swinging.

He swung and he swung until he could not hear anything but crumbling drywall and Mom's panicked voice—*let's put the hammer down, good, yes, we'll get you into pajamas, you're tired, sweetie, we'll deal with this in the morning, it's okay, it's okay.* And, of course, the blank indifference of a house with holes he had created.

———

The first friend Cameron hurt was the sixth-grade class pet. A sparrow, named Pauly. It had started as "Polly," but two weeks after Mrs. Macintosh rescued it from the parking lot outside the playground, the vet pronounced it male. Pauly was a tufty, fuzzy brown. His wings were clipped, so they could let him out of his cage when the classroom door was shut.

Pauly would perch on Cameron's outstretched arm, like he couldn't tell the difference between Cameron's skin and the plastic tree Mrs. Macintosh bought at the pet store. This was three years after Dad left, and Mrs. Macintosh told Mom that Pauly was a good outlet for Cameron, that a pet at home might help with his anxiety. Cameron didn't want one.

In the spring, Mrs. Macintosh took the sixth-grade class—Pauly included—on a camping trip in the mountains.

For two nights and three days they stayed in tents, spread across one of the most popular campgrounds in the Rockies. Mrs. Macintosh showed them how to tell the habits of native animals based on scat. *That's the scientific term for shit*, Ronnie said. The class rode horses and watched birds with binoculars. Cameron liked bird-watching best; he learned about the different species native to Colorado. Their habitats. He drew anatomical diagrams over the blue lines of his spiral notebook and cartoons of house sparrows perched in aspen trees.

On the last night of the camping trip, the teachers packed the bus for the three-hour morning drive, and the parent chaperones went to bed. Mr. Howard, the teacher on duty, was asleep in front of the campfire. *Come out on my signal*, Ronnie had said earlier. *Tom has a bottle of whiskey.*

At Ronnie's signal, Cameron unzipped the tent and slipped out. He was curious how the rest of the kids broke rules, and how this looked different from Cameron's own nighttime rebellion.

Ronnie was waiting at the edge of the woods. Hushed laughter blossomed from a dense cluster of trees, and when Ronnie saw Cameron, he waved and disappeared into the woods.

"Shut up," Tom was saying from the trees, and Cameron followed the sound of his voice, shining Dad's heavy metal flashlight across the walking path. "Are you trying to get us caught?"

The sixth-grade class sat in a circle. Girls on one side, boys on the other. Cameron joined the boys' side, slightly outside the perimeter of their shoulders, between Ronnie and Brady Callahan. He was surprised at how easily he blended in, how his legs folded underneath him. Sitting on the forest floor, he almost looked like everyone else.

Tom had set the bottle of whiskey in the middle of the circle—the same whiskey Dad used to drink late at night in the living-room armchair.

Tom swigged straight from the mouth of the bottle and passed it to Brady, who took a swig, coughed, and passed it to Beth. Soon, Ronnie was clutching the bottle; in the dim moonlight Cameron saw Ronnie sniff the rim of the bottle, discreet, before lifting the neck of it to his chapped lips. He swallowed. Sputtered, and passed it to Cameron.

The moment the liquid touched his tongue, Cameron knew he was going to vomit. The taste was so familiar—it had been in the air all those mornings, as Cameron dressed for school, dried and sticky against the rim of Dad's glass in the sink.

He didn't have time to stand up, to turn around, or to direct the spew away from his body. He threw up in his lap, all over his jeans, one hand cupping his own vomit and the other still holding the bottle of whiskey.

The girls squealed. Everyone else started to laugh. Even Ronnie joined in. Cameron could sit in their circles. He could whisper so he didn't wake the teachers. But he couldn't laugh like that.

Cameron stood up, dropping the bottle, and stumbled away.

"Where you going, faggot?" Tom hissed, a distant voice on Cameron's heels. "I thought you were used to swallowing."

Cameron let the forest hold him. He left Dad's flashlight in his pocket, where it sank like a stone, and imagined he could melt into the pools of darkness between each solitary tree. Maybe there, wrapped in night, he wouldn't have to be the kid with jeans covered in stomach acid and whiskey. He should have turned on his flashlight, because the forest was pitch black, but he didn't want to see anything. He wandered along, vision blurry and salty, stumbling over roots that protruded from the ground like the limbs of the dead.

So alone. He was so alone. Cameron found a spot on the forest floor and curled up there, trying not to think about Dad and how huge he must have been, hitting that girl over and over again with his sweaty Dad hands. And then Cameron was stumbling back to the campsite, where everyone had gone to sleep; he didn't know what time it was; he didn't know whether hours had passed and, if so, how many. He could see everyone's tents, like a little village in the moonlight. Next to Mrs. Macintosh's tent, Pauly's cage.

For a while, Cameron stood beside Pauly's cage. Pauly slept, nestled into his own neck. Usually, Pauly made Cameron feel peaceful, but he could not fathom peace tonight.

Mom had always told Cameron it was important for a man to be gentle. Anger was unfamiliar to him. He picked up a stone from the ground near his shoe and squeezed it so hard its edges were sharp against the bones in his hands. He felt no better.

Quietly, Cameron unlatched Pauly's cage. Pauly's eyes opened. Like Cameron had done so many times before, he stuck his arm inside, making sure to keep his fingers as still as possible, marble Statue fingers. He waited. Cicadas sang their unflinching songs.

Pauly shifted his weight. Hopped lightly onto Cameron's outstretched arm.

It occurred to Cameron that Pauly's body was just like all the others in the world: the same stupid things kept him alive. Connected bones and muscle and tissue, and blood running through it all. These things were inconsequential—ephemeral, transitory, so easy to take.

Something collapsed inside Cameron. He was cupping Pauly's quivering back with his right hand; he was thinking how nauseating this world was. Pauly's wings were flapping now, he could sense something was wrong, but Cameron held them close to the bird's fragile frame. Cameron was filled with something that felt too old for his body—it built and built and built, it was deeper than a sadness or a rage, it was a hunger and he could not rid himself of that bubble, that thrash. In one easy motion, Cameron curled his left hand over Pauly's chaotic beak and his right across Pauly's neck. He twisted, just once.

Later, Cameron would read a statistic saying that suburban house cats killed 3.7 billion birds a year, and he would feel a little better. He would read about sparrows, members of the passerine bird family. They didn't need much food to survive. Then, he would Google *How many sparrows exist in the world*, and he wouldn't find an answer, only that there were billions, too many to count. He would find a Bible quote. Matthew 10:31: *Even the very hairs of your head are numbered. So don't be afraid: you are worth more than many sparrows.* He would dig out Dad's copy of *The Map of Human Anatomy* and he would read about a different inch of the human body every night.

Mrs. Macintosh made the announcement the next day, as they were disassembling their tents. *Sometime in the night, Pauly escaped*, she said. *He's back in his natural habitat now.*

Cameron remembered only fragments of the rest of this night. How the sun peeked nervously over the tips of the mountains, then cracked over the earth like an egg, running yellow over dewy morning. He remembered digging a shallow grave at the edge of the forest, just out of sight of the campground, while the other kids huddled in their sleeping bags. He remembered Pauly's spine, thin as a toothpick, snapping between his fingers, oily feathers warm against his unfurled palm, and the distinct feeling of lightness that followed—like he had rid his own body and Pauly's of the sickness that plagued the forest.

———

In the drawing at the back of Dad's closet, Lucinda's eyes were open.

She stared up at the ceiling, eyes like an abandoned home. Angry black slashes cut across her cheeks. Her hair was matted—charcoal had been ground violently into the paper, knotting her usually sleek hair in clumps. She was not smiling. Her neck was out of line with itself, like a horror movie. The background was black, pools of powder charcoal spread around her angelic, deformed head. In the top right corner, Cameron could make out a small, rigid bump. The carousel's platform.

Two smudged wings jutted from the outer corners of her lashes. Those smiling eyes—it was Cameron's thumbprint. His signature.

For the first time in three and a half years, Cameron started to cry. The tears were hot on his cheeks. They dripped onto the portrait, creating lakes where there had been only paper. Cameron could only do such realistic portraits of things he had seen, and Lucinda dead on the carousel was one of them.

Russ

Ronnie Weinberg had given them Lucinda's diary.

I saw my art teacher with it, Ronnie had said.

Your art teacher?

Mr. O, Ronnie said. He teaches at Jefferson High.

Can you tell me exactly what you saw?

The diary was wrapped in a sweat shirt, and he carried it out to the parking lot. He put it in the glove compartment of his car.

You're sure? Russ asked, though he'd slid behind the receptionist's desk and one hand was already dialing the lieutenant.

———

The art teacher drove a dented Honda Civic. Detective Williams had wrenched open the door in the Maplewood Memorial parking lot. He would later claim the glove compartment was open already—they could see the purple suede book, lying in a sea of technical manuals and spare change.

They zipped the evidence tight in a plastic bag. Pulled off their latex gloves, clapping powder from their hands, which Detective Williams streaked across the thigh of his black pants.

Upon later examination—the diary was only half full, with little girl poems scrawled uselessly across each page. It told them nothing. But toward the end, a ragged edge: one page had been ripped out. They'd searched the car carefully. Found nothing.

They brought the art teacher in anyway. Took him back to the station house, where news vans waited, hungry and insistent. Russ refused each flash, staring into the recesses of the bright white lights, and thought: he had made two promises. One to his wife, and one to a ghost. He'd promised both he would protect the people they loved most. Russ thought of Cameron, how he'd pushed him on the swings at the very same playground Lucinda had been found on—that child gaze, alarmingly old. Russ knew, if it came to it, which suspect he'd relinquish to the greedy hands of the police: Ivan. He refuses to think too hard about why.

———

Now they have the art teacher in the same seat Ivan occupied yesterday. A sterile conference room. Various acquaintances of Lucinda's shuffle in and out of the station house, each bearing useless information. Outside, news vans speculate.

Can you explain the notes we found in your car? the detective asks the art teacher.

The girls in my sixth-period class, the teacher says. They think it's funny to pass notes about me. I think it's inappropriate. I confiscated them.

One note reads, and I quote—*Do you think he'd paint me like one of his French girls?* Can you explain this, sir?

I told you. It's this group of girls. Beth DeCasio and her friends. Kaylee, Ana. They think it's funny. I don't.

Okay. So—was Lucinda Hayes friends with these girls?

Yes.

Is it possible she could have participated in these games?

Yes, I suppose so.

Did she ever hint at an inappropriate relationship with you?

No.

Are you sure?

I mean, it could have been any of them. I don't know.

So you're saying: Lucinda could have written these suggestive notes, which you then took and kept in your car along with her diary, which just happens to be missing a page?

I didn't know the diary was missing a page. I was bringing it here. And about the notes, I don't know, okay? I don't know.

You expect us to believe that?

I don't know anything.

When Lee's trial began to take shape, during the intricate volley of he-saids and she-saids—before they'd known that Hilary would refuse to testify, before Russ could fathom that his friend would simply pick up and leave—Russ confronted Lee.

Lee had gotten out on bail. Mostly, he stayed in the house with the curtains drawn shut. Outside, Lee was a pariah. A criminal. Dangerous. He was all these things inside too, but Cynthia's form of cruelty was different from the points and stares the population of Broomsville showered on him as they ushered their children out of sight. Cynthia was cruel in the only way she knew how. Disregard.

Amidst the confusion of the trial, Cynthia took a part-time job at the craft store downtown. She could be seen through the window from the coffee shop across the street, picking through bins of beads, searching for crippling deformities—tumors bulging from smooth glass surfaces, bubbles in the center of gold-flecked orbs. She could be seen in the park for hours in the afternoon, pushing Cameron on the swings, his little hands frozen red, nose runny, in desperate need of a hot bath. She could be seen everywhere but her own home, where a monster took residence in her bed, beneath the quilt her grandmother had sewn by hand in a pattern Russ could dictate from memory. The force was under strict orders not to visit Lee.

Russ rang their doorbell like any other visitor. He had sat in the car outside for twenty-five minutes, hands in his lap, trying so hard to remember. All those lazy afternoons on the cliff, meals on that checkered tablecloth, never-ending games of gin rummy. How can you let all that go, even in the face of such incriminating evidence? You can't. You can't.

Lee opened the door, wide. Not surprised to see Russ, sheepish on the porch. Russ followed him inside, and they sat in the cluttered living room. Russ perched—dainty, like a woman—on the arm of the leather chair.

His heart, a patter. A gallop. A roar.

Please, Lee said, from the other side of the room. You're my best friend, Russ. You have to help me. The evidence has to go. They're trying to use the type of soil on her shoes to convict me. Please, for Cynthia. For Cameron. You have to help.

Lee walked right up to Russ. Came closer, closer. That gallop—that roar—Russ could kill this man. His oldest and dearest. But Russ kept still as Lee put one warm palm to Russs's stubbly cheek. Cupped it there.

Protecting, always protecting.

———

Russ went in after hours. Late in the evening. It wasn't hard to get into the evidence room, one of the Broomsville Police Department's many failings. Russ knew the password from watching the receptionist type it in, and she kept the swipe key in a safe beneath her desk, which remained consistently unlocked.

It didn't take Russ long to find the box. He pulled only the essentials: The bloodied blouse. (Plaid, silver buttons.) The pair of cheap cotton panties. (Unstained, but catalogued anyway.) Two high-heeled boots. (Both covered in the soft soil that caked the plains surrounding the stretch of highway Lee had patrolled, alone, on the night in question.)

Russ drove around aimlessly, evidence of Hilary Jameson's assault shoved in his trunk like a body. Broomsville was so small that night, as Russ wound through suburban streets. All the houses were the same; new developments from the same contractor. Year after year. In the dusk, the peaks of the houses were miniature mountains. Russ drove in circles for hours until, finally, he stopped behind the public library.

He left the car running. Pulled the clothes from their evidence bags and shoved them to the bottom of a dirty trash can by the light of a moth-clouded streetlamp. As he left the incriminating evidence to the bottom of the public garbage can, Russ thought mostly of Cynthia and Cameron. It didn't seem fair, how loving someone made their precious things your precious things, too.

On the drive back to his hollow house on his snoozing white street, Russ remembered the security cameras at the police station. When the evidence was discovered missing, two weeks later, Russ took a sick day. He huddled beneath the throw blanket on his living-room sofa, sure they'd come for him the way they came for Lee. Rattling handcuffs. But no. If Lieutenant Gonzalez had watched the security tapes, he never said a thing.

———

Now Russ stands by the coffee machine. In the conference room, the art teacher's head is in his hands.

Intimidation before interrogation, Detective Williams tells Russ, though Russ can see through this forced conviction: Detective Williams has no faith in the art teacher's guilt. The man has been cooperative, if shaky, and he has an alibi—a weekly night class for painting students. He hadn't swiped out of the Broomsville Community College art studio until after eleven o'clock the night Lucinda died, and stoplight cameras showed him headed straight home.

I found the diary in my classroom, the teacher tells them, and it sounds like the truth. Lucinda must have left it there. I took it to my car, to bring in after the funeral.

Detective Williams pounds the table when he asks questions. Scare tactics. Russ is used to cold weather—he has lived through thirty-six Colorado winters now—but looking at the teacher on the other side of the mirrored glass, Russ is chilled to the bone.

Fletcher, someone says. Fletcher. You okay?

Russ stumbles backward.

Fletcher? Where are you going?

———

Everything ended the night before Hilary Jameson was assaulted. Russ will think of this night every day for the rest of his life, and when he does, he will feel a shocking combination of regret and yearning.

Patrol was slow. Russ and Lee sipped black coffee. They'd been doing this lately—joining one another voluntarily for the overnight shifts, the ultimate insomniac pairing. This night, they idled in the car beneath the shadow of the cliff, both too tired and dazed to make the climb up for sunrise, though this had been the original plan, the only reason Russ had come along for Lee's graveyard shift. The houses around them slept, peaceful and stagnant. Russ and Lee kept awake with a game of Would You Rather.

Would You Rather: hear one song for the rest of your life—"Eye of the Tiger" or "Bohemian Rhapsody"?

Would You Rather: have sex with your cousin in secret, or never have sex with your cousin but everyone thinks you did?

Would You Rather: have sex with Detective Williams or the lieutenant?

What the hell? Russ asked.

If you had to choose one, Lee said. Life or death.

Death, Russ said, and they both laughed.

This is a dumb game, Lee said.

It is, it's really dumb, Russ said.

So they sat. Neither turned on the radio. July—trees danced in a casual breeze. Russ's uniform pits were damp, so he rolled down the passenger's-side window. Night had folded itself over the world, a blanket.

Lee shifted in the driver's seat, rested his right hand on the middle console where they kept cigarettes and condoms and cinnamon gum. Russ's hand, also on the console, had been fidgeting with a Styrofoam cup. Digging half-moons with his nails into the white. When the cup dropped to the floor by Russ's dirty work boots, his hand stayed.

Russ and Lee had had ten years' worth of conversations sitting in these two nylon seats. Now, frenzied July wind streamed in, the same mountain air dipping from Russ's mouth and into Lee's. Vice versa. He and Lee had had hundreds, thousands of conversations in the car, but perhaps none as important as this.

Whatever Russ had known about himself before this night—it shifted inside him, rearranged itself, rose up to choke him. He could have rolled up the window, he could have turned on the radio, he could have used the hand on the console to take a sip of cold coffee. He did none of these things.

Instead, Russ left his hand. As it was—bare inches from Lee's hand on the middle console. They both stared through the glass windshield at the rolling dawn landscape, so conscious of their traitor heartbeats, their own Judas fingers.

He can't remember who was at fault. Who leaped those two inches of space.

Butterfly: skin. Lee's thin pinky finger curled over Russ's pinky finger. Smallest digit on smallest digit. And that unfamiliar desire, blazing and determined, the desire to curl more than pinkies—whole selves—to curl bodies around bodies. The desire to eat someone whole. Smell, taste, swallow.

Fill. It was paralyzing and perfect, crippling in its singularity. Here is what I have been alive for all this time, Russ thought. This touch.

They sat this way, rigid in squeaky seats, pretending to count smeared insect carcasses on the windshield while instead counting seconds as they passed. Pinkies on pinkies, children making a promise they would never keep.

Minutes. Twelve, thirteen. All shaking insides.

Then, the call: a Toyota pickup speeding down I-25. Twenty over the limit. Lee tore his hand away, Russ revved up the engine, and they drove away from that unremarkable spot. When the shift was over, the sun rose over the mountains, bleeding an inky orange across the sky. Neither man could look at the other.

And the next night, Hilary Jameson. Four broken ribs in a ditch on the side of the highway.

Russ knows nothing of love. The lethal grip of it: a stillborn blue.

Jade

The Arnauds have repainted their house. It's a pastel yellow now. They also redid the garden in front—a stone path leads up to the porch, where two hand-carved rocking chairs sit next to a rustic wooden table. I bet Mrs. Arnaud spent hours poring over the Pottery Barn catalogue at their sunny kitchen counter. *Cette couleur?* she probably asked Mr. Arnaud, and he probably kissed her forehead, slow like he used to. I bet the Arnauds speak in quiet French before bed, Mrs. Arnaud in a clean silk nightgown, hair falling natural in her face.

Chunks of half-melted snow litter everything. I take the new path up to the door, but I hesitate before ringing the bell. Nostalgia stops me.

Nostalgia is my favorite emotion. It's like, you think you know how to deal with the passage of time, but nostalgia will prove you wrong. You'll press your face into an old sweat shirt, or you'll look at a familiar shade of paint on a front door, and you'll be reminded of all the time that got away from you. If you could live it all again, you'd take a long moment to look around, to examine knees against knees. Nostalgia puts you in this dangerous re-creation of something you can never have again. It's ruthless, and for the most part, inaccurate.

I feel very small, standing on Zap's stoop in my white dress and my army coat. This isn't a bad thing.

When I ring, Mrs. Arnaud answers immediately, still wearing her tailored black ensemble.

"Hi, honey," she says. "Please, come in."

———

WHAT YOU WANT TO SAY BUT CAN'T WITHOUT BEING A DICK

A Screenplay by Jade Dixon-Burns

INT. BEDROOM—DAY (LATER)

Celly watches from the doorway as Boy sits on the edge of his bed, pressing his thumbs deep into his temples. He looks up.

                    CELLY
    Hi.

                    BOY
    What are you doing here?

                    CELLY
    I came by to make sure you're okay.

                    BOY
    Thanks. I appreciate that.

The two stare at each other in silence.

```
                              CELLY
                     (gesturing to the bed)
         Can I . . . ?


Boy shrugs. Celly scoffs, hiding her hurt.


                         CELLY (CONT'D)
         I know there's a part of you that wishes we
         were young again, that we hadn't lost our
         way or whatever.


Boy watches the lines in his palms. Tracing. Avoiding.


                         CELLY (CONT'D)
         I want you to remember how we got here,
         okay? The love that drove us to become the
         people we are. It meant something.
                            (pause)
         Right?


Boy finally lifts his head. He looks at Celly, earnest now.


                              BOY
         It meant everything.
```

Zap used to be messy. When we were little, he'd throw school papers in piles on his desk. His soccer cleats would leave mud cakes at the bottom of his closet, and his jeans were always splayed across the floor, like he'd stepped out of them and they were waiting there, patient, for his legs to fill them again.

I consider doing our secret knock—two sets of quick raps, a horse's patter—but we are old now. Instead, I knock twice, firmly.

"Come in," he says.

Zap sits on the edge of his bed. His arms are crossed and his elbows rest on his knees; his body makes a perfect box. His shoulders form an angular T, and his head is bowed and limp in the center, thumbs pointed up toward his face.

"Hey," I say. Voice too high. "It's me."

His bedroom is spotless. He's painted the walls—one is red, the other three white. On the red wall, he's hung a bulletin board, which he's covered in pictures of him and various friends. The boys' soccer team, crowded around a campfire. Leaning out of jeeps. They're all very tan from a summer of lazy drinking on docks and joyriding dirt bikes through the mountains.

He got a new bedspread. It's black, and looks scratchy. The sheets and the comforter are both tucked in at the corners.

"My parents called you, didn't they?" he says, without looking up.

"They're worried."

I'm still standing in the doorway. I take a tentative step forward, hoping he'll invite me in. He doesn't. The seconds pass, miserably slow, honey slinking to the bottom of a jar.

"I don't know what they want from me," he says, gaze still fixed on his hands.

"I don't know, either," I say.

It occurs to me that Zap and I have not been alone in the same room for nearly two years. It also occurs to me that two years is a very long time to avoid someone—to form new ways of speaking, to kiss girls with flat stomachs. To clean your room.

Zap lifts his head. His eyes are puffy and ringed in tired circles. Under his gaze, I feel gigantic. My dress grabs me in all the wrong places and I cross my arms to cover the scabs from picking.

"Sorry," he says. "I don't know what to tell you."

"It's okay."

"I don't mean to sound rude," he says. "But I'd really like to be alone."

And then I notice it: in the corner where he used to keep his Hardy Boys collection is a model airplane. It's hand-painted and landbound in a clear glass case. When we were younger, Zap never expressed an interest in model airplanes, or airplanes at all.

This breaks my heart. I guess that's the difference between loving someone—really loving someone—and doing it from afar. It's like, you can know every detail. You can memorize how he sits in class, with his legs all casual out to the sides. You can count the lines on the palm that shoots upward in math class, and you can know those knuckles. But those hands have created something delicate, a miniature and impeccable combination of glue, paint, and sticks. This took care, precision, and a certain level of tenderness—all of which you didn't see.

———

A year and a half ago, the Fourth of July. That's when it really ended for me.

Amy was off with her friends and Ma dragged me to fireworks—I could tell she felt bad for me, but not in a way that encouraged her to be nice. She spent the night telling me how I shouldn't be wearing such short shorts, they weren't flattering on a girl my size, and when was I going to start using the gym membership she paid for every month?

The night was thick with mosquitoes. Kids pranced around on the shore of Windfall Lake, waving sparklers and lighting bottle rockets—this was the public part of town, where you went if you didn't know anybody rich. Ma brought two bottles of champagne for herself, which she stuck in an old cooler from the garage. When she left to find a Porta-Potty, I dumped my soda in the grass and poured a healthy amount of champagne into my cup, which I hid behind my lawn chair. If Terry saw, he didn't care.

"I'm going for a walk," I told Ma when she came back. She lowered herself into the lawn chair. Examined her nails.

Jenna Lindhauser was throwing a party. I hadn't been invited, of course, but I knew where Jenna's house was, from the carpool schedule years ago. If the lake were a clock, Jenna's house was at the three—Ma and Terry were at the six. I circled around, winding my way through the treelined suburbs, slapping my arms every now and then to scare the mosquitoes. By the time I reached Jenna's house, the fireworks had started, cracking and popping over the lake. The side gate was propped open with a slab of concrete; from behind the house came loud music and laughing. It smelled like barbecue. It didn't matter that I hadn't been invited—no one would notice me. They never did. Maybe that's why I went to the party in the first place. For that warm, unsettling feeling of fading into the background. Or simpler; masochism.

Zap's friends sat around a picnic table on the deck. He was probably in the crowd down by the water—the fireworks crackled red and blue and yellow, wilted trees over the lake, doubled in their reflections.

I drained the warm champagne from my cup, thankful for the calm that came over me in its wake. I needed another drink. Jenna's house was bright lights and marble, and I wound my way through the dining room, then the living room, in search of the kitchen.

On the way, something stopped me. In a small, dimly lit hall off the dining room, animal sounds came from behind a cracked door.

I knew what sex sounded like. I'd watched internet porn (albeit minimally). Soon, I would do it myself: only two months later, I would have sex with a nineteen-year-old named Jason who was staying in our hotel on our family vacation to Ohio. It would hurt, but I wouldn't bleed. He would pull my hair. He'd make me leave right after because his parents were coming back from the casino. I would never hear from him again.

I didn't know what I'd find at the end of this unlit hall, but it would be personal, intimate. Something I wasn't meant to see. I would follow anyway, for the sake of it. That's what I do. I push people. I make them angry. I do things no one wants.

The door was cracked open, and I peered in through the half-inch sliver. They were on the bed.

I recognized his toes. The second toes poked out farther than the big ones. And the calluses along the sides of his feet, from years of running in soccer cleats—flat and white, built up along Zap's bones.

Lucinda was perched on top, wearing only a pair of denim shorts. Her back was smooth. Her shoulder blades had ridges in all the right places, two flat pans covered in soft, doughy skin, and the flawless curve of her lower back. She was tiny around the middle, only a few inches thick in profile. She shook her hair out to the side and lengthened her back, brown nipples hard, cupcake breasts arched to the ceiling.

Lucinda bent her head over him. Fast breathing. Gasps—a moan. Her hair was a sheet of gold as she bobbed up and down, her mouth sliding over him, her legs split to either side like she was going to devour Zap, consume his very being. It was almost pretty to watch. Like an absurdist painting of a crime scene: horrendous and exquisite, so much of both that you can't look away.

As Zap groaned under the spell of Lucinda Hayes, I stood behind the door, champagne sloshing in my gut, and thought: This is how it feels. This, here—her full lips wet around him, ice-tray teeth and warm tongue—this is how it feels to lose someone.

Now, forty-five minutes after Lucinda's funeral, Zap presses his palms to his eyes and I shift my weight in his bedroom doorway. There are plenty of things I want to say, but most of them are irrelevant.

"How well did you know Lucinda?" I ask.

"What do you mean?" he says.

"I mean, you knew, right?"

"Knew what?"

"About her secret."

"Secret?" he asks.

"About her and Mr. O."

"Come on."

"She was fucking the art teacher."

"Stop it," he says.

"I can see her bedroom window from mine. I can see everything."

"You're lying."

"I'm not."

I regret this immediately. Partially because it's a lie. Mostly because I derive a sick pleasure from the way his face contorts.

This gives me a surging satisfaction, mingled with disappointment in myself and, of course, guilt. Ma always says I have serious inclinations toward sadism, and for the first time I understand what she means. Part of me did it to see if he would call me out. If he would say, *You're lying, Jade Dixon-Burns, because I know you. I've seen you. I remember you and you are a liar.* But we've pulled very far apart—for the first time, probably ever, Zap takes my word at face value. He believes me.

"You're wrong," Zap says halfheartedly. "It was that freak. That freak that always stood outside her window. I saw you two this morning, coming into the funeral. You're trying to protect that pervert."

"Jade?" comes a quiet voice from behind. Mrs. Arnaud's arms are crossed.

"Thank you for coming over today," she says, but it's not in her usual husky voice. She's heard me.

I calculate the distance between me and Zap. It's no more than five feet, but I swear, I've never felt further from someone. It's like what Zap used to say about Alpha Centauri, the closest star in the sky. It looks so close, he would tell me, but did you know it's actually 4.37 light-years from the earth?

It should have ended a month before that Fourth of July. Late May, sophomore year. The same semester we built the fort.

It was past midnight. I'd never gone to Zap like this before, and we were already beginning to fall apart, but I had a red stain in the shape of Ma's palm ironed across my cheek and the acute sense that spending the night alone would crack something irreparable inside me. One of Ma's fat rings had broken the skin just below my eye. I didn't cry—salt water wouldn't help.

I'd stumbled to Zap's house in a pair of broken flip-flops, drowning in self-pity and the memory of Ma's vodka-laced voice. *Useless little shit.* I rubbed my arm where I knew it would bruise. I read somewhere that if you pushed hard enough on an unformed bruise you could stop it from flowering. This doesn't work on me. My skin is too thin. Poor circulation.

Zap answered the door in a black T-shirt and a pair of blue plaid boxer shorts. His skinny white legs stuck out the bottom. I rarely saw Zap's knees; they were round and knobbly, naked outside the familiarity of his pants. He didn't seem surprised to see me. He made a shushing motion, pointing upstairs. Mr. and Mrs. Arnaud were long asleep.

We tiptoed up the creaky stairs and into the guest bathroom, which had a gold soap tray and embroidered towels. Zap clicked the door shut and flicked on the lights—the bulbs were harsh. Hot on my face.

"My God, Jay," he whispered. "What did she do to you?"

"I'm fine," I said. "Doesn't even hurt."

I poked the small cut under my eye to show him how much it didn't hurt, but my finger came away bloody. When I sucked on the nail, I tasted iron.

"Jesus," he said, pulling one of the embroidered towels off the rack and running a corner under the faucet.

"Don't," I said, when he tried to lift the spotless white towel to my face. "Your parents will notice."

"Here." Zap pulled his black T-shirt over his head. The static made his hair stand on end. "I have a million of these. We'll just throw it out, okay?"

He wet the sleeve and pressed it to the lacerated skin. The fabric was cool.

"It was the TV remote," I said. "I got the wrong batteries."

"What?"

"Ma freaked out. Said she'd given me specific instructions, and if I couldn't get a pair of fucking double A batteries how was I supposed to do anything? I told her to stick the triple As in her vibrator."

Zap opened his mouth the way he did when he laughed really hard, though he wasn't laughing.

"I don't need your pity," I said.

"It's not pity," he said. "I'm just worried."

We stood in the midnight glow of the vanity lightbulbs that lined the bathroom mirror, and he pressed the cloth against my face. I'd seen Zap shirtless plenty of times, at the pool in the summer. He looked more naked here. I'd never noticed the way his skin changed color from his neck to his chest. A ripening peach.

"What's this?" His hands moved to my arm.

A straight red line branded across my bicep, already purpling.

"The upstairs banister."

Zap ran a thumb over the tender skin, shaking his head. It wasn't disbelief—he expected this from Ma. We both did.

"Do you still want to leave here?" I asked.

"What do you mean?"

"Remember? You said we would move away. Go to New York."

"I remember."

Zap's thumb wandered my arm, roving over goose bumps so softly I looked down to make sure I wasn't imagining it. I wasn't. His thumb was there, his nail clean and neatly cut, knuckle wrinkled in folds.

Zap had three chest hairs. I'd never noticed them before. His stomach was a slate, his torso a triangle. A trail of hesitant fuzz crept from the seam of his boxer shorts, painting a straight line to his belly button. For the first time, I recognized Zap for what he was: a man.

We both watched his hand crawl up my arm. The heat. The surface of his fingers slid up my shoulder and across my collarbone, into the hollow of my neck, up to the base of my skull until he was holding my jaw with gentle cupped hands that didn't know where to go from there. His fingers shook. Small earthquakes.

I'd never touched someone like that. I explored his waistband, tentative. He pressed against my stomach with parts of his body I knew existed but had never considered. And then we were all hands, all motion, breathing too fast, not knowing how to move forward or back. I pulled my shirt over my head. Unclasped my bra. I stood there in my jeans and flip-flops, letting Zap see all the parts I could hardly bear to look at myself. The bathroom mirror taunted me, but I wouldn't look, for fear I'd start crying. I reached into his shorts and held him, stiff and heavy, silk in my palm.

Zap stopped. He opened his mouth, like he couldn't figure out how to push us back to a moment before all this, a moment before we were both unclothed in the bathroom and he was hard in cotton boxer shorts—he couldn't figure out how to tell me he hadn't meant for this to happen.

I hadn't meant for this to happen, either. He never gave me the chance to say it.

"Jay," he said. "We can't."

"Why?"

"I don't . . ."

"What?"

"I don't want to."

That was enough.

For a long time following, I'd repeat these words to everyone I could, if only to wear them out, wring them of meaning. Take out the trash. I don't want to. Ms. Dixon-Burns, why don't you write the answer on the board? I don't want to. Take your sister to school. I don't want to. Talk to me, please, Jade, I'm only trying to understand you. I don't want to.

And that night, before I stormed out the front door with my bra unhooked. Please, just put your clothes back on. I don't want to. Don't you understand? I don't want that. I don't. I don't want to.

Cameron

Things Cameron Wondered as He Stood Outside The Hayeses' House at 3:37 p.m.:

1. How do you know if you deserve the world's sympathy?

———

In his memory, Lucinda stood at the Thorntons' kitchen sink.

From Cameron's spot behind the oak tree, Lucinda was framed in the oval pane. She watched her own reflection as she washed dishes, baby Ollie crawling across the kitchen floor, sucking a plastic block, while the old gray dog gnawed a slobbery toy in the corner. Lucinda wore a tight athletic shirt: her ribs curved out like a pair of wings sewn tactfully to a caterpillar's body. Once, Cameron read that no two butterfly wings were the same, and this made him want to feel Lucinda's unique contours.

The thought made Cameron hard against the zipper of his jeans. He reached down to adjust his erection, and his hand brushed against the lowest branch of the oak tree—the tree made a tinkling sound so loud, Cameron's stomach burst with shock.

A set of wind chimes dangled from the branch he'd hit. They clanged together, deafening. Cameron tried to grab them, to drown out the song with his skin, but it was too late.

Lucinda pushed aside the red cherry-print curtain above the kitchen sink. She cupped her hands to the window and peered into the darkness. Cameron held so still. He imagined his bones were melting, then hardening again, that he was a figurine made of misshapen glass.

Lucinda's face disappeared from the window, and Cameron counted to six before the sliding glass door suctioned open. Lucinda stepped barefoot onto the back porch, an hourglass silhouette with arms crossed tight against her torso.

"Hello?" she called.

Cameron shrank behind the oak tree, wishing he could sink right into the whittled bark. The metal wind chimes were cold in his hand, kissing one another noiselessly. Television chattered, numb in the background, as the light from the living room illuminated Lucinda's form.

The space between Cameron and Lucinda was tense and palpable, a rope held taut. They could have walked it with bare feet. They didn't. Instead, Lucinda turned and padded inside, suctioning the door shut behind her.

The crickets rubbed their legs together, screeching and yelling in their acoustic cricket language.

———

The Hayes family was holding a reception.

Cameron stood on the street and watched the pulsing crowd of black-clad bodies mulling around the Hayeses' home. They pulled tinfoil off casserole dishes, wiping leaky eyes. He couldn't see Lucinda's family from the sidewalk; he guessed they were at the center of the crowd, wringing their hands, wishing to be alone with themselves but too afraid of the quiet to ask. Cameron wondered who would clean their house after everyone was done stomping through. An aunt, maybe, or a dependable cousin would vacuum around the Hayeses' feet, sucking up the mud and slush the chattering mourners had dragged in.

There was a police car parked in front of the house, and a tall, straight-backed figure sat inside, watching people come and go. Cameron deliberated briefly, then walked up the driveway.

He did not know what he was looking for inside Lucinda's house, but her smashed charcoal face was etched into the foreground of Cameron's vision. He needed evidence, proof that he had not imagined her.

When Cameron slipped inside, the crowd was so thick that no one glanced his way. He had never been in Lucinda's house in daylight. People ate noodles with plastic forks and the place smelled vaguely of tuna. By the bathroom, two women were talking about Lucinda's parents.

"They're in the living room, yes. They're talking, but not much."

Cameron recognized no one; for the first time, he was relieved to be in a crowd so big. Before anyone picked him out—before someone from school caught sight of him and started whispering—Cameron slipped into the side hallway and climbed the stairs, leaving the chaos behind.

There was a pressing quiet upstairs in the Hayeses' house, a purposeful and intrusive emptiness that settled on the green shag carpet and the ridges of the photo frames. Suffocating. Usually, Cameron liked silence, but this was unbearable compared to the noise downstairs. Malicious.

Cameron wanted to examine this untouched part of the house, to document it in ways he had not from the outside. It hit him—sweet, explosive—that Lucinda had breathed the air trapped upstairs, and it was getting recycled into his own lungs, sacred air that wouldn't exist after the Hayes family had opened the doors and windows enough times.

When he reached Lucinda's bedroom door, he pushed it open fast, to ensure he wouldn't turn back.

In the white light of 3:39 p.m., Lucinda's bedroom was just a room.

Four lavender walls and beige carpet with a coffee stain near the vent. Tracks ran up and down the carpet where the housekeeper had pushed a vacuum. Lucinda's computer was gone, and there was a perfect frame of dust where its torso used to sit.

Someone else had made her bed. Lucinda never fluffed her pillows—no, she always left the indentations from sleep, where the weight of her head had cast its skull mark.

———

The porcelain ballerina balanced on the edge of her dresser.

Cameron had seen the ballerina up close only once, when Lucinda had unzipped her backpack in the hall by her locker—the ballerina had been in the front pocket, inexplicably accompanying Lucinda to school. Cameron's proportional estimates had proven accurate: the figurine was no bigger than his hand. Her left leg made a triangle of empty space in conjunction with the right, held at a perfect ninety degrees, as she balanced on the tip of a porcelain slipper.

Now, Lucinda's ballerina was light in Cameron's hand.

The bed could have been anyone's, her desk could have been anyone's, her dresser could have been anyone's. The pens sat, bored, in a cup on the nightstand. Cameron clutched the ballerina, desperate for something that was distinctly Lucinda's. He was a continent, standing in this anonymous bedroom. He was a continent and Lucinda was a sailboat, circling, circling. He could not move; he could only watch her pull further away.

He needed more.

Lucinda's closet door was open. There was her favorite pair of jeans, the ones she wore with flat shoes, accentuating bluebird ankles. An old pink shirt with the word "LOVE" embossed across the front. The dress she'd worn to last year's Halloween party. Green velvet.

Cameron ran his fingers along Lucinda's velvet dress—it was liquid, running down his knuckles and over his hands, so familiar he swore he could taste her. Salt. Chemical perfume across her clavicle. Bitter on his tongue.

He slipped the dress off its hanger. Pressed his mouth to the fabric.

———

The Hayeses' upstairs bathroom was shiny and neat. Cameron draped Lucinda's dress over the rim of the bathtub.

White lace drapes failed to keep out the day—it tore through them, heedless. The shower curtain had a girlish striped pattern, and the toilet-seat cover was made of fuzzy pink yarn. Two toothbrushes with white film crusted down their necks leaned against the rim of a plastic cup, and the voices downstairs came up through the floor, muffled, a distant murmur.

In the mirror, Cameron looked hollow. The three naked bulbs that lined the ceiling made his face pale white, with thick, sagging shadows, like a sick person from a movie. His hair stuck up in a thousand funny places, and a leaf clung to the collar of his button-down shirt. Maple. He plucked it off and dropped it in the sink, where it sat, morose with all its veins.

Cameron snaked his belt out of its loops and dropped it on the bath mat. He unbuttoned his shirt—bits of skin revealed themselves like secrets. Someday his chest would have hair like Dad's, but now it was white and smooth and bare, nipples interrupting like unexpected punctuation.

His shirt puddled on the floor. Cameron slid out of his dress pants, bunching each pant leg around his ankles, then wriggling clumsily out of them.

He examined himself: Cameron was a boy in a pair of plain white boxers from the drugstore, the kind that came three pairs in a bag. He was a human body. Just that. What went on inside was irrelevant. He didn't hate himself. He only investigated a body with all its anatomical parts, all the related bits and pieces, a body that knew what felt good and what felt bad.

Lucinda's green velvet dress had a zipper in the back and a tag across the seam. *Eighty percent cotton. XS. Machine washable.*

She had worn the dress to last year's Halloween party. Cameron hadn't been invited, but he knew from the photos plastered to Beth's locker that Lucinda and her friends had dressed up as the seven deadly sins. Seven girls with heart-shaped faces smiled into the camera, crouching, a line of paper dolls with stick-straight hair and vodka eyes. Lucinda had gone as envy.

Cameron eased his feet in first. He reveled in the parting velvet, how it let him inside. Surrounded him. Slippery. His shoulders were broader than Lucinda's—when he pulled the dress up past his chest, a rip tore down the side. The dress wouldn't fit over his arms. The sleeves were too tight and the shoulders bunched, then settled around his elbows.

The dress was a green horizon line across Cameron's chest.

Shooting heat. A plunge. The same heat as when he looked at Rayna Rae's centerfold, or when Nicole Hartley sat so close to him in science class that her silky brown hair stroked the back of his hand as they wrote in lab notebooks. Cameron was set ablaze. Set to explode.

He gripped the edge of the sink so tight the rim left ruler marks in his palms. His reflection in the mirror pulsed in and out. In. Out. He was so dizzy. He sat on the knitted toilet-seat cover and pressed his nose into his forearm—he smelled like Lucinda's musty vanilla closet.

Cameron was very worried he would vomit. He peeled the dress off and kicked it into a puddle on the floor, stumbling panicked into his own pants, belt, shirt. The ballerina figurine sat poised on the counter, witness to the whole scene.

He needed to leave.

Shoving the ballerina in his pocket, Cameron considered the dress, lying crumpled and torn on the tile—it felt wrong to put it back in Lucinda's closet, so he stuffed it under the bathroom sink, folding it morbidly over a damp, rusty pipe.

The angles in the Hayeses' house were all wrong. The stairs were too steep. The upstairs was drenched in that oppressive emptiness, the downstairs bustling with the show that went along with it.

He yearned for sunlight, for a space that did not belong to his desolate love.

———————

Cameron's Collection of Statue Nights had documented a lot of afternoons, evenings, and nights, but he only saw Lucinda touch herself once.

Cameron knew this night was different from the others in his Collection of Statue Nights when Lucinda pressed an ear to her bedroom door. She murmured into the phone. She wore a baggy gray T-shirt and a pair of cotton shorts with small blue flowers embroidered across the seams, like the tiny blossoms that sprouted between sidewalk cracks.

Lucinda climbed onto her bed. She lay on her back and bent her knees, tapping bare feet against the comforter, laughing and shaking her head *no* to the person on the line. After four minutes and twelve seconds, Lucinda reached her hand into the seam of her pajama shorts.

She pulled the shorts halfway down; Cameron could see the V of her hips, where they melted into the hill of her pelvic bone. He couldn't tell which underwear she wore, but the insides were lacy black. A small patch of shocking dark hair sprouted from beneath her stretching palm.

Cameron tried to look at something else, anything else, as Lucinda started to explore, slowly at first, hand twisting in tender circles. But in the entirety of the neighborhood, Lucinda was the only light and the only motion.

Lucinda's hand moved in circles. Her back arched. She was starting a fire somewhere he could not see, a flicker of blue heat that rumbled up. Her long, thin toes were flexed, her legs spread butterfly against the bed. Cameron wondered, at what point do two people stop being two people—when do you become one entity, one conjoined thing that pulses together? When do you become one motion, building to reach, furthering, furthering? He didn't know the answer, but he wanted to be that with Lucinda as she bent toward the warmth of her own fingers, her lungs expanding and contracting, the back of her head pressing hard into the pillow, dainty neck so stripped and vulnerable. If Cameron could have asked Lucinda anything in the world right then, it would not be who she was talking to, or why she did this for the voice on the other end of the line.

He would ask: *Where does that bring you, my girl—can I hold you by the neck, be a part of this creature thing?*

———

In his entire life, Cameron had done only one landscape painting, and that was Pine Ridge Point.

Everything above looked bigger from Pine Ridge Point, and everything below looked smaller, and Cameron thought this was how the world should have been shaped all along. Good things always came from above. For this reason, he could not imagine a better place to go when it was time for things to end. There was a place like this in Hum, he was sure, and he'd spend all his evenings there, watching the sun bow and retreat. Lucinda would sit next to him in her favorite purple skirt, blooming full.

Look, Cameron would say. *Don't you see how weightless we are?*

Jade

"How'd it go?" Ma says as I kick off my boots at the front door. "You look terrible."

In my bedroom, I move aside a mountain of dirty clothes and flop into the ball of blanket stuffed between the mattress and the wall. I lie like this. Time hovers over me, unsure of itself.

"Hey."

Amy stands outside my door. She has changed into a plain flannel shirt—she looks younger than I've seen her in years. She's taken off all her funeral makeup, and for once, you can see her freckles. Her orange hair is pulled into a sloppy bun, and she pads across my carpet, feet bare. When we were kids, I used to read Amy a book before bed; she'd climb into my bed in her pilled Little Mermaid nightgown, sucking her thumb as she tucked herself under my arm. Amy almost looks like this now, with the eyeliner gone, hair knotted at the base of her neck.

"Go away," I tell her. "Did I say you could come in here?"

Amy ignores me. She sits on the foot of my bed, crossing her legs beneath her.

"I'm sad," she says.

WHAT YOU WANT TO SAY BUT CAN'T WITHOUT BEING A DICK
A Screenplay by Jade Dixon-Burns

INT. CELLY'S BEDROOM—DAY

Sister sits on the edge of Celly's bed, her back against the headboard.

> SISTER
>
> I'm sad.

> CELLY
> (fed up)
>
> Jesus.

> SISTER
>
> What?

> CELLY
>
> You think sadness is something you can hide behind. I'm tired of it.

Sister's eyes well.

> CELLY (CONT'D)
>
> It's not just you. It's everyone. Everyone's grief. You can't truly grieve over someone you didn't understand, Sister. None of you

```
can. And I won't. So please, don't ask me
to.
```

———————

"I'm sad," Amy says.

"I'm sorry."

"Come on. You're not sorry."

"Fine. I'm not."

She glances at the dead moth in my windowsill—it's been there for months, and every day it gets lighter in color as the sun turns it slowly to dust.

"Do you think he did it?" she asks. "The art teacher? You had him in school. You know him."

"I don't know, Amy. Why are you asking me all these questions?"

"Just looking for the truth."

"Fuck the truth."

"You don't get it, do you? You can't just say 'fuck the truth' and sit there like you don't care. Lucinda was *murdered*. That's a huge thing."

"I guess."

"So that's why the truth is important. And why I'm sad."

For the smallest second, I want to tell her about Zap. I want to unload the past two years on Amy, the pretty sister, the one with the light step, the one with friends, the sister free of *violent outbursts due to insecurity*. I want her to carry some of the weight, to help me hold up my own miserable head. But Amy and I aren't like that anymore.

She picks at a cuticle.

I reach for the stereo on my nightstand and turn on "Death by Escalator." This does it. Amy gives me her classic glare, and over the deafening drums and screaming vocals, she glides out of my bedroom. The music is so loud I can't tell if she slams the door.

I am very alone.

I pull open one curtain.

Usually when I watch Lucinda's window, it's with a combination of fascination, hatred, and jealousy. Today is different. There's guilt, of course, but more than that. Three days ago Lucinda was brushing her hair in front of the mirror and untangling the laces of her ballet shoes, and now her body is being processed in the basement of the Broomsville County Hospital. I think how lonely it must be down there, and I wonder if, wherever Lucinda is now, she can feel how much everyone loves her.

Pulling the curtain wide, I watch the reception going on below. People mill around the main floor of the Hayeses' house, and upstairs, Lex lies alone on her bed. The door is shut and a striped towel is stuffed beneath the frame. She has an arm over her eyes. Next door to Lex's, Lucinda's room should be empty, but it isn't. A figure slides clumsily into view.

I know the wrinkled collar of his shirt. And the way he walks—cautious and hunched, like he doesn't think he deserves to be standing.

The clock reads 3:41 p.m. Before I can question why Cameron is in Lucinda's bedroom instead of downstairs—or why he's gone to this reception at all—he disappears into the part of Lucinda's room I can't see from my window. He doesn't reappear until ten minutes later, when I see him fast-walking down the driveway, sweat-shirt hood pulled over his forehead, arms crossed like he's holding something heavy.

Sadness washes over me for the first time since all this started. I think of Zap and his grown, foreign shoulders, of Mr. O locked in a holding cell, of Lucinda sneaking out her bedroom window late that night. And finally, of Cameron. How he waited—he calculated that full minute before sprinting after her in the night. I think he loved her, he really did.

Everyone's looking for the truth. I'm so afraid I'll have to pry open its grave.

"Jade." Ma comes into my room moments later, as I'm picking the polish off my nails. It comes off in chunks of shining, glittering black. "We're giving to the church garage sale to raise funds for Lucinda's family."

She holds a giant plastic container filled with my old stuff, dug up from the depths of the basement.

"Now?" I say.

"Now," she says. "We'll bring it all over tonight. Last chance for anything you want to keep."

She leaves the container open next to my bed.

Old clothes, from seventh and eighth grade. Outdated bell-bottomed jeans, the occasional stuffed animal. I dig through the junk—I don't want to remember this time in my life, or really, any time in my life.

And then, at the bottom of the box: the third sign from Lucinda Hayes. The Token.

It's a small gift box, from a cheap pair of department-store earrings. Pearly pink, lined with foam. When I pull the box out, I refuse to cry. *Don't, don't, don't.*

The shell feels exactly how it used to, curled gracefully in my palm. The shell Zap gave me so many years ago, the one that lived under my pillow, with memorized ridges and folds, which I'd touch just to remember: *One day, we'll go away together. One day, we'll get out of here. One day.* It is smaller in my hand now, and only slightly less beautiful. This afternoon, the shell is just a shell from a beach in France. A doll's ear. Whispered promise, lost to the wind.

The Token.

You're supposed to act after three signs. You have to. A third sign is a last chance.

On my bike, Broomsville isn't so limiting, or constrictive. Just a corner of the world, with whitewashed people and fuming mountains. The houses race backwards, a suburban conveyer belt, until I've reached the highway that winds up into the foothills.

I remember all those playdates with Lex and Lucinda. Lucinda was never cruel to me—just indifferent. And who am I to hate someone for not giving a shit? As Broomsville rushes past, I recall shy smiles and vague offers of lemonade, Lucinda handing me the remote so I could pick the last half hour of television before Ma came to retrieve us. Small things that did not count as friendship, but had to count for something.

And I remember what Cameron said, about places you go when you're feeling locked inside yourself, and I go there—not for me, or Zap, or even Cameron. For her. This stupid, perfect girl with the inexplicable misfortune of being dead. I go because I am alive, and she is not, and there must be some cosmic reason for this.

It's this cliff, up in the mountains. It's very calm.

Russ

When Russ comes home from the station, Ines is standing at the refrigerator. The rusty door hangs open, the only light in the house. The page from *Love in the Time of Cholera* is still trapped beneath a magnet, faded, with curling edges. From behind, Ines could be anyone. Her hair hangs in a sheet down her back.

Russ had left in the middle of interrogating the art teacher—no explanation. A frantic need to get out from beneath the station lights.

Ines? Russ asks now, soft.

When Ines turns around, tears bubble in her lashes. Something is terribly wrong. She looks very sad to Russ, who holds his car keys too tight in his fist. The kitchen, all shadows.

What's wrong? he asks.

Russ, she says, a quake. There's something I need to tell you.

Ines slumps against the refrigerator door, next to a crusty bottle of mustard and a liter of flat Pepsi. Russ, she says again, this time an apology, a word she has knitted, soft, just for him. Behind her, a solitary bell pepper wilts in the vegetable drawer.

———

They'd started meeting months ago, at the Hilton Ranch hotel bar, to talk about Ivan. Marco had just started his program at the community college, and he knew all about tuition loans and applications—maybe this was the next step for Ivan. He could put all his philosophy to practical use. Marco suggested social work.

It just happened from there, Ines tells Russ. I am sorry.

Russ gathers his keys, wallet, jacket. Before he leaves, he asks his wife one thing.

Do you love him?

Though Russ knows the answer. Maybe instead, he should have asked—Do you love me? But Ines is weeping into her hands now.

Do you love Marco? Russ repeats, one hand on the door.

A stranger asked me that just last night, Ines says. I did not know until then, but yes, I think so. I think I do.

———

Russ took Ines up to the cliff in the mountains. Lee's birthday, five years after he left.

They got out of the car on that winding forest road, and Ines was shivering, so Russ gave her his police jacket. They made the hike hand in hand. When they got to the top, Ines gasped. Russ had almost forgotten the beauty of the place, the reservoir spreading beneath the cliff, glassy and sanguine. The city on the other side, unimpressive clusters of beige homes.

It's beautiful, Ines said.

I know, Russ said. This used to be my favorite spot.

Used to be? Ines said.

Russ nodded, left it at that. He wrapped his arms around his wife's waist and breathed in her familiar scent. Top of the scalp. Ines, so warm against his torso, fleshy and malleable. It was late afternoon; the sun pierced the sky like an open sore. It hadn't rained in over a month, and the reservoir was slowly ebbing to a cracked, dry crater.

Russ tried not to think of Lee, as Ines kissed his neck. But the memory of this place. He laid Ines down on a flat stretch of dusty earth and lowered himself on top of her. She laughed, pinned beneath him. Right here? Out in the open?

Only if you want to, Russ said, and he traced the side of her cheek with a hangnail thumb.

I want to, she told him.

Russ gave a part of himself to the woman in the dirt, the same lactic muscle that had loved and snapped before. She took that fragile, aching thing. Kissed it lightly. When Russ came, he cried. Collapsed on top of her. Ines held his face in both hands and sucked the tears from the corners of his eyes.

They never spoke of it again, and they never went back to the cliff. Ines didn't ask what had cracked Russ open. She had made her move in this long game they played, this strategic withholding of crucial information. Russ was thankful she had not asked, that she had left that vast black-hole distance between them. Secrets remained secrets. Wife remained wife. Someday, he would tell her, Russ vowed, as they shuffled back down the mountain, sticky and bleary and stunned. He thought of that night, in California. Tell me about the people you've loved. Someday, Russ would, and when he brought her back up to the cliff in the mountains, it would just be the two of them—Ines and Russ and the wind over the lake. No ghosts.

———

The night Lee fled, he did not go straight from the car dealership to the highway. No, Lee pulled into Russ's driveway, hat yanked low on his forehead. Green T-shirt, cargo shorts. Flip-flops.

They stood in the front hall of Russ's house. This was before Ines, of course; Russ had not cleaned the kitchen in months, and the mice chattered through the walls and cupboards.

Where will you go? Russ asked, when the silence had crept between them and placed one clammy hand on each of their throats. No air.

West, Lee said. Does it matter?

It did not matter.

Take care of my boy, will you? Lee said.

Okay, Russ told him. Okay.

There was nothing else to say. A hug would have been unbearable, a handshake too distant, so Lee just shrugged at Russ.

All right, then, Lee said.

And he was gone.

Only when Lee's car had groaned out of the driveway and Russ's house was its filthy self again—then, Russ wanted to ask. How could you do it? It wasn't a question of whether Lee had committed the crime. No, he wanted to ask: How could you do this to me?

He wanted to know how Lee had hidden such devastating darkness, how he had allowed that darkness to briefly escape its chains. How, in this newly shifted world, Russ could understand the nature of violence. Because Lee's specific violence—futile and needless—was something Russ could not possibly forgive.

Now, Russ does the only thing that will calm him: he gets in his squad car. Revs the engine, which sputters in the cold. Changes the radio to the local

FM station, where the news reports about the investigation—substantial leads, still no arrest.

Russ's phone rings four times in a row. His pager buzzes on the dashboard. Russ should go back to the station house, but instead he turns onto the road that will take him to the mountains.

It is Ivan Russ thinks about now, Ivan and his sermon on evil. If evil does not exist, how do you explain that broken little dove on the playground carousel—how do you explain Lee Whitley?

The mountains are cool and angular in the distance. Russ takes the highway route—he will not pass the station. Instead, his parents' old house, just off the shoulder of Exit 265.

He thinks of Ines and the home they have tried hesitantly to build: Of the corners of their house, where balls of dust and hair have clumped and a halfhearted vacuum refuses to reach. Of the tattered T-shirt Ines sleeps in, even after Russ bought her that silk nightgown for Christmas. When she opened the package she stroked it gently, said thank you, and put it back in the box. Russ has not seen it since. Ines, and how she eats her food without looking up, scooping each bite evenly onto her fork. Ines, and their separate worlds, lived together on the couch at night in distant but companionable silence—Russ, because he wants a body near his own; Ines, because of her brother. Both, because it is easy enough.

Russ's hands and feet steer him forward. Past the reservoir. Up into the foothills.

The mountains are on their knees, begging him home.

Cameron

Mom was in the kitchen. Through the back window, she looked like anyone else: another neighbor picking fat leaves off a potted basil plant. Through glass, she didn't seem so sad. Just old, and very tired.

Cameron took the usual route into his bedroom: hoisted himself from the planter beneath his window until he was holding the ledge with both hands, like someone falling off a cliff. He kicked his legs against the side of the house for traction and heaved himself through the open window frame.

He took off his muddy shoes beneath the window. Creeping down the hall in browning socks, he listened to make sure Mom was still in the kitchen. She'd turned on the radio, soft jazz, and the deep grumble of a saxophone slid through the narrow hall. Mom did not sing to herself. She did not hum.

Mom's room was messy. Floral sheets were balled up at the foot of her bed, and mugs with hardened teabags at the bottom gathered on her nightstand, where she kept her current books: *The Secret About Positive Thinking* and *Child Psychology and Development for Dummies*. Cameron knelt next to her bed and pulled the wooden box from underneath.

The .22 was in its hiding spot. It lay in its broken lockbox, buried treasure.

Cameron picked it up, careful not to touch any dangerous parts. Mom had stored a box of Aguila copper-plated bullets in the small compartment underneath the main carriage of the box. Cameron left them there— judging by the weight of the handgun and the tension on the trigger, it was still loaded.

Cameron edged the gun carefully into the back waistband of his jeans. The .22 was safe between his pants and his boxer shorts. Metal was still cold through cotton.

Before Cameron left, he checked Mom's bathroom. If Lucinda was ever going to come back to him, he hoped she would come back now. But the bathroom was just the bathroom, with grime gathered in the sink and the cracked yellow bar of soap lying in its plastic tray.

———

I don't understand how you draw from memory, Mom had said once, as Cameron spread his art supplies across the living-room floor. He'd been working on a portrait of a dancer. *How do you hold on to all the details?*

Cameron had shrugged and said, *I guess I can't figure out how to lose them.*

———

Now, Mom sat at the head of the kitchen table, late-winter light falling over her in gracious yellow rays. She hovered over a rectangular sheet of paper. One feather hand was cupped over her mouth. She'd turned the stereo off, and now she was bent over the version of Lucinda smashed on the carousel.

The painting of Hum hung right above Mom and Lucinda—a reassurance.

Cameron pulled a chair from the left side of the table, scraping it across the hardwood floor. He sat next to Mom, and together they examined the portrait of Lucinda.

Even here, Lucinda looked very beautiful. Mom thought so, too. He could tell from the way her eyes roved over black patches, places where Cameron had etched the charcoal so dark he'd pressed cavities into the skin of the real, living girl. And the white parts, where the sun from the kitchen window hit her clean paper skin, where her contours filled themselves out, where her jaw jutted out over her neck. Those staring eyes—even here, crevasse and unseeing, Lucinda was a vision. She was a brilliant combination of light and dark. Shadow and its resulting counterpart. She was luminescent.

"Cameron," Mom said. "Tell me what this is. Please, sweetie. I need to hear it from you."

"I'm sorry," Cameron said to Mom, because he was. "I need to be alone in my room for a little while."

Mom didn't answer, only shook her head at ruined Lucinda. Her jaw was trembling, and her hands were wrapped tight around a mug of tea to stop their shaking.

Cameron didn't like to touch, but he stretched his arm around Mom anyway. He tried to hold her up, but her sinewy arms and neck and collarbone all sank toward the table. At his touch, Mom's eyes filled. Cameron pulled away. He didn't want to make her cry.

He wanted to tell her good-bye and that he loved her, but instead he studied her gaunt profile. Cameron remembered how Dad used to watch her, and he tried to see the same. Mom had such graceful lines.

Cameron cupped a palm to the back of her neck, like how you were supposed to hold a baby, then left Mom at the table with her sadness.

The outer edges of Broomsville were flat and open. Run-down houses sprouted off the highway, with their beat-up trucks and collapsing barns, threadbare American flags waving to empty space. People out here lived differently: they sat on old couches and watched fuzzy television and drank homemade iced tea. The houses faded into the landscape. The people faded with them.

Cameron walked these roads to get to the base of Pine Ridge Point. Half an hour, just over a mile. His black ski jacket was layered over his sweat shirt, layered over the gun.

He climbed without thinking. He refused to look back as he scuffled up the side of the hill in his stiff dress pants, his shiny black funeral shoes sliding across the rocks. Pebbles toppled down the mountain behind him, miniature landslides.

It was only 4:45 p.m. when Cameron reached Pine Ridge Point. He'd wanted to watch the sky melt to black, but it would be an unforgiving blue for another half hour still. Cameron had that sacred feeling in his bones—a feeling you could only get at the top of a mountain, when the wind was blowing and you were alone.

If Cameron could answer Janine now, he would tell her yes, he was much happier alone than with other people. With other people, you couldn't feel like this—like a part of the lake, spread hapless beneath you. Still as a photograph. You could only wonder how it felt to be a mountain. To stand, so sure like that.

In the other direction, red roofs were speckled white with dandruff snow. That was Broomsville: a set of Monopoly pieces placed carefully in clusters around the sprawling plains. And beyond that: more plains. And beyond that: the horizon. And beyond that: he didn't know. The ocean, somewhere. More people. He thought of Dad, but not for long.

Cameron staggered, panting, to the edge of the cliff. The drop was only twenty feet—below that, landing after landing that led down to the water. Cameron sat on a small rock, near where the land turned into air, and pulled the porcelain ballerina from his pocket. She had survived the climb. Pristine. He balanced the ballerina in his palm, which was covered in red soil, and he thought about how somewhere out there, beyond this festering town, other people had killed. He wondered what they killed for. Compulsion, maybe. Or like in the movies: people killed for sex, or for money.

Cameron was relieved to think that if, indeed, he had killed—it had been for a monstrous love.

———

Two days before she died, Lucinda loved him in the yard.

He'd been a Statue only twenty minutes when she slid open her bedroom window and popped out the screen.

Cameron had always believed you could sense when things were over. Inside you. In the air around you. Now, the streetlights were humming, and Cameron had the distinct notion that after this moment, he would exist in a different era.

Lucinda lifted her right hand and held it there, a solemn wave. Her lips curled up, into a smile meant only for him.

Cameron had never felt so full. They were connected, they were undeniable.

She was a bird, perched and curious. He stretched his arm out. He waited.

———

Pine Ridge Point was like the middle of your favorite song—between the bridge and the chorus, where you held your breath and waited for the inevitable boom of music to take you away. Wind rustled through the branches of the pine trees, soft hands on sharp needles. Everything converged in a rattle, a combination of consonant melodies, a series of songs for Lucinda.

Cameron could hear all the words she would not say. The shoulders she would not touch. The strawberries she would not eat. The number of times a day she would not blink. The glasses of lemonade she would not drink, the white nail polish she would not spread across her fingernails, the millions of shades of reds and oranges and pinks she would not see, tucking themselves quietly into bed behind the mountains.

Things Cameron Asked Himself:

How do you explain the badness inside you?

White flame sun in his pupils, Cameron pulled the .22 from his waist-band. He swore if he lived through this day, he would not say another word to another human for the rest of his life, not even if that word was "sorry."

Jade

Kids at school refer to the cliff in passing. It's a revered make-out spot—the cliffs are tall, but not dangerously so. It overlooks the reservoir, and at night the moon hangs over the water like a single burning bulb. Last year, I came up here with Jimmy Kessler. His mouth was a suction cup, and he tasted like sour milk. When I got home, I took a long shower—the water ran cold as Ma pounded on the door.

It's the golden hour now. The sun looks like melted sugar. Irises grow more layers. Purple mountain majesties.

When I get to the base of the cliff, I lean my bike against an aspen. My legs burn as I take the first few steps up the steep, dry path. Powdery red dirt covers my heavy boots.

By the time I reach the top, sun is coming down in rays so thick you could grab them by the fistful. They filter through naked branches, scattering shadows across the plateaus.

Cameron sits on the edge, feet dangling into the abyss. He does not look any particular way. His back is stiff, unnaturally so, and he stares into the unknown space below, the hood of his winter jacket folded over his forehead. It drowns him.

I imagine, just for a second, how it would feel to be with him.

Cameron would do it differently. It would still hurt. But he wouldn't say, *Hey, you should probably go; my parents will be back soon.* He'd be shaky. Nervous. And afterwards, he'd wrap his arms around you and kiss your forehead and you would lie there until you weren't out of breath anymore. Cameron knows how to watch. Because of this, I imagine he's much different than Jason from Ohio, or Jimmy Kessler, or even Zap. Cameron would look at you like a painting he doesn't want to understand: He would study each brushstroke. He would see something embarrassed, something raw and cracked and fragile, and he would trace these things with artist's hands.

Cameron will never watch me this way. I don't want that. But it's funny, to suddenly be able to picture this, knowing someone so minimally. It's tangible.

———

"Hey," I say.

Cameron is barely visible behind the curtain of his hood. One hand is clenched inside a pocket.

I ease down next to him, swinging my feet in time with his. My boots hit the underside of the cliff, and a few pebbles chase one another over the edge.

"Hey," he answers.

"I saw you that night," I say. "Before *and* after. I saw you come back without her."

"Please go," he says.

"You followed her to the park. You staggered back. You looked drunk. You threw up in the bushes in front of the Hansens' house. Remember?"

He's crying now. Tears fall fast, but he doesn't move otherwise, not a muscle.

"Want to know something?" I say.

"Sure."

"I wanted her dead."

"That's a pretty terrible thing to say."

"I know. So I didn't tell anyone what I saw."

"You don't owe me anything," Cameron says.

"Not you," I say. "Her. I came here for her. Anyway, we're not all that different, you and me. Wanna know something else?"

"Sure."

"You can only see fifty-nine percent of the moon from the earth's surface. No matter where you go, in the entire world, you'll only ever see the same face. That fifty-nine percent."

"Why are you telling me this?"

"I'm just saying. We know this fact, but it doesn't stop us from staring."

The night I got home from that grisly scene at Zap's house—*I don't want to*—I stood in front of my own bathroom mirror. Studied myself, in my ripped-up concert T-shirt, with jeans that cut too tight across my bulging hips and skin that puffed out like the head of a cupcake. It was a searing hatred. A whole and incapacitating contempt for the very cells that made me up, for the way those cells replicated without my permission, how bones grew without my knowledge and skin acquiesced, folding over them in this intolerable manner.

I took a safety pin from Ma's sewing kit in the linen closet. I lifted my shirt and poked my ribs 815 times, not hard enough to draw blood but enough to leave a connect-the-dots across each flabby rib, a poem in braille I would never learn how to read.

This can't be it, I thought. *This can't be love.*

This rotten love was stuck to my skin, humid, dewy. That night in the bathroom, I could not fathom the possibility of peeling it off, allowing new, pink skin to breathe. So for years I wore it like a cloak, this decaying love. An excuse.

Now, on the cliff, I find there are no excuses to be made.

———

Cameron pulls a small object from his pocket.

The thing looks out of place in Cameron's palm. It's a tiny girl made of porcelain, lying on her side against his reddened lifelines. A ballerina. I would recognize the figurine anywhere. It has the most unrealistic face and this awful smile—the kind of smile you know is a cover for something else.

"Where did you get that?" I ask. "Did you take it from the Thorntons' house?"

"What?"

"That ballerina. It belonged to the baby Lucinda and I used to watch. Ollie Thornton."

When I go to touch it, to examine the figurine, he lifts the hand that isn't holding the ballerina. It rests, palm up, on a rock wedged between our two bodies.

His pointer finger is laced lazily through the trigger of a small black handgun.

I've never seen a gun before. It occurs to me that we are children.

Cameron

The ballerina figurine belonged to Ollie Thornton.

As February fifteenth came pouring over Cameron—the last time he would ever live his Collection of Statue Nights—he wished he could stop the wave of memory, the lost chunk of time he'd spent the last three days reluctantly trying to retrieve.

As he remembered February fifteenth, Cameron allowed himself to think only of Hum. Lucinda would be sitting on the edge of the bed. The sheets would be white and crisp. She would tuck her hair behind her ear with one of those thin, gorgeous hands. Cameron's favorite hands in the world. Outside, the birds would whistle their welcome.

Finally, he imagined Lucinda would say. She would smile. A ghost. Sublime. *You're home.*

———

The day she died, Lucinda left her diary on top of the drinking fountain in the art hallway.

The purple suede book sat on the cool, vibrating metal. When Cameron found it, he felt both ecstatic and horribly average. Ecstatic because it was the key to her, and average because he knew he would not open it. The diary belonged to Lucinda and only her; he would not take that away.

Most everyone had left school, except a few teachers who graded quizzes in empty classrooms. A group of girls rounded the corner and faded out of sight—they laughed like girls, shrill voices echoing off linoleum and trophy cases.

Two nights earlier, Lucinda had seen him in the yard and raised one slender hand in solidarity. For over a year, Cameron had watched, a presence that didn't partake in her existence. Steadfast observer, devoted spectator. But the diary would change this—she'd left it on purpose. Cameron was sure. She was raising her hand to him. This time, she was beckoning him in.

He slipped the diary into his backpack and walked home like usual.

"Well, don't you look happy," Mom said that night, smiling at Cameron, curious but wary. She'd cooked dinner from a sealed bag, one of those pasta packets you emptied into boiling water. "Any particular reason?"

Cameron couldn't tell her how it felt to be loved back.

It felt like a seed in a pot.

It felt like the right shade of yellow.

The last stroke of paint on an exquisite masterpiece.

By nine fifteen that night, Lucinda had curled in the fetal position on her bed, spine facing Cameron. He clenched the diary tight in his hand. He hadn't opened it, of course. He wouldn't betray her.

Lucinda's family watched television in the living room—Lex was sprawled on the floor with a bowl of ice cream. The house was dim.

He had practiced what he would say when her mother answered the door. *Is Lucinda home? I have something of hers.* Lucinda would pad barefoot down the stairs and she would lean on the doorframe. They would be two people facing one another in shaky, unpredictable conversation.

Cameron hated the thought. He wanted to leave her like this, perfect on top of the blankets, with a sheet of glass between them. Cameron clutched the diary to his stomach, thinking that he loved Lucinda most when she was just far away enough to exist tenderly, unaware of her audience. He loved Lucinda most on these quiet Statue Nights.

Tonight was different. Lucinda unspooled her limbs. Stepped gingerly from her bed. She put on her winter coat (yellow, like a down comforter), and walked to the window.

She cranked the window open, peering out at Cameron with green almond eyes. Pulled out the screen and slid one leg through. She breathed heavily—from fifty feet away, it could have been crying or panting. She climbed from the bedroom window onto the roof of the porch. Wrung her hands. Gathered her nerves. Jumped.

Lucinda landed on the frozen ground with a delicate thud, feet away from Cameron. Up close, she looked different. Much older than fifteen. She walked much older than fifteen, with a showgirl swing in her hips.

He could have reached out. He could have touched her. He could have said, *Come be with me.*

But Lucinda glided across the lawn and through the back gate, inching it carefully shut behind her. Cameron counted, as slowly as he could, blowing on his hands for warmth. *Sixty-three. Sixty-four.* She was not turning around; she was not coming back to him.

He followed.

———

Cameron tracked her all the way down the block: a fairy under the occasional streetlamp. The glow of her cell phone light blue in her hands.

Lucinda wore her favorite skirt with a pair of sparkling black-and-silver tights. The skirt was purple—the one from school-picture day. Golden hair trailed down her back, a swaying sheet that danced with Cameron. He followed her until they reached the elementary-school playground.

Cameron stopped at the edge of the playground, but Lucinda kept walking: to the far back fence, near the Thorntons' yard. She gazed up. She had stopped beneath the big oak tree where Cameron stood on Tuesdays, watching Lucinda rock baby Ollie to sleep.

Cameron lingered by the tennis courts, clasping the diary, as Lucinda reached up to the lowest branch of the tree.

Wind chimes.

The wind chimes Cameron had accidentally hit—they tinkled through the brisk night. This time, with purpose.

A back door slid open, then closed. A figure tiptoed out of the light. Cameron tried to sink deep into himself, to become a Statue. He'd never been so mortified. Those wind chimes.

Cameron would remember this moment as proof: Lucinda turned around, looked back at him in the shadows. Direct eye contact. That searing, alpine gaze. *Bear witness*, she seemed to say.

———

A grown man was hopping over the Thorntons' fence, was meeting Lucinda under the wild oak, was taking her by the hips and drawing her close and brushing her hair out of her face with fat adult hands, he was kissing Lucinda on the mouth in the moonlight, and the wind chimes were singing their aluminum praise.

Mr. Thornton. He wore a wool coat, unzipped. Shiny shoes. A button-down shirt with no tie, the first few buttons undone to reveal a spouting of chest hair. Mr. Thornton was kissing Lucinda on the mouth, pressing his forehead against hers, and wrapping father hands around Lucinda's shark-fin hips.

And with him: the limping little dog. Mr. Thornton clicked off its leash and the dog—happy to be outside and free—sniffed lethargically around the trunk of the wind-chime tree. Mr. Thornton zapped the extendable rope up into the leash like a tape measure, holding the big square of blue plastic by the handle. This was Mr. Thornton's ten o'clock walk—Cameron had always gone home when Mr. Thornton brought the dog outside, afraid of sharing his nighttime space.

Cameron stayed behind the tree. The bark ran up and down the tree in patterns he could have molded with his hands—faces that glared, faces that judged, and some that watched, unsurprised, as Lucinda kissed Mr. Thornton back.

They whispered things Cameron could not hear. It occurred to him how you could watch people all their lives. You could watch them sing along to music, but you'd never hear what song. You could watch them drink cups of tea before bed, but you'd never know that bitterness on their tongue. You could watch them talk on the phone, but they could be in love with the person on the other end of the line. Sight was useful, and also beautiful—but it was not necessarily truth. The truth was a rock lodged deep in Cameron's gut, and before he could turn around, before he could leave her diary on the ground next to the tennis courts for the cold to freeze over, Lucinda and Mr. Thornton started to yell.

Cameron only caught the loudest words.

"You wouldn't," Mr. Thornton was saying. "I know you wouldn't."

It happened in one instant, so trivial and seemingly unimportant that Cameron would not understand how, already, death had appeared.

Mr. Thornton was digging his man fingers hard into Lucinda's shoulders. She was yanking herself away, Mr. Thornton was reaching for her, she was stumbling backwards, taking quick steps across the lawn. She turned around and ran toward the playground, and Mr. Thornton ran after her.

He caught up with Lucinda at the carousel. In one swift blow, his arm, heavy with that sorry little dog's leash—a flash of sharp blue plastic tucked in his palm—cracked against the side of her head.

A small scream as she fell. Quickly silenced.

Cameron wanted to yell out. No: He wanted Lucinda to call for him. To acknowledge that she knew Cameron was there, that he was watching, had always watched. That Cameron loved her and he would help. But Lucinda only lay on her stomach on the carousel, the back of her skirt flipped up with the force of the fall.

It did not look like death at all. Mr. Thornton was kneeling in his suit, shaking her, begging, but she was limp. Gone. Minutes passed, and Mr. Thornton sprinted, panicked, back to the fence, where the dog sniffed calmly around the bushes, and then into his house. The faces in the tree grimaced at Cameron as the scene swirled around him—chaos, midnight, matted gold hair.

———

Cameron stood in the shadows with the diary, as Lucinda lay with her head turned grotesquely sideways. For the first time in his life, Cameron had what he wished for: he was invisible.

———

Miraculously, the snow. The sky's kindest form of mourning. Cameron let the flakes land and rest on his hands, his neck. He begged them not to melt.

When he could no longer feel his skin, when the snow had given his entire body a coat of fur and his jacket was soaked through, when his mouth was filled with the snot that had run from his nose, Cameron dared to move again. To leave her. It was not Lucinda, lying with her eyes open on the carousel: just a girl in a bleeding blanket of white.

As he walked away, he heard the click, then slam of a door. The night janitor. Cameron's only friend in the world. From his angle by the door, the night janitor would not see Lucinda until he crossed the parking lot in the morning, at the end of his shift. So Cameron took up his usual spot on the street— tonight, he was Tangled, so he did not nod. The janitor shrugged, as always. Raised his palms to the sky, like *Yes, yes, I know it's cruel.*

Cameron left him to the discovery.

———

Now, on the cliff, with Jade staring terrified at the gun by his side, Cameron remembered flashes of the rest of that night: the floor of Dad's closet with Lucinda's diary tucked, damp and sacred, between his shirt and his belt. He remembered making terrible slashes with charcoal. *Realism is made up of what you see*, Mr. O always said, and Cameron had hated him for this.

So with his legs dangling over a brutal formation of rocks, Cameron remembered the side of Lucinda's face, and he hated Mr. Thornton's massive hands, foreign and unexpected all over her. He was sad, he was so sad, because Lucinda was not alive and she was not loving him. She was not loving anyone—but she especially was not loving Cameron. He didn't know which devastated him more: that Lucinda was gone, or that she was gone and the reason had nothing to do with him.

Jade

Ma once told me I have a heart made of stone. I've never forgotten this. Often, I imagine my heart sitting heavy in my chest, a rock sunk to the bottom of a muddy lake.

Cameron lifts the small black handgun, and I have the brief, stupid thought that this will save me. You can't hurt someone made of minerals.

I have no idea what just happened. But I sense it, clear and electric: danger. I am in danger.

Cameron's head is thrown back on his neck like the beginning of a laugh. He fiddles with the gun, hands in his lap, bitten nails traversing the barrel, the magazine, the trigger. The gun is small, less than five inches long, but it looks massive in Cameron's hands. The air smells like iron. Urine.

The wind picks up, and my hair snaps across my shoulders. At the sudden motion, Cameron sits straight again. Laces his finger through the trigger.

What do you want? I try to ask myself, because I think it might be over. I want to see New York. I want to write something like lava, like gravity. There are things beyond the border of Broomsville, and I want to know how they taste. Somewhere, there is a person who will stand with me under the bathroom fluorescents, and when they say *I want you*, they will mean it.

I want to be unafraid of death, but my heart is not made of stone, it's made of the same thing as everyone else's. I want to be unafraid of memory.

For the first time, my future is manifest, material—hovering just feet away from me, in the hands of a boy who barely understands he holds it. I could reach out and touch it.

"Mr. Thornton," Cameron says. "I remember. It was Mr. Thornton."

I first saw the ballerina on Eve Thornton's dresser. It always looked out of place—the thing is too delicate to look natural anywhere in the Thorntons' house, which is still packed in boxes from their move two years ago.

For a short period—maybe a month—they moved the figurine to the table next to Ollie's crib. This was around the time Eve got really sick: she spent days locked in the bedroom with curtains drawn, leaving me or Lucinda with the baby.

Once, during those first weeks, Mr. Thornton came home drunk. I could tell he was wasted from how he whistled under his breath, off pitch and unnervingly cheery. I was in the living room with Ollie when he came in, tie hanging open, the first three buttons of his shirt undone. He sang to himself in the doorway, eyes closed, arms held to support an invisible girl in an invisible waltz while Puddles ran excited circles around his legs.

Ollie cried. Loud. Every day. Eve got sicker and sicker, until she was gone, for the most part, just a locked door at the end of the upstairs hall.

A few days after the waltz, the figurine disappeared.

I didn't think anything of it.

Now, the signs from the dead. Not signs at all. Just the world, turning as it does.

"Cameron," I say, careful to keep my voice even. "I don't think you're some-one bad."

Lying flat in his palm like a peace offering or a cold fish: the gun. A few more words of explanation: *I saw,* Cameron said. *He hit her, and then she was so still.*

One motion, exaggeratedly slow—I slide my hand over the gun. When Cameron looks at me, it feels like surrender: he does not protest. The gun is heavier than I expect, metal warm from where it has kissed his skin.

"Come on," I say, thinking of the inconspicuous times Mr. Thornton had asked Lucinda to babysit instead of me. "Let's get you home."

———

It's like all those nights with Ma. Her purple wine teeth, the chill of the wall behind me, the endless wait for the blow to come. Sometimes it comes, sometimes it doesn't—but in those moments of wait, there is always fear. Fear and I do such a familiar dance. Even tonight. But now, I help Cameron stand up and I do not feel like my usual self, cowered in a corner, waiting for the punch or the slap or the shove to take away the scared. No; I am taller. I am the one who holds.

Ma's bruises spread across my legs, and I poke them, bare in the cold.

Pain. Bearable.

———

We stumble down the melting mountain. Cameron can hardly walk: he smells like musty soil and urine. It's soaked through his pants and down his leg. I hold the gun, Cameron leaning against me.

We are an accident. Strangers. Both at fault, in theory. In actuality, the irony makes my hands tremble. Cameron doesn't notice. He's breathing fast, a panting dog, and his hair is stuck to his forehead. His breath is stale—I turn away.

It's almost funny: you think you matter to someone. They're the center of your universe, the sun you revolve around. You'd give anything for their details. You inch closer, closer, with tentative steps. You can walk as far as you want, but it won't matter. You're not even on their map.

We are not the killers. We are silly kids. Casualties.

Russ

Russ stretches out of the car. He has been here too long, at the base of the cliff, forehead on the steering wheel, counting heartbeats. His legs are sore from sitting; when he climbs out, feeling returns to his thighs. Pocketing his keys, Russ slams the door and raises his arms above his head. The pull of muscle wakes him. The evening is so cold—he should have brought his gloves, maybe a hat. A semi truck rumbles past, and Russ coughs in the exhaust.

The sun has just begun to set. The color: snowy tangerine.

Russ scuffles up the hill. He'd like to see that view—the lake, ghostly serene, and the pinprick Broomsville lights lapping at his back. But Russ has not climbed this mountain in a very long time, and after a few yards he is panting. He wishes he had brought some water; freezing air aches in his throat. He can see his own labored breath.

A sound. Voices.

Russ is only halfway up when two figures appear at the top. One limps, the other supports. A boy and a girl—young. Hey! Russ calls, but neither of them answers.

The boy wears a hoodie. His slacks are wet around the crotch. The girl holds a gun.

When she sees Russ, the girl waves him forward. He scrambles to meet them on the incline, hands raised in a practiced surrender. Don't shoot. The girl holds the gun by her side, almost a foot from her body, fist clenched around the barrel in a clear effort to avoid the trigger.

Their faces sharpen: for a second, Russ sees Lee. Lee, those woman hands, the way he'd suck beer from the neck of a bottle and sweat clumped in beads that ran down the back of his scarlet-burned neck. Before Russ can consider that Lee has finally come back for him, the boy comes closer. Cameron, of course. A dark patch on his jeans—he is half comatose.

The girl gives Russ the gun, and Russ nimbly empties the bullets into his pocket. No one speaks.

Russ picks up Cameron like a daughter who has fallen asleep in the car. The boy is not heavy, but he is wet with his own urine, which leaks through the sleeves of Russ's coat and onto the strong arms beneath as they take baby steps down the mountain.

It wasn't him, the girl says. Jade. Her hands are clasped in her lap as they wind down the foothills, past the stadium and the crumbling gas station. The polish on her fingers is picked at, a frame of black around each nail. A dark smear of marker slashes across her inner wrist. Cameron, in the back with Jade's bike, stares out the window. Russ thought about putting the tarp from the trunk beneath Cameron's soaking pants, but humiliation was not the game.

Did you hear me? the girl says. Cameron didn't kill Lucinda. It was her neighbor.

I believe you, Russ says.

As they near the station, he flips open his cell phone. Russ's hands remember the number. Old choreography.

Cynthia? he says when she picks up. I have him. He's okay.

When it's over—when they've gotten the story from Cameron, who speaks in a shuddering voice, with tears racing brakeless down his cheeks—Cynthia comes to Russ by the drinking fountain.

Russ, she says, battle-beaten beneath fluorescent lights. Thank you for bringing him home.

Russ steps forward, wraps himself around her. Cynthia's smell— lavender and lemongrass. After so many years.

They stand this way for minutes, absorbing one another's twin sadnesses, and Russ wishes with all his might that it were possible to go back to that day in the garden, to put his hands around Cynthia's sun-sweating face and help her pull every single plant from the ground.

———

Russ stays late for the paperwork while Detective Williams handles the neighbor and the chief handles the news vans. After a round of congratulations, everyone else has gone home. Russ is exhausted—he wanders into the break room for a cup of gritty coffee.

The break room looks exactly like it did seventeen years ago. Russ imagines Lee sitting across from him at the folding card table, holding a hand of aces and smiling, fake innocent. Lee would put down his cards—they'd both burst into booming laughter. Come on, Lee would say. Rematch. I know you can do better than that. Russ would shake his head, joking angry. In his chest, a flight of springtime geese moving back north for the summer. Flapping home.

Tonight, the memory feels less like a stab wound and more like a memory. Distant and unchangeable. A sighing reprieve. Russ stands at the gurgling coffee machine and thanks the years between then and now, a road the length of the country that separates Russ and that young fool self.

Jade

---

*E*verything happens for a reason, Mrs. Arnaud used to say. Zap told her this was stupid. *That phrase gets you nowhere*, he would say. It's a logical fallacy. It's like believing in the tooth fairy, simply to make you feel secure in your own existence. Sayings like these are safety blankets, he used to say. They're pretexts.

I partially disagree. I don't think everything happens for a reason. Some things do, of course. There's a reason Lucinda died. I don't know it, and neither does Cameron. This is an impossible consolation.

———

While we wait for Cameron's mom at the police station, the receptionist gives him a clean pair of scrub pants. He comes out of the bathroom, too dazed to be embarrassed, and sits next to me on a chilly bench in the police department's waiting room.

Cameron's sadness is a palpable thing, radiating from his curved spine, from the shadows beneath his baggy hood.

I take his hand, lacing my fingers between his. Cold sweat. We don't speak. When Cameron's mom comes bursting in, harried and tear-streaked, Cameron's hand unclasps from mine, and it feels like waking from a long night of satisfying sleep. A parting that I recognize—for the first time since Lucinda died—as a sort of grief.

———

Ma picks me up at the station.

I'm waiting outside with my bike. She doesn't say anything, just loads the bike into the trunk of the car, exerting more physical effort than I've seen from her in years. She slams the back door. Claps the slushy grime off her hands. Cars rush past the station and we stand in their tail wind, irreconcilable figures trying to ignore the nightfall breeze. Ma doesn't have a jacket.

"Officer Fletcher called," she said. "You were with the Whitley boy, huh?"

"Yeah."

"You should have talked to me first. I would have driven you here."

"No, you wouldn't have."

"Don't take that tone with me."

I'm about to tell her to fuck off when she steps forward, and then we're hugging. I can't remember the last time Ma and I touched like this. She smells like old cigarette smoke and orange Tic Tacs. I wrap my arms around her—plastic bra straps dig into her back, creating rolls I could grab in my fists.

It's over quickly. I walk to the side of the car, where Amy sits in the back; she's saved me the passenger's seat. When I slide in, Amy rolls her eyes and taps her long nails on the door's inner handle. She tries to crane her neck to see into the police station without looking too interested.

"I'll tell you later," I say to Amy. Tonight, we will curl up beneath my comforter and I will recount the story. I will tell her about Zap, the ritual, the gun, and the sunset sky. Amy will listen, twirling that red hair around her fingers. When I'm finished, she'll press her chest against my back and we will lie there, our separate heartaches shaped different but wearing matching clothes.

After I called Ma to pick me up, Officer Fletcher pulled me aside and said: *You should know—you're the hero of this story.*

———

Once Ma goes to bed, I sneak out the back door.

Terry has assumed his usual position on the couch. They've been playing the same things on the news, over and over again. *One of the victim's neighbors, not yet identified, is now in custody as a prime suspect. Sources say the victim was engaged in an illicit relationship with an older neighbor.* They zoom the camera in on Lieutenant Gonzalez, who coughs into his uniform sleeve and says things like: *We're doing everything in our power to bring justice to the Hayes family.* Police cars have crowded the street in front of the Thorntons' house. The neighbors across from us have gathered in their driveway, pajama-clad and curious, gossiping by the mailbox as lights flash red and blue across their faces.

I sneak out of the neighborhood in the opposite direction. First, I go to see Howie.

His stench dissipates in the winter. In the summer, pools of urine soak in the heat, and fermented clothes stick to his unwashed skin. But February—it's not so bad. Howie is slumped against his usual wall, atop a mangy blanket. His face is badly sunburned, turned a glossy, cracked red. His right hand is splayed out, palm facing up: even in sleep, Howie knows how to ask for help.

"Howie?" I say, not loud enough to wake him. "It's me. It's Celly."

I crouch down, wrapping my army parka close to keep out the wind.

"I gotta tell you something," I say, though it's useless. He can't hear me. "My name is Jade Dixon-Burns."

A line of ants crawls across the concrete, marching organized, one by one, somehow alive in the cold. I smash an ant with the thumb of my knitted glove, then regret it, rubbing its guts off with a crumpled sheet of newspaper.

"I'm seventeen years old. I'm not moving to Paris. Also, I'm not in love. You should know that—I'm really not in love."

Howie doesn't answer. Just lies there, unconscious, stuck in the stupor of last night's whiskey.

I thought maybe I'd feel lighter, or like a better person. In reality, I am only myself.

I walk slow all the way home, taking the long way through the field behind my house, which has become a wall of night. I'm wearing fleece sweat pants and an old pair of insulated snow boots. Mittens with holes in both thumbs. It's bitter out.

When I get to the middle of the field, I feel very old.

This place used to feel so much bigger. Endless, really. When Zap and I came here to watch the sky, it was like gazing at the edge of the world. Now, you can see the twinkling of the houses on the other side of the field, boring people living their boring lives. Although I'm not sure what to make of this darkness, it certainly is not infinite.

Cameron

After Cameron was home and showered, wearing clean sweat pants, he thought of sitting in front of Dad's friends. The only relief had come when Russ Fletcher asked: *Cameron, you watched her every night. How did you miss the signs of this? How did you miss an entire illicit relationship?*

The only explanation: Lucinda had hidden it until she couldn't anymore. She'd known Cameron was there, counting his own exhales on the lawn. In that notion, he found just an ounce of comfort. *U terrify me.* She had written of windows, of glass—and not necessarily of Cameron.

Cameron thought of last August. Of Lucinda standing in Mom's bathroom, dabbing Mom's gardenia perfume onto her wrists, Mr. Thornton's animal laugh echoing from the driveway.

Russ

W hen Russ gets home from the longest day, he does not expect to find Ines. She is knitting in bed, eyes puffed and pink.

At first, he is angry. Then, only tired. Russ sits next to her and the mattress sinks.

Are you okay? Ines asks.

I lied to you, too, Russ says.

When? Ines asks.

That day in California, Russ says. When I told you I had never loved someone before.

Ines throws her legs from beneath the comforters and pulls a pack of cigarettes from the nightstand. Russ has never seen Ines smoke. They lean out the bedroom window, and she lights one for each of them. Ines in her nightshirt, Russ in his starchy, pressed police uniform.

It started seventeen years ago, he tells her, and from there, he is racing. He tells Ines all the things he has never spoken of, pinkies on pinkies and how a gesture so small could feel so explosive. By the time they get to Cameron, hours have passed, and they're both slumped against the wall beneath the bedroom window.

Ines does not speak for a while. Russ wonders if she is angry. If maybe

she has always been angry, and this he has mistaken for passivity, compla-
cency. No way to know. Russ has always been the one with the badge, the
one with the gun. Her only weapon: silence.

Come on, Ines says. I think we need some air.

She pulls him into the bathroom. Opens the window and wriggles the
screen from its frame, gesturing with the pack of cigarettes. Russ realizes,
pathetic, that he has never been on his own roof.

They sit on the shingles. The bedroom comforter keeps them warm.
Ines tells Russ her own stories: how she got to America. A drive by herself
in a used Camry she would later sell to one of Ivan's friends, and a border-
control officer who glared and waved her through. She tells him again how
Ivan had never been a criminal back home, but he couldn't find a job here
after his own tourist visa had run up, and he needed money to keep working
with the church. Ivan had just begun when Russ and his friends busted the
house on Fulcrum Street.

She tells him what she has spent her days doing, these past few married
years. Skyping home, planning a trip back, arguing with Ivan and petition-
ing for his citizenship, this man who loved the country that had imprisoned
him, who had brilliant ideas about how he would fix it. She would stay for
the church, she'd promised Ivan. They were helping people. They were trying to find the money for a better space, and they already had donations
from the parents of the children she tutored. There is a new church opening
where a Rite Aid used to be, and Ines has been campaigning for the funding
to share the space with the owners. Ines has already told Marco all of these
things—he has listened. Listened, inquired further, listened, empathized,
listened, known her.

Do you hate me? Russ asks her.

A little bit, Ines tells him. But maybe you should hate me, too.

I guess.

I will be leaving, she tells Russ. You understand?

I know, he says.

Did you truly think that Ivan did this? Did you truly think he could
have killed Lucinda?

Probably not, Russ says.

I like to think you never believed it, Ines says. You made him a monster.

Probably, Russ repeats.

They smoke the whole pack of cigarettes as the sun rises up from the plains, washing everything in glow and gold. From the roof, Russ can see all the way to the end of the cul-de-sac, where housing developments turn to open fields. Though he knows that Ines will leave, and that this will needle its own pointed hurt, he takes Ines's small hand and rests it on his abdomen, beneath his shirt, which stinks of the day. She does not protest. The reassurance of palm skin—gentle, a salve—right where a rotting secret used to be buried.

———

Russ wakes at three in the afternoon. Ines is long gone—she did not come to bed with him.

When Russ goes downstairs for coffee, he finds her everywhere. Yarn: a trail of Ines. Up the stairs, across the front hall, a tangled pile covering the dining-room table like moss. Ines, in colors like fuchsia and mustard and forest green. Russ goes from room to room, opening all the blinds in the house to better see.

Years of carefully stitched Ines, undone and shapeless, one last act of defiance. She has unraveled it all, the whole closet of hand-knitted sweaters, blankets, hats, socks. In this sense, at least, Russ knows his wife—this is her mercy, and her revenge.

Weeks
Later

Jade

I see Zap in the cafeteria.

He nearly runs me over as I'm carrying my brown-paper lunch bag to the courtyard doors. He mumbles, *Sorry*, ashamed. I say, *It's okay*. Zap isn't wearing his glasses. He's nearly blind without them—he must have gotten contacts. His face looks much smaller in their absence. Naked. He wears a soccer jersey with his name printed in all caps across the shoulders.

———

WHAT YOU WANT TO SAY BUT CAN'T WITHOUT BEING A DICK
A Screenplay by Jade Dixon-Burns

INT. HIGH-SCHOOL CAFETERIA—DAY

                    CELLY
      I'm sorry. For what happened.
                (beat)

After the funeral.

                    BOY
It's okay.

                    CELLY
Just tell me one thing. Did you ever know
me?

                    BOY
Of course. Of course I did.

                    CELLY
Then how did we get here?

Boy runs his fingers through his hair. Thinks.

                    BOY
We grew into different things.

Celly bows her head. Acceptance. Boy gives a small wave and
lopes away.

———————

"Wait," I say, because Zap is already hurrying away.

"I'm sorry," I say to his back. "For what happened after the funeral. At your house."

"It's okay," he says over his shoulder. "They caught the real guy."

"I know."

We both nod, two people stuck in different places at the same time.

"See you around," he says. He lifts his chin at me, in the way boys do when they're trying to look casual. This makes me laugh, but he can't see because he's already gone, absorbed into the group of sports kids standing by the windows.

There are a million types of love in the world. I think of that night, in the bathroom, how Zap's thumb wandered tender over bruises. How do you classify that sort of love—young, fleeting? I keep trying to distill the difference between friendship and love—in an effort to figure out how you can lose both at once—but maybe it doesn't matter.

It was love. It was there. It was enough.

I leave my brown bag on a ledge by the courtyard and push through the lunchtime clusters toward the music wing.

The practice room smells like brass and linoleum. You could shout in here, and it would echo. The drums are lined up against the wall, the piano exposed ivory in the center of the room.

Zap's trombone case is lined up with all the other trombone cases. A label near the bell reads "ARNAUD."

The seashell is jagged in my pocket.

I take it out, hold it up to the light. It is pearly and transparent. Fossil. I leave the seashell in the nook where Zap keeps folded sheets of music. The shell rests against a tattered page, so seemingly insignificant. Offshore.

As I let the door bang shut behind me, I try to ask myself how I feel. This is stupid, I know. Emotions shouldn't have names. I'm tired of bothering with them.

Mostly, I feel uncaged.

———

"She left us something," Aunt Nellie says, when I walk into the Hilton Ranch one night.

"Who?"

"Our Tuesday-night lover-girl. Melissa found it in Room 304. We thought maybe you'd know what it means."

Aunt Nellie hands me a folded scrap of paper, and before I can open it she says, "Someone threw up in Room 101. You'd better hurry."

I wait until I'm in the elevator. The note is no bigger than my palm, just a corner of notebook paper. On it, Querida has scrawled in smeared pencil.

yo me perdí de noche sin luz bajo tus párpados
y cuando me envolvió la claridad
nací de nuevo, dueño de mi propia tiniebla.

—*Neruda*

Google tells me:

I got lost on a lightless night under your eyelids
and as lucidity enveloped me,
I was born again, master of my own darkness.

—*Neruda*

———

Cameron opens the door in a pair of Jefferson High School sweat pants that ride an inch above his ankles and a gray T-shirt stained at the neck. He looks how I expected. Gaunt. Eyes darting in all directions.

"Come on," I say from the stoop. "I want to show you something."

"Right now?" he says.

"Right now."

He puts on the same jacket he wore on the cliff, though it's warmer outside now, and the Velcro covering the zipper has balls of lint caught in its teeth. Behind him, his mother stands in a baggy sweater, arms crossed. She looks like someone who is constantly cold.

"Jade," she says. "It's nice to see you again."

"Hello, Mrs. Whitley."

"I have something to give you. Wait right here."

Cameron and I sit, both bumbling and gawky, while he ties his shoes. I've only come over here once since the truth came out, and then, we sat on the couch. We watched six episodes of *Full House* until I said, *It's getting late; I should go*. Cameron looked at me with these huge, weird eyes and said, *Come back soon, okay?*

When Cameron's mom returns, she presses a purple brochure into my hand.

"Take a look at this," she says. "Just an idea. It's a summer program I did when I studied ballet, around your age. Cameron says you want to be a writer, and I've heard their program is good. They give out scholarship money where it's needed."

The brochure is for a summer arts program at NYU. *A summer of artistry and diversity in the heart of New York City*, it reads. The words alone make my throat itch, so I fold the flyer and stuff it in the pocket of my jacket so she can't see how softly this touches me.

"Thank you," I tell her.

"When will you be back?" she asks.

"An hour. Two, tops."

I have Ma's car, and as we slide in, I turn the radio all the way up. I wish the Crucibles were playing, but they're not, just some shit pop song I don't recognize. Cameron presses his forehead to the window as we merge onto the highway. Headlights whiz by, fast-moving light. Comets.

I steer us into the Hilton Ranch parking lot and pull my all-access key from the pocket of my army parka. Cameron follows, feet shuffling and dragging, in through the revolving doors and to the elevator bank.

When we get to the room, Cameron glances back, furtive.

I know this room will be clean, because I did it myself and no one has reserved it since. I triple-checked the log. Trash bags are tied tight around plastic cans, the bed is tucked, neat and trim at the corners. Pillowcases fluffed. I've even Windexed the mirrors and folded a towel into the shape of an elephant at the foot of the king-sized bed.

"Smell it," I say, as Cameron follows me inside.

"Smell it?"

"Clean, right?"

"Very clean."

I perch on the edge of the bed and pat a flat swatch of comforter.

"Sit," I tell him, and he does. His snow boots are thick and rubbery against the checkered pattern of the carpet.

That's the thing about hotel rooms. They level the world. Every single one is the same, and inside, you can become what you'd like. You all sleep in the same scratchy sheets, you all stand under the same underpressurized showerhead, you all dry your legs with the same starchy towels. Doesn't matter who you are; in a hotel, you become no one and everyone, all at once.

Cameron lies flat, and I do, too. The green-shaded lamp on the nightstand is the only light in the room. Together, we watch the amorphous white ceiling like dazzled stargazers, finding constellations in the asymmetrical cracks, nubs of drywall gathered in clumps. We lie like this until it's an hour and forty minutes since we left his house.

"We should go," I say.

"Yeah," Cameron says.

I drive him home.

WHAT YOU WANT TO SAY BUT CAN'T WITHOUT BEING A DICK
A Screenplay by Jade Dixon-Burns

INT. HOTEL ROOM—NIGHT

Celly and Friend sit on the edge of the freshly made bed. The pillowcases are fluffed. A towel is folded in the shape of an elephant at the foot of the king-sized bed.

                         CELLY
            I have a question.

                         FRIEND
            Yes?

                         CELLY
            Are you angry with her? With Lucinda?

                         FRIEND
            Not angry, no.

Friend watches her for a moment. Celly falters under his gaze.

                         CELLY
            Everyone has more going on inside than
            you'll ever know. You couldn't have seen
            this, no matter how hard you tried.

                         FRIEND
            It all feels a little pointless, then,
            doesn't it?

                    CELLY

Maybe the point is this.

                    FRIEND

This?

She looks up at him, unwavering.

                    CELLY

Everyone's running around, trying to
understand themselves and each other. But
there are moments like this. Moments when
our little human bubbles collide. We rub our
boundaries together. We create friction.

                    FRIEND

And then what?

                    CELLY

We spin away again. We'll always feel the
shape of the people we've touched. But
still, we spin away.

                    FRIEND

That's sad.

                    CELLY

It's not so sad. It's just life. It's how
things go sometimes.

Russ

Russ walks into the station wearing his only pair of blue jeans and a T-shirt from the softball league he quit seven years ago.

He marches straight to the back office, where the gold plaque on the door reads "Lieutenant Gonzalez." He does not knock. The lieutenant is hunched over a stack of paperwork—caught off guard, he looks ten years older. The bags under his eyes are a purpling blue. Russ decides that he does not hate the lieutenant. Just pity.

Fletcher, the lieutenant says. Didn't I give you the week off?

I'm leaving, Russ says.

He places the grocery bag on the edge of the lieutenant's desk. A stack of paperwork slides as the lieutenant pulls out the accoutrements of Russ's police career: pants, belt, jacket. His badge. RUSSELL FLETCHER. His gun, with the bullets packed separately in a Ziploc. The lieutenant lays Russ's things across his desk, then shakes his head.

Are you sure you want to do this? the lieutenant says. In the corner of his mouth, the faint hint of a knowing smirk.

I think so, Russ says.

You know, the lieutenant says, you did have some potential, Fletcher. Even after all that mess with Lee Whitley.

Thank you, Russ says, and then he lies. It's been a pleasure.

———

After, Russ drives deep into the mountains. The roads are thin up by the timberline. Precarious. They snake across the cliffs—real cliffs, in the heart of the Rockies. No plateaus.

Russ rolls down the windows, even though it is February. The trees are naked, except for the pines; their needles stand erect, having shaken off that thin, misleading layer of snow. Russ turns on the radio. "Eye of the Tiger."

He starts to sing along, quiet at first, then louder, louder, until he is yelling—he is hollering—*and the last known survivor stalks his prey in the night*—the bright sun is simple nourishment to his skin.

When the song is over, Russ pulls to the shoulder of the winding mountain road. He gets out of the car and breathes alpine air, sharp, retreating. He looks down at his hands, which are red and barren in the cold, but resolutely his own.

———

At the end of Fulcrum Street, Ivan is sitting on his front porch. He reads a book, a bottle of Coke wedged in the crook of his elbow. Russ pulls up in his new car, a Subaru with no sirens or lights.

I thought you might come by eventually, Ivan says.

Russ walks up to the porch, and Ivan beckons him forward. Russ sits, awkward, on a wicker chair, which creaks beneath his weight. The floral cushion is fraying.

I quit my job, Russ tells Ivan.

Yes, Ivan says. Ines told me you were considering it. Good for you.

I kept thinking about what you said, Russ says. A long time ago, do you remember? You were right. I felt like a puppet.

Sometimes you need to do something new, Ivan says.

I found a good option already, Russ tells him. Teaching a six-week gun-safety course. The job travels all over Colorado.

That sounds great for you, Ivan says, and he sounds sincere.

They sit. A brooding good-bye.

I came to tell you I'm sorry, Russ says. I'm sorry for everything.

I appreciate that, Ivan says.

As Russ gets back into his car, it occurs to him that throughout this ordeal—Ines and Marco, Lucinda Hayes, Lee Whitley back from the dead—and despite all Ivan's hulking religion, his scary peaceful understanding of his own being, Ivan has been the only one telling the truth.

———

Even after he has cleaned up the yarn, Russ finds traces of Ines everywhere. Long black hairs littering the bathroom counter. An old T-shirt that fell behind a bookshelf, covered in dust. A single purple sock in his own drawer. Nail clippings by the bedroom trash can—frail, mooning slivers.

Russ runs. He takes off down the sterile Broomsville streets. In the weeks since Ines left, Russ has bought a new refrigerator. Read a whole novel. Applied for the gun-safety teaching position.

All he can do now is push—move his body, sweat it out, keep inching forward. For now, he focuses on his own limbs and the miracle ways in which they serve him. The freedom of the open Colorado sky.

A twilit periwinkle. Edgeless.

———

When Cynthia opens the door, she takes an instinctive step back.

Russ, she says, composing herself. Come in.

The house looks different now—it has taken on Cynthia's colors and scents. No remnants of Lee. Since Lee left, Cynthia has redone the living room; the couch is on the opposite wall, reupholstered. She has spent a lot of money on new hardwood floors.

Tea? Cynthia offers.

She puts on the water before Russ can answer.

He tells her the house looks great, and Cynthia thanks him. They hover over the kitchen table, and Russ picks up a framed photo from the window-sill. In it, Cameron is gangly—ten years old, maybe eleven. He stands in front of the Denver Art Museum, his arms raised in triumph.

Good picture, isn't it? Cynthia says. That was Cameron's first trip. He's always loved that painting by the window, and they opened a temporary Van Gogh exhibit. Cameron spent hours looking at it.

She puts the tea in front of Russ and invites him: sit. The water burns a patch on Russ's tongue.

I brought something, Russ says.

From the pocket of his sweat shirt, Russ pulls out Lee's old deck of cards. Tattered, yellow around the edges.

Is that . . . ? Cynthia trails off.

I thought I could teach Cameron how to play gin rummy, Russ says.

For a pulsing moment, Cynthia squeezes her eyes shut. Tilts her head to the light. Russ watches as she stands, shaky, and calls down the hall for her boy.

Cameron

Cameron sat on the stool in Mr. O's office, trying to make an apple stem look three-dimensional.

"It looks good," Mr. O said. "You're getting there."

He patted Cameron on the shoulder, twice, and went to check on the rest of the class.

Cameron drew an apple in a bowl. *Why don't you try still life?* Mr. O had said when Cameron came back to school. Mr. O had been spending most nights at Cameron's house, in Mom's room. Even though this had been awkward and embarrassing at first, he felt better with Mr. O just down the hall at night. Safer. Russ Fletcher came over some nights too, and when Mom was in the other room, he told Cameron stories about Dad, stories that made Dad seem like the sort of guy Cameron could feel okay about missing.

Cameron had spent two weeks at home with Mom, driving half an hour every day to see a psychiatrist—a nice woman named Maura, with curly red hair and tortoiseshell glasses. She asked him questions like *How do you feel when you first wake up in the morning?*—the sorts of questions he'd always wanted to ask someone, but hadn't known how. The potted plant behind her head sprouted up like alien hair.

Ronnie was afraid of Cameron, but that was okay. Cameron didn't miss him. Everyone at school looked at him funny when he walked down the hall, even though Detective Williams had found the bloody dog leash in a gym bag that Mr. Thornton had stuffed into a trash can at his office in Denver, along with Lucinda's cell phone. Mrs. Thornton was back in the hospital. Baby Ollie was with her grandparents in Longmont. Some people said Cameron had caught a murderer, and some people still swore Mr. O did it, even though he'd never even been accused and the school district was threatening to sue the police department on his behalf.

Cameron heard Lucinda's name less every day.

Now, he drew an apple in a bowl. It was nice, he thought, to see what he was drawing as he drew it. Even though it didn't breathe, the apple was difficult to replicate. It had its own contours, bits where it rose and fell in very lovely ways. He found it refreshing to draw something that was actually in front of him. Something with weight.

———

Things Cameron Would Not Dare to Touch Again:

1. The drawings of Lucinda. Mr. O had taken them to his own house, to keep them in a safe place where they could not make anyone Tangled.
2. The Collection of Statue Nights: he stored this Collection in a part of his head that he only visited when it was safe. When he was in bed, alone with thoughts of her. Just in case of sleepwalking, Mom put a child-safety lock on the drawer that held the kitchen knives.
3. The .22 handgun. The cops had confiscated it, at Mom's request.
4. The Tree. Cameron decided to forget this place he loved to go, even though the dirt and sticks had formed a pattern and that pattern was imprinted in his brain.

   He hoped it would rain.

———

Cameron missed his friend, the night janitor. He had put an end to his late-night wanderings, and lying in bed with the window locked shut, Cameron often thought about the man in the jumpsuit. If he could go back to Elm Street now, he'd walk right up to the janitor. Press his heavy head to the janitor's chest and let the big man hold him. He wouldn't ask why the janitor had never mentioned seeing Cameron on February fifteenth, on the other side of Elm Street. That's what friends did, and in the night janitor, Cameron had found a real one.

At night, he imagined telling the janitor each day's small lesson. Today: Untangling wasn't always the answer. Your insides were a labyrinth, and there was no use trying to unfurl it all. Tangled was a natural way to be, and you could only try to understand that knot inside—how it had formed, and where it was loosest, those inches of slack where you could find some relief.

———

It was early March now, a rare eighty degrees. Colorado did that—shifted so quickly from winter to summer you could hardly catch your breath. Mom was pulling weeds in the garden, hands on her hips in her beat leather gardening gloves. Upstairs, Mr. O was painting in the studio he'd created in the attic for him and Cameron to share.

"Can we take a trip?" Cameron asked from the patio table.

"Where do you want to go?"

"Somewhere that isn't so dry."

"We'll go to the ocean," Mom said, peering at him from under her straw sun hat. Cameron thought about salt, how it could sterilize an open wound.

Every day, Mom and Cameron sat down to talk, as the psychiatrist recommended. Some days they had lots to say—others, they simply existed together.

How do you feel when you first wake up in the morning?

Sometimes, Cameron thought of Lucinda. When sunlight splayed across his comforter in angular rays, when he was still hazy from sleep: Lucinda would be sitting on her bedroom floor, the purple diary open in her lap. Swaying and tapping her pen, dancing to a song only she could hear. Cameron felt okay, remembering her like this—lost in some melody, building like a flooding body of water. Someday, Cameron would turn sixteen, seventeen, eighteen, and Lucinda would still be there, stuck behind the glass of her window. Fifteen and luminous, moving like a high branch in summer wind.

By the time Cameron brushed his teeth, Lucinda would be gone.

A collection of memory.

A figment of his sleep-sweet mind, smiling even as her face morphed into Cameron's own reflection in the window's glass. As if to say: *yes, of course, once you knew me.*

Acknowledgments

This book would not exist without my parents, Arielle Kukafka and David Kukafka. Mom, thank you for your wisdom and optimism, your certainty about my path. Dad, thank you for your guidance, reasoning, and unbridled pride. Thank you both for your investments in my education, sacrifices, and absolute support. I love you.

Thank you to Dana Murphy for being my dream agent, fairy godmother, confidante, life coach, and outstanding female friend. Your passion for this book beats ferociously at the heart of it. And to the lovely ladies of The Book Group—Brettne Bloom, Elisabeth Weed, Julie Barer, Faye Bender—thank you for raising us both.

Dazzled thanks to Marysue Rucci for your incredible insight, unparalleled enthusiasm, and deep understanding of this book, in shape and in heart. Some days I still pinch myself, I feel so lucky to work with you. Thank you to Zack Knoll for thoughtful, astute edits and tireless work backstage. Thank you to Jenny Meyer for fulfilling my dreams of being published abroad, and to Kris Doyle and his team at Picador UK. Thank you to copy editors Jonathan Evans and Molly Lindley Pisani, to Allison Forner and Alex Merto for the beautiful cover design, and thank you to everyone at Simon & Schuster—Jonathan Karp,

Cary Goldstein, Richard Rhorer, Ebony LaDelle, Dana Trocker, Sarah Reidy—for believing in my work.

Thank you to Sarah McGrath, my generous and unflappable mentor, for teaching me how to really read (in turn, how to really write). To Barbara Jones, for being the first person to tell me I was "in the ballpark," and Stuart Krichevsky, for pushing me out on my metaphorical big-kid bike. Thank you to Geoff Kloske, Jynne Martin and my Riverhead family for cheering me on—sometimes even physically.

Thank you to NYU's *Gallatin Review* for publishing excerpts from this book in the short story "Zap." I'd like to thank the following writers for their work and insight: Lord Byron (*She Walks in Beauty*), Gabriel García Márquez (*Love in the Time of Cholera*), and Pablo Neruda (*Soneto LVII*). Credit and thanks to Kevin Oliver for the translation of the Pablo Neruda poem, "Soneto LVII," found on page 337.

Thank you, of course, to my brothers and sisters—Laurel Kukafka, Joshua Kukafka, Talia Zalesne, and Zachary Zalesne. Thank you to Avi Rocklin and Jim Wright; to Shannon Duffy, Pete Weiland, and Maddy Weiland; to Lisa Kaye and Aiden Kaye.

To some wonderful friends: Steph Bow, Chris DiNardo, Ellen Kobori, Kaitlyn Lundeby (#1 fan!), Emily McDermott, Lauren Milburn, Tae Naqvi, Alissa Newman, and Raka Sen.

A special thank-you to Hannah Neff for growing with me for so many years in so many ways. Thank you to Tory Kamen, for getting it.

And thank you, Liam Weiland, for being exactly the person you are. The softest words I write are always for you.

Lastly, to each and every reader of this book—thank you. You humble me.

About the Author

DANYA KUKAFKA is a graduate of New York University's Gallatin School of Individualized Study. She currently works as an Assistant Editor at Riverhead Books. *Girl in Snow* is her first novel.